BOOKS BY JENNIFER L. HART

Southern Pasta Shop Mysteries:
Murder Al Dente
Murder À La Flambé

Misadventures of the Laundry Hag Mysteries:
Skeletons in the Closet
Swept Under the Rug
All Washed Up

Damaged Goods Mysteries
Final Notice

Other Works
Who Needs a Hero?
River Rats
Stellar Timing
Daisy Dominatrix
Redeeming Characters

MURDER À LA FLAMBÉ

---

a Southern Pasta Shop mystery

JENNIFER L. HART

MURDER À LA FLAMBÉ

CHAPTER ONE

"Hey, Jones, come taste this sauce. I need to know if it's worth going to war over." I dipped the wooden spoon into the red concoction and brought it to my own mouth, blowing to cool the scalding liquid.

Malcolm Jones, my devilishly handsome significant other, quirked a jet-black brow. "I didn't realize red sauce violated the Geneva Convention." His crisp New Zealand accent always made me shiver.

I held the wooden spoon up to his lips. "Not *war* war, just a battle of wills with Aunt Cecily."

"Andrea, no sauce in the world is worth that." Despite his protest, he leaned down and tasted my fresh batch of tomato basil sauce. I got a little shiver as I watched his masculine lips close around the spoon.

"Well?" I had to clear my throat, my voice thicker than Alfredo.

"It's delicious, as always. But why would you have to battle your aunt over it? Isn't it a family recipe that you already serve in the shop?"

The shop he referenced was my family's pasta shop, the Bowtie Angel. My Christmas present from my Sicilian great-aunt and my grandfather had been a transfer in ownership from them to me. Technically, I, Andy Buckland, was the sole proprietor of the only ethnic eatery in Beaverton, North Carolina. But a month later I was beginning to feel as though the passing of the torch was more symbolic than anything else.

"Not exactly, it's lighter. I made it special to be served over fried risotto. I want to expand the menu to include appetizers. And dessert." As a culinary graduate and former celebrity chef, I was always playing around in the kitchen. While the family recipes we currently served were comforting, I couldn't hold myself back from being creative.

Jones leaned back against the counter and crossed his legs at the ankle. He was garbed in his customary black on black, though his feet were bare. "Appetizers and dessert sounds more like a restaurant than a pasta shop."

I turned to fuss with the window box full of herbs Jones had made for me. "Well, not a restaurant in Beaverton, obviously. The town council would probably have me flogged for even suggesting it. But maybe if the new dishes go over well enough, we could do a restaurant in Raleigh or Charlotte or even Asheville. Celebrity chef–owned restaurants are all the rage."

Though I'd turned away from him, I could feel Jones's piercing blue gaze boring holes into the back of my cranium. "Are you planning to move, Andrea? Is that what this is about?"

I turned again and wrapped my arms around him. "Of course not. This would still be my home base, obviously. Kaylee just started school here. Do you really think I'd up and leave now?"

Kaylee, the baby girl I'd put up for adoption when I was barely more than a kid myself, had recently come back into my life. I'd lived with the regret of giving her up for adoption every day of the past sixteen years, so Jones knew there was no way I'd pull up stakes now that I had her back. "It's just pie in the sky, anyway. No one wants to be fed by the Death Chef."

His forehead creased. "Is that what's troubling you, your reputation? Because I've offered to investigate—"

I held up a hand to stop him mid-offer. "The last thing I want is to stir that all up again."

Among his many other talents, Malcolm Jones was a licensed private investigator. He'd offered before to find out exactly how the linguini and clam sauce recipe that I'd made a hundred times before had given food poisoning to my live studio audience during my debut cooking show. We both harbored the suspicion that someone had tampered with the dish in order to discredit me but hadn't found a way to prove it.

My arms fell to my sides, and I plunged my hands into the soapy water to start tackling the mountain of dishes. When he'd first made the offer to go digging, I'd waved him off. My life was in Beaverton now, and it seemed pointless to stir the pot, since it was unlikely I'd ever go back to celebrity cooking.

He turned me back to face him, ignoring the suds I dripped on his immaculate kitchen floor. "Talk to me, love. What's eating at you?"

"I heard Flavor TV declared bankruptcy." Flavor TV was the small cable station that'd aired my disastrous debut. "They've been buried under lawsuits since last spring. All those people out of work. I feel like it's all my fault, you know? I need to prove to the world that I'm a competent cook, not the Death Chef."

My eyes watered, and I swiped at them with the long sleeve of my sweater. The pity party had turned ugly. I thought I'd matured beyond the overwhelming need to prove myself. Not even a year ago I'd helped save the Bowtie Angel from going under and caught a killer at the same time. I had a job, my family, and Jones. It should have been enough, more than enough, so why wasn't I happy?

Jones opened his mouth, but the doorbell rang before he could say anything. He gave me a level stare, and I could almost hear his sultry New Zealand accent in my head saying, *This isn't over.*

Turning back to the dishes, I tried to decide if the fried risotto should be flat like pancakes or round like meatballs. The balls could be stuffed with fresh grated cheese, something soft that melted well, like fontina. I was always in favor of adding more cheese to any Italian dish, something that didn't go over well with my very traditional aunt.

Jones was right to be wary of Aunt Cecily. She was a stubborn old battle-ax from the old country, and it was rumored she put the Evil Eye on people who displeased her. In our small southern town, she was a living legend. Only a fool would cross her. Though I was 99.9 percent sure she wouldn't actually curse her own kin, I wasn't willing to bet my best cheese grater on it.

Expanding the menu at the Bowtie Angel wasn't just good for me though. My sous chef, Mimi, was a skilled pastry chef, and expanding meant she could use her expertise right where she was. Otherwise, she might grow bored and start up her own pastry shop after her citizenship came through. Having her make cannoli and tiramisu for our customers would keep her happy and hopefully on my payroll a little longer.

I'd set the colander in the drain board when it occurred to me that Jones hadn't come back yet. Curious, I dried my hands, gave the Crock-Pot of tomato basil sauce one more turn with my wooden spoon, then strode out into the living room.

The sound of angry male voices carried through the spacious front room. I paused, deciding to peek around the corner instead of striding into plain view. Jones had his back to me, blocking the visitor from my line of sight. The front door was still wide open, a cold gray January evening looming ahead.

"Malcolm, be reasonable." I frowned as I recognized the voice as belonging to Jones's father, Mr. Tillman. Jones was, as he'd tactfully put it, "born on the wrong side of the blanket" and hadn't known his father until he moved to Beaverton last spring. So far, he hadn't been impressed. Mr. Tillman's life had been turned upside down, and he had taken to drinking like he could medal in whiskey guzzling. Needless to say, he wasn't a regular visitor.

"I am perfectly reasonable," Jones said. Anyone who didn't know him well would think he wasn't at all affected by the conversation. Over the last year, I'd picked up on his subtler cues, and the crisp way he bit off each word clued me in that he was furious. "This matter is none of your concern."

Mine either, and I doubted the men would be pleased to find me eavesdropping. I was about to tiptoe downstairs and check on the load of towels I'd put in the laundry earlier, when Mr. Tillman's words froze me to the spot. "None of my concern? My only son is married and living with another woman on my property, and it's none of my concern?"

Rochelle. Somehow Mr. Tillman had found out about Jones being married to Rochelle, the two-timing bigamist hussy, and was having a royal conniption over it.

"First of all, you're in no position to pass moral judgment on your bastard son's actions. Pot calling the kettle black and all that rubbish."

I flinched at the cutting word choice. Poor Malcolm had serious daddy issues. And mommy issues. And abandonment issues and trust issues. I could so relate. That was why we were perfectly dysfunctional together. However, being caught spying on them would most likely throw a big fat monkey wrench into our cozy little setup. I tried to tell my feet to move forward and take me out of earshot, but they refused to cooperate.

"Secondly, the marriage was never legal because she was *already* married."

"So why did she show up at my office today looking for, and I quote, 'her husband?'"

Seriously? I was floored by this, but Jones took it in stride.

"Most likely her other husband finally had enough of her philandering and deception and divorced her, and she thinks I have a rich father. Money is all Rochelle ever cared about. Well, other than herself."

He hadn't spoken to me about her, beyond the basic facts. Married, then heartbroken when he'd found out about her trickery. His quick recap was concise and to the point, almost as though he were assembling a case for the grand jury. I knew she'd cut him deeply though. I could hear the hurt in his voice.

"It's not as though you'll inherit from me, not carrying on with that woman right under my nose."

I bristled at that. That woman? As in me, myself, and I? What was so wrong with that woman? I was freaking fabulous—just ask me.

There was a thud and a grunt, and for one horrifying moment I thought Jones had walloped his father. As much as the old jerk deserved it, I didn't want my significant other brought up on assault charges. The last thing the Tillman family needed was more public tongue wagging. A door slammed, and the sound of footsteps headed my way. Jones had physically shown his father the door and was about to bust me as Little Andy Spies-A-Lot. Scurrying for the kitchen, I dove for the fridge and pretended to look busy. I grabbed the first thing my hand closed on, kicked the door shut, and picked up my chef's knife.

"Hey," I said brightly, using my *everything is just hunky-dory* tone.

"You heard all that." It wasn't a question.

I picked up my chef's knife and set the random cold objects on a cutting board. "Shoot, how'd you know?"

"You were about to mince my film containers."

I looked down and sure enough, two black canisters were laid out side by side on my cutting board.

"Rats," I grumbled. "It was totally an accident, I swear. I wasn't trying to spy. I just sort of got stuck there, you know?"

His expression lightened. He crossed the room and rested his cheek against my hair. "Thank you."

I blinked. "Whatever for?"

"For giving me a reason to smile."

I glanced around the kitchen, but everything was staged well and could be left unattended for a bit. "Come on to the bedroom, and I'll give you a few more reasons to smile."

* * *

A while later, I slipped on one of Jones's black button-down shirts and a pair of thick gray socks and padded into the kitchen. Since the sauce was done, I shut off the Crock-Pot and filled a pot of water for dinner. After salting the water and setting it on the stove to boil, I snagged the fresh linguini I'd brought home from the pasta shop.

"That's a great look for you," Jones murmured as I reached for the wineglasses, his shirt riding up to expose my pasta-enhanced backside. "I wish I had my camera."

Thank the powers that be that he didn't. I cleared my throat and tugged the shirt back into place. "Sorry, all my stuff is in the wash."

"You can bring more stuff over, you know," Jones said as he opened a bottle of red wine. "You're practically living here now."

He had a point. I'd brought everything of importance over, including my grandfather's smelly old dog, Roofus, who spent most of his time sprawled on the blindingly white living room rug, snoring like a buzz saw. "I could, but I don't see the point when you could be evicted at any time."

Jones shrugged. "It's Lizzy's place. She's free to move in whenever she wants—though I don't think she'll want to until after the wedding."

"Any idea when that will be?" Jones's half sister, Lizzy Tillman, was engaged to Kyle Landers, who also happened to be the father of my daughter, Kaylee. Though they'd been engaged for over a year, Lizzy seemed reluctant to set a new wedding date, since the death of the pastry chef at her engagement party had put the kibosh on the original date.

He shook his head. "Your guess is as good as mine."

The water had reached a rolling boil, so I added the pasta while Jones sliced a loaf of fresh Italian bread. I stirred in silence, lost in my own thoughts.

Though the house we inhabited was perfect for Jones and me, it wasn't truly ours. If Lizzy decided to elope with Kyle next weekend, we had nowhere else to go. The Victorian on Grove Street where I'd grown up had been put on the market. I'd sold my condo in Atlanta, and my assistant was currently residing in the small room over the pasta shop. Lizzy and I had a tumultuous history, and I knew she didn't like me shacking up with her half brother any more than her dad did. What if the two of them decided to oust Jones out of spite? I wouldn't put it past anyone in the Tillman family. "I probably should start looking for my own place anyway."

Jones didn't answer, and I glanced over my shoulder, frowning. Had he heard me? Before I could ask, my cell phone blared. The ringtone was a classic, "Baby's Got Back."

"That would be Donna. She was at the town council meeting tonight and promised to call in with the gossip. Will you drain the pasta? I'll be just a minute."

"Take your time." Jones headed toward the stove without giving me any eye contact.

My cell was buried beneath a million other random things in my tote bag. I dove in with both hands, shoving aside the new menu samples, my iPod and earbuds, wallet and change purse, coupons and about a dozen recipe cards, tubes of lip gloss, stray scrunchies, bobby pins, leather driving gloves, and the sunglasses I thought I'd lost. I plucked out two key rings, one to Mustang Sally, my cherry-red classic muscle car, and the other to the pasta shop. I'd just grabbed hold of the Droid I was looking for, when the music stopped. Drat, I really needed to talk to her too. Not only was Donna Muller my best friend since kindergarten, she was also a Realtor, and I needed her to get a jump on the spring listings and find me a primo place to live.

I waited to see if she'd left a voice mail, but to my surprise, the phone started jiving again in my palm. I answered by saying, "You're a persistent wench—I'll give you that."

Instead of bantering back in our usual style, Donna gasped. "Oh my god, Andy, did you hear?"

She sounded out of breath, her voice higher than normal. What could have her in such a state? My grandfather and Aunt Cecily had attended the meeting on my behalf so I could have the evening off. Did something happen to one of them? "Hear what? Is it Pops? Or Aunt Cecily?"

"No, they're fine. It's the florist shop next door to the Bowtie Angel." In the background I could hear people shouting and the sound of sirens.

I frowned. "You mean Mrs. Bradford's place? What about it?"

"Oh, Andy, it's just terrible." Donna sniffed. "I came out of the town hall, and well, it's on fire."

Tomato Basil Sauce

You'll need:
3 tablespoons extra virgin olive oil (basil or garlic infused adds a stronger flavor)
2 garlic cloves, crushed
1 pound tomatoes, seeded and diced
1 tablespoon sugar in the raw
1 teaspoon molasses
Sea salt and freshly ground black pepper to taste
10 fresh basil leaves, chopped

Coat a saucepan with 2 tablespoons of the oil, and warm over medium-low heat. Add the garlic, and cook, stirring, until soft, not browned. Add the diced tomatoes, molasses, and sugar. Season with salt and pepper. Turn the heat up slightly to medium, and simmer the sauce for 30 minutes, stirring occasionally. Stir in the basil and the remaining olive oil. Toss with hot pasta, and serve.

**Andy's note: Fresh tomatoes and molasses cut the acidity in this sauce, and the flavors combine even better if you let them simmer on low in the Crock-Pot for several hours.

CHAPTER TWO

———

It seemed like the entire town of Beaverton was out watching Mrs. Bradford's business burn. Luckily, the octogenarian owner and her assistant had both been at home when the structure went up. The volunteer fire department had arrived in time to contain the blaze so it didn't spread to the Bowtie Angel or any of the other nearby structures.

Since the roads were slick and I was distraught, Jones had driven me into town in his behemoth SUV. He parked in the municipal lot, and we watched as the flames died down.

"What do you think caused it?" I asked Jones.

"It could be anything from one of those pluggable air fresheners left on too long to mice chewing through the electrical wires. It's too soon to tell," he murmured. "After the structure cools, the fire department will send an investigator in to determine the point of ignition."

I worried my lower lip. "If this had happened later at night when no one was awake to notice it, it could have spread to the pasta shop. And Mimi would have been inside." As part of her salary, Mimi had taken up living in my great-aunt's studio apartment over the pasta shop.

"But it didn't. Don't borrow trouble, Andrea." He raised my hand to his lips and placed a soft, reassuring kiss on my knuckles

My heart rate had just started to slow when someone rapped on the passenger's side window. I jumped in my seat, jerking my hand back, but sighed when I spotted the familiar face. "Oh, it's Donna. Let her in before she freezes."

Jones hit the automatic locks, and Donna moved around to the backseat. She was paler than usual, her typical healthy glow noticeably absent.

"Are you okay?" I reached over the seat to squeeze her hand reassuringly.

Donna shook her head quickly back and forth. "No. When I first came out, I thought it was the pasta shop. I was halfway up the block when I realized it was the florist's place."

"Did Pops or Aunt Cecily see?" I asked, afraid my older relatives would have heart failure if they thought our family business had gone up in flames.

"No, they left early to meet Kaylee and her mom for dinner in Lumberton."

Thank the heavenly father for small favors. "Where's your car?"

Donna gestured toward the town hall lot, and the exit was currently being blocked by a fire truck. "In there. I'll have Steve come get me."

"Then he'll have to take the kids out too. It's easier if Malcolm drives you home."

"Just me, not us?" Jones raised an eyebrow.

"I want to see if I can find Mimi, make sure she's all right," I told him. "Will you meet me back here after you drop Donna off?"

"You didn't bring a jacket. Take this so you don't freeze." Jones shucked his black leather coat and handed it to me.

I slid my arms into it, absorbing his body heat and unique male spice. "Thank you. See you in a few."

I leaned in and kissed him, then slithered out of the vehicle and strode toward the congregation being held back by several uniformed police officers. Over the crowd, I spotted the sheriff's hat and called Kyles's name until he strode over.

"Have you seen Mimi?" I asked when he was within earshot.

"We evacuated her from the pasta shop in case it went up. Last I saw, she was headed to the intersection of Main and Elm."

I thanked him, and he turned back to work. Another thought occurred, and I caught his arm. "Are we going to be able to open tomorrow?"

Kyle frowned as he thought about it. "I don't see why not, though part of the street will probably be closed off for several hours."

"Okay. Kaylee's first day of work is tomorrow after school. I didn't want to cancel on her."

Kyle's expression softened the way it always did when someone mentioned our daughter. "I'll make a point to stop by and see her at work—tell her how I used to do that for her mama. Bet she'll get a kick out of that."

"Don't go giving her ideas about boyfriends," I warned him. "We weren't a sterling example of young love, and we don't want her following in our footsteps."

Kyle's eyes widened. "I hadn't thought of that. She's too young to date, isn't she?"

I did a palms up. "You'll have to ask her mom about that."

Kyle didn't like that answer. I could practically hear the shotgun being ratcheted back, but then he pointed over my shoulder. "Oh look, it's your new neighbor."

"What new neighbor?" I turned in the direction he was pointing, and my jaw dropped. "No. Freaking. Way."

"Do you know her?" Kyle's head swung back and forth between the two of us.

"Lacey L'Amour," I said between clenched teeth. "What in the sweet cannoli-filled afterlife is she doing here?"

The blonde bombshell pivoted in our direction, and our eyes locked. She scanned me up and down, a small smirk on her collagen-injected lips. My eyes narrowed, and my lip curled in an involuntary sneer. She wore a scarlet dress that was cut almost indecently low and four-inch heels, which she somehow maneuvered across the icy walkway. Beaverton wouldn't know what the heck to do with her ultra-urban self. Several of the men stared openmouthed while their wives glowered with crossed arms. I couldn't have been more surprised if it had started raining marinara as she approached. "What are you doing here?"

Several heads turned in our direction, but Lacey air-kissed me on either cheek. "*Oui, c'est moi.* So good to see you, Andee."

Liar, liar, well, unfortunately something was already on fire. She didn't like me anymore than I appreciated her. She'd always been a phony, more flash than substance. Her well-displayed charms and saccharine-infused tone made my eye twitch.

"So you two are…friends?" Kyle looked doubtful.

"We went to culinary school together." Unfortunately.

"*Oui*." Lacey nodded forcefully as though Kyle would doubt my statement if she didn't back me up. But that was classic Lacey L'Amour, spotlight hog extraordinaire. She'd been so ticked when I'd been tapped for my own cooking show on Flavor TV. Of course that had been a catastrophe, and from the glint in her dark eyes, she was thinking the same thing.

"Hey, I know you." Missy Elliot from the grocery store snapped her fingers a few times. "Didn't you win a season of *Chef's Showdown*?"

"No, sadly, I was only ze runner up." Lacey pouted prettily. "But you would be amazed by what even zat can do for your career."

"Almost as good as learning how to cook, huh?" I muttered, my tone caustic.

Her eyes flashed, just a glimpse of the poisonous snake, coiled to strike. "Oh, Andee, let's not have ze sour grapes, no?"

"My grapes are just fine, thank you very much. What are you doing here, Lacey?" Dread filled me as I recalled Kyle calling her my neighbor. "You haven't moved here, have you?"

"*Oui*." She tipped her chin up and thrust out her breasts until she looked like the prow of a ship. "I've bought *la petite restaurante*. We will open this weekend."

Dread coiled in my gut like heavy cream turned rancid. "Are you talking about the old pub house? The building right there?" I pointed to the storefront directly across the street from the Bowtie Angel.

"*Oui*." The word dripped with satisfaction. "I'm sure you are up for a little competition."

In fact, I wasn't. While the Bowtie Angel made a small profit, enough to pay Mimi and keep the doors open, we weren't enough of a draw to go up against a competing ethnic cuisine restaurant right across the frigging street. By the evil smirk on her pouty face, she knew it, too.

"Of course." I pasted a bright smile on my own puss so she wouldn't see my unease. "The more the merrier."

* * *

"Why Beaverton?" I griped to Jones the next morning as I added Arborio rice to the sizzling pan in our kitchen. I planned to have the risotto ready so Kaylee could help me try out the new appetizer later that day. Since the fire marshal was still investigating the blaze, I'd decided to do my prep work from home. We couldn't serve it to the customers that way, but it would be good practice for her and allow me to tweak the recipe as needed. "Lacey has no connection to this town, so why set up shop across the frigging street from me?"

"I don't know." Jones poured himself a second cup of coffee.

I stirred a little too franticly and several grains of rice went flying. "Damn it."

He set his mug aside and wrapped his arms around me. "It'll be all right, Andrea."

I knew better than to cook while I was angry. Short tempers led to ruined meals and on occasion, injury. I slowed my frenetic stirring and leaned back into his embrace even as I said, "You don't know her like I do. She's crazy."

I could hear the smile in his voice as he murmured, "Then you're well matched." I shot him a scathing look, and he held up his hands in defense. "Sorry, couldn't resist."

Jones was right. I *was* acting like a lunatic. The rice had begun to emit a nutty aroma, and I added the wine to the pan, careful not to slop this time. I tried to focus positive energy into my food instead of the whirlwind of frenetic emotion that had me gasping for air.

Jones set his coffee cup aside. "Talk to me, love. What is it that has you so worked up?"

I took three deep breaths and ladled some hot stock into the pan. "I don't know, exactly. I just feel so unsettled, and having Lacey here chafes like a sandpaper thong."

His lips twitched. "Quite the image."

"It's the best I've got. She never could cook. Do you know she was sleeping with several of our instructors back in school?"

Jones raised a jet eyebrow. "Is that fact or rumor?"

"Fact. Someone reported her to the program coordinator. Three instructors lost their positions, though she didn't get booted out. Her food is bland and tasteless, though she does know presentation."

"I know," Jones said, surprising me.

I frowned and added another ladleful of stock to my pan. "You do?"

"I saw her on that cooking competition."

My jaw dropped, and I glared at him. "Are you kidding? You, who refuses to watch television, who had *no clue* who Regis Philbin was, saw Lacey frigging L'Amour on TV?"

He shrugged in an offhanded way, as though that wasn't a big fat hairy deal. "It was on in a bar I frequented while doing surveillance. Watching the program was a good cover."

Though his explanation made sense, an irrational flare of jealousy kindled in my chest. "I see." I didn't, but what else could I say?

Jones, being Jones, knew exactly what was bugging me. "Would you like me to watch your show? I know for a fact that Donna still has a copy—"

"No!" Talk about jumping from the frying pan into the fire. The last thing I wanted was Jones having the visual of my horror-stricken face as my live studio audience upchucked my linguini and clam sauce. "Not exactly my finest hour as a chef. Plus, you already have all the behind-the-scenes information. Let's not beat the dead horse, okay?"

"As you wish." With one last lingering kiss, Jones set his empty coffee mug in the sink and turned toward the cellar stairs. "Call me if you want a ride into town. It's icy out this morning."

I smiled my thanks. He really was a gentleman, helping me in and out of the SUV, when I slowed down long enough to let him. For the next twenty minutes, I focused on my risotto and had just put the double batch in the refrigerator to cool when my cell phone rang.

"Where are you?" Aunt Cecily asked.

Her terse greeting was par for the course. Since I'd known her all my life, Aunt Cecily didn't scare me. Much. "With Jones, at his place. Where are you?"

"Where you should be, making the pasta."

Crud, I'd forgotten to tell her that we were delaying opening because of the fire. Officially, Aunt Cecily was retired, but that didn't stop her from coming in to "supervise." Translated roughly, she showed up to boss me around. "I'll be there soon."

"You come now," she said and hung up before I could argue.

"Ugh," I said to the empty room. Even though Jones had offered to drive me in, I hated tearing him away from his darkroom. Mustang Sally was garaged for the winter, since as pretty as she was, she was a crappy snow car. When I'd lived in Atlanta, I'd taken public transportation whenever the weather was iffy. I still needed to talk to Donna and, on impulse, texted her to ask for a lift.

Fifteen minutes later, her shiny new Escalade was parked in the driveway. I said a quick good-bye to Jones, who was monkeying with a few prints he had contracted with a gallery in New York. If all went well, he might have his own show over the summer and be able to live off his art instead of following cheating spouses around to seedy bars and hotels that rented rooms by the hour.

"You doing okay?" I asked Donna as she helped me load my food into her cargo net.

"Better than yesterday, at least. Everything's relative." She shrugged. Dressed in her Realtor duds, a smart black pinstripe pantsuit with a dove-gray shell and pearl earrings, she was a knockout. The lime-green bubble jacket and pink mittens she wore to stave off the cold ruined the effect.

"Vanilla Ice called. He wants you to stop raiding his '90's closet," I teased. "Where's your good coat?"

She sighed. "Dry cleaners. Pippa was playing dress-up and spilled grape juice all over it. It was either freeze or go out looking like a blast from the past."

"Well, at least the car looks professional." Donna had been driving her mom wagon, complete with car seats for her twins and stale french fries, to showings until her husband had convinced her to lease the Cadillac SUV.

"Plus it will smell like Italian food when I pick up my clients, which hopefully will leave the subliminal message of home and hearth."

"Speaking of which…" I trailed off, unsure if I should bring it up.

Donna and I had been friends long enough that she knew what I was asking without my having to actually ask. "Are you saying you and Jones are in the market?"

"Just me," I clarified.

She slowed to take a hairpin turn. "Wait—is something wrong with the two of you?"

"No. We're great." I frowned. "At least, I *think* we're great."

One pink mitten waved in circular motions. "Okay, I'm going to need more information here."

"As a Realtor or as my BFF?"

She grinned "Both. That way I can give you my professional opinion and still ask you if you're off your meds in case the need arises."

I laughed, though it came out as a sort of wheeze. "Fair enough. Bottom line, I just don't know how much longer I can live off Lizzy's largess. Jones doesn't talk about what comes next, doesn't want to make any plans beyond dinner tonight. He just says we'll deal with that when the time comes. I still don't know if he plans to stay in Beaverton indefinitely. I told you, he might have that gallery show in New York. But I own the Bowtie Angel now. Kaylee's mom moved closer so she could get to know Kyle and me, and there's you and Pops and Aunt Cecily too. I can't just up and leave."

"What do you want?" Donna probed.

"Honestly, I really don't know. For the most part, I like the way things are now, but I know they can't go on forever this way. Lizzy and Kyle will get married eventually, and then she'll want to live in her house. But he won't make any future plans no matter how many times I bring it up. It's so frustrating. And—"

I cut myself off, but Donna pounced like a kitten on a ball of string. "And what?"

I cleared my throat. "There are times that he tends to um...forget me."

"What do you mean?"

"You know, he goes down into his little man cave and then sort of forgets I exist. I spend as many evenings alone as I did when I was single."

"Did you say anything to him about it?"

"How can I? He's working on making his dream come true at the same time he's working his regular job. I want him to succeed, and I'm trying to be supportive. You know the domestic PI stuff wears him down. He can't talk about it, confidentiality and all, but there are only so many cheating spouses you can follow without becoming completely jaded."

Donna's lips parted, but her cell phone rang. "I can't figure out the stupid Bluetooth connection on this thing. Could you get that for me?"

I fished it out of the cup holder, glad to leave the subject of Jones for a while. "Donna Muller's phone."

"Hey, Andy, it's Steve." Donna's husband had a deep, authoritative voice, perfect for a cop.

"Hey, Steve. What's going on?"

"Donna asked me to call when we got the fire marshal's report in."

There was a pause, and I cleared my throat. "Well, she's driving right now, but I can pass it along. Did he find anything?"

"Yeah, just don't go spreading this around town. And tell Donna I said the same thing. Preliminary evidence indicates it wasn't an accident. Further inspection is needed, but by the looks of things, it was arson. Someone meant to burn the florist shop to the ground."

Mushroom Risotto

You'll need:
1 1/2 cups Arborio rice
1 pint baby bella mushrooms, chopped small
1 quart chicken broth
1/2 cup white wine
1 medium shallot, diced
3 tablespoons butter
1 tablespoon vegetable oil
1/4 cup fresh grated Parmesan cheese

Heat the stock and mushrooms to a boil to cook the mushrooms, and then lower the heat so that the stock stays hot. In a large, heavy-bottomed saucepan, heat the oil and 1 tablespoon of butter over medium heat. When the butter has melted, add the diced shallot. Sauté for 2 to 3 minutes or until it is slightly translucent.

Add the rice to the pot, and stir it briskly with a wooden spoon so that the grains are coated with the oil and melted butter. Sauté for another minute, but don't let the rice turn brown. Add the wine, and cook while stirring, until the liquid is fully absorbed.

Add a ladle of hot chicken broth to the rice, and stir until the liquid is fully absorbed. When the rice appears almost dry, add another ladle of stock, and repeat the process. Continue adding ladles of hot stock and stirring the rice while the liquid is absorbed.

Continue adding stock, a ladle at a time, for 20 to 30 minutes or until the grains are tender but still firm to the bite, without being crunchy. If you run out of stock and the risotto still isn't done, you can finish the cooking using hot water. Just add the water as you did with the stock, a ladle at a time, stirring while it's absorbed.

Stir in the remaining 2 tablespoons butter and the Parmesan cheese, and season to taste with sea salt.

**Andy's note: It's important to stir constantly, especially while the hot stock gets absorbed, to prevent scorching. Add the next ladle as soon as the rice is almost dry. As it cooks, you'll see that the rice will take on a creamy consistency as it begins to release its natural starches.

CHAPTER THREE

———

"Arson?" Pops scowled as he repeated the word. He was in the small office in the Bowtie Angel, having stopped in to do the bookkeeping for the week. "But why would anyone want to burn down a florist's shop?"

I'd asked Donna's husband the same thing. "The most likely reason is for insurance purposes. You did the books for Mrs. Bradford, right?"

My grandfather's expression turned even darker. "Now hold on just a minute there, Andy girl. Are you saying that Mrs. B would burn down her own business, putting our place and everyone on the street at risk?"

"No, I'm just asking a question. Don't get your dander up, Pops." The southern colloquialisms flowed after I spent any time talking with Pops, who couldn't seem to speak without an aphorism or two tossed in like radishes in a salad.

He harrumphed at me and folded his arms over his flannel-covered chest. Three hundred and sixty-five days a year, Pops wore flannel, even changed into it after Mass on Sundays. What was it with men and the limited wardrobe? "So, what was the question again?"

Even though the office door was closed and there was no way anyone out front could hear us, I lowered my voice. "Was the florist shop struggling financially?"

Pops shook his head. "No, in fact Mrs. B is one of the savviest businesswomen this town has ever seen. She got on board with online ordering before most of the townsfolk had computers, and she does steady business. She wasn't getting rich off the place, but she turned a tidy profit every year."

"Was she getting ready to retire?"

"Nah, she's like your Aunt Cecily and me. She'll work 'til she's dead."

I drummed my fingers against the desk. "Well, I'm out of ideas. It doesn't look like anyone profited from that fire. So who set it and why?"

Pops shrugged. "Maybe just a vagrant passing through."

I barely stifled an eye roll. "There aren't any vagrants in Beaverton, Pops. We don't even have a seedy part of town. Beaverton—don't blink, or you'll miss it."

"Not if Mayor Randal has his way. You know he had the gall to propose we open up to franchises again at last night's meeting? His daddy is rolling in his grave at the thought of a Starbucks in this town."

If it had been anybody else, I would have told him to stop talking dirty, but since it was my grandfather, I just said, "Starbucks are good, Pops. Great coffee, fast."

Pops's spidery eyebrows drew together. "We make a perfectly good pot of coffee at home, and it don't cost us no four dollars, neither. What's wrong about that?"

I sighed. There was no use trying to drag Pops into the twenty-first century. He was part of the old guard, and if it was good enough for him, it was good enough for the likes of everyone else.

"I have to get back to the kitchen. Kaylee will be here soon."

Pops grinned at the mention of his great-granddaughter. "She sure is a pip. Last night at dinner she told the funniest story about her old house and how it was supposedly haunted by a cross-dressing ghost. Had us all in stitches. She reminds me of her mama at that same age."

I bit my lip. When I'd been Kaylee's age, my own mother had been on the verge of committing suicide. It had been a dark and twisted point in my life, knowing something wasn't right but not sure what to do about it. Even before her death, my mother had a way of making me feel as though I constantly disappointed her. I'm sure Dr. Phil would have a field day with my issues, but all I said to Pops was, "Glad you had fun."

I returned to the kitchen, where Mimi was taking the test batch of risotto balls from the pan. I moved over to inspect them. "Looking good."

Aunt Cecily stood at the stovetop, heating a batch of red sauce. Her brows drew together, but she said nothing about our latest endeavor. Much like Pops, Aunt Cecily had to be dragged kicking and screaming into anything she considered progressive. If she had her way, we'd have a herd of goats tethered out back for making our own cheese.

I moved toward the sink to tackle the mound of dishes that had piled up. Dishwashing would help me compose myself before my daughter arrived. Kaylee had opened up to Pops and Aunt Cecily better than she had to either Kyle or me yet. It made sense, as they were also her family, but they hadn't been responsible for her being put up for adoption.

After a great deal of discussion, Kaylee's mom, Kyle, and I had decided to keep her relationship to us under wraps. She'd lost her adoptive father a few months ago and would have a hard enough time transitioning to a brand new life in Beaverton. Outside of our inner circles, which included Lizzy, Jones, Kyle's parents, Donna, and Mimi, no one else knew that she was our biological daughter. I hadn't wanted town gossip to upset her or interfere with the very delicate getting to know each other stage. I'd asked her to work in the pasta shop after school since it was such a big part of my life and the perfect cover for our ruse.

Though she'd seemed relieved that not everyone would know the sordid details of her life, she'd been a little cold with me the last two times I'd seen her. I thought she liked spending time with me, but she clammed up if I asked anything too personal. I'd spoken to her mother, wondering if Kaylee resented my choices or blamed Kyle for not coming after her. All she'd said was that Kaylee kept her own council about it, that she'd always been private, and there was nothing that would move her to open up until she was good and ready.

Chip off the old Rossetti block. All the women in my grandmother's family had two things in common—a massive stubborn streak and a penchant for Italian cooking. I was hoping the latter would help break the ice that had formed between us and help counteract the stalemate.

The back door opened and Kaylee came in, pink-and-black zebra-striped backpack slung over one shoulder. I smiled in greeting and reached for a dish towel. "Hey, I'm glad you're here."

She nodded, accepting my words and looked around the cluttered work space. "What should I do?"

"Let's stow your backpack and coat in the office, and then I'll show you around. Do you like Italian food?" Oddly, I hadn't thought to ask that ahead of time.

She shrugged. "It's okay."

Not a promising start. To my surprise, she went right to Aunt Cecily and kissed her on the cheek. Aunt Cecily's customary scowl lifted, and she nodded in approval as she murmured a greeting in Italian.

The office was empty, so I figured Pops must have gone out through the front. Though he'd spent years working a desk, the man didn't sit still for very long, and it wasn't unusual for him to shoot the breeze with whoever stopped in for a bite. "You can leave your stuff in here."

Kaylee nodded and obediently set her bag down. "Kind of small."

"It serves its purpose. Pops doesn't need much room to do the books. Half the time he takes the paperwork home with him."

Kaylee's blue-eyed gaze roved the small space. "So this is really a family business?"

I nodded, proud of our legacy. "Three generations. Well, four, now that you're here."

She looked at me directly for the first time. "Where's your mom?"

"She died." Things were too uneasy between us to dig up the unpleasant details.

She looked away. "Like my dad."

Her adoptive father had been killed in a car accident a few months ago. From the little I'd been able to piece together, he'd been the parent closest to Kaylee. "I'm sorry about that. He was a good guy."

Emotion flashed across her face, and I took half a step back at the anger she put on full display. "You didn't know him."

Crap, I hadn't wanted to upset her. "You're right. I didn't."

She looked at her boots. "He wasn't my real dad anyway."

I wanted to tell her that biology didn't change anything. I was sure the father she'd known had loved her, but her mood was so volatile, and I was afraid of overbalancing the applecart. Instead of addressing her comment, I cleared my throat and took a page from Aunt Cecily's book. "Time to make the pasta."

* * *

"You look all done in, Andrea," Jones said when he came into the pasta shop a few hours later. "Is something amiss?"

"Nothing Shakespeare couldn't turn into a stellar play." I sighed and put the last of the uncooked pasta into a Tupperware container.

"Kaylee?" my insightful boyfriend asked.

"Yeah." I sighed. The few hours she'd been at the Bowtie Angel had been productive, at least in terms of business. The town had congregated to talk about the fire and to come see the new girl. After I was sure she could handle it, I left her out front to talk with the ladies from the Rotary Club and clear tables. My presence had grated on her though, so I'd sent Mimi out front to help her.

"What can I do?" Jones asked now.

Instinctively, I knew he wasn't talking about scrubbing the sink full of pots. "I don't think there's anything to be done right now. She's wary around me, and her emotions are all over the place."

"She's a teenage girl," Jones pointed out.

"She's good at it." I sighed and went to the sink. "It'll come in time. Hopefully."

"How did the risotto balls do?"

That was the one bright spot to the afternoon. Though I couldn't bring in already made food to sell in the restaurant, I'd sent some home as free samples with a few family friends. "Really well, actually. Even Aunt Cecily liked them. And you know she doesn't like anything."

"That's overstating things a bit." Jones grinned. "Are there any left?"

"The bag on the counter is for you."

Jones peeked inside. "Smells divine. You're truly a visionary, Andrea."

"Comments like that will definitely get you laid tonight," I said just as his sister pushed open the door from the kitchen.

"Andy," she said to me in a cool voice.

"Lizzy," I answered in what someone who didn't know me might have considered a mild tone. Though I wanted to tell her that this area was for employees only, I was trying to get along with her, for Jones's sake. Not to mention as Kyle's significant other, she had every opportunity to badmouth me to Kaylee if she was so inclined. The last thing the relationship between Kaylee and me needed was an assist from my high school nemesis. So I took out my irritation on a particularly stubborn pot instead.

Lizzy turned away, pretending I didn't exist. "Malcolm, can I talk to you for a minute?"

"Let's go out back." There was a small patio behind the pasta shop, which Aunt Cecily had used as her private garden when she lived here.

I waited to the count of ten, trying to convince myself that I should give them their privacy. Jones would tell me anything important, right?

Maybe, but if I could leave it to chance, I wouldn't be a Rossetti.

So I sneaked into the ladies' room, crept into the handicapped stall, put one foot on the toilet seat, the other on the bar, cracked open the window, and shamelessly eavesdropped.

At first I couldn't hear much over my own pounding heartbeat. They weren't directly below the window and spoke in normal conversational tones, which didn't carry well. I was about to give up, when a familiar name froze me to the spot.

"When I saw Rochelle earlier..." Jones said, the rest too low for me to pick up.

He had? Where? And when? And how the hell come he hadn't told me he was going to see his ex, the woman he'd loved enough to marry?

Cripes, it was true what they said about eavesdropping— you never heard anything you wanted to hear.

"Are you in here, Andy?" Mimi's voice called from the bathroom door. I made to get down, and my sneakered foot went right into the toilet.

Much cussing ensued, but I did it quietly so as not to alert Jones and Lizzy. "Be out in a second," I called to Mimi.

If she wondered what the splashing was about, she didn't comment. Smart woman. I sighed as I looked at my soggy pants leg and dripping sneaker. Put a whole new spin on the term "I put my foot in it this time."

Holding my leg under the power dryer, I did the best I could to de-saturate myself, wondering the entire time if Jones was planning to tell me about the meeting with his ex. It must have been accidental. Like he bumped into her at the grocery store or something. Except he never went to the grocery store without me. Post office maybe? Nah, if he had, someone would have mentioned it to me. Had she gone to the house? My molars ground together at the thought of Rochelle at our house, even if Lizzy's name was on the deed. If she had been in our living space, he damn well better tell me.

Another possibility occurred, one I didn't want to consider but wouldn't leave my mind. What if he'd sought her out? Went to her office or met her at a café? Not in Beaverton, because after almost a year in town, everyone would recognize him on sight and there would have been a stampede on Main Street as the gossipmongers fought to be the first to tell me that Jones was out with another woman. No, he was too smart for that.

Why was she here? Maybe she wanted to hire Jones as a PI? Or it could be there was some unfinished business from their relationship, some joint bank account or distribution of furniture. Custody of a dog, some simple explanation. But if that was the case, why wouldn't he tell me?

You're being unreasonable, I told myself. What could he have to say to her anyway? Every time her name came up, he looked away, obviously ashamed of the way she'd fooled him. I frowned, a wad of paper towels clutched in my fist. At least, that had been my impression of why he'd never let me see his face. A horrible possibility crossed my mind, one that actually caused me physical pain.

What if Malcolm Jones was still in love with his ex? And what if she wanted him back?

Fried Risotto Balls

You'll need:
1 batch your favorite risotto, cooled overnight
4 oz fontina cheese, grated
1 cup all-purpose flour
2 eggs
3 cups Italian-style bread crumbs
Vegetable oil for frying
Take pinches of the cheese, and shape into small balls
for the filling. Beat eggs with a tablespoon of milk and set aside.

Take a small handful of rice, and shape into a shallow
cup in the palm of your hand. Place one of the cheese balls in the
center of the rice, then enclose the rice around the cheese, and
roll into round balls. Set out three shallow bowls, one with flour,
one with the egg mixture, and one with the bread crumbs.

First roll the balls in the flour, then coat with the egg
mixture before rolling in bread crumbs. Set the coated rice balls
on a baking sheet when they are completed.

Heat the oil in a large pot or deep skillet.

Carefully slip 3 to 4 balls into the hot oil at a time, and
fry until golden brown. Drain on absorbent towels, and keep
warm until you are ready to serve.

Top with a fresh basil and tomato sauce and serve hot.

**Andy's note: Hands down one of my all-time favorite
appetizers. It's a decent amount of work, then again, everything
worth doing usually is.

CHAPTER FOUR

———

I'm not in the habit of hiding my emotions. Some women can continue to function when something's on their minds, but I don't happen to be one of them. Anxiety and frustration leaks into almost everything I do and spills over into every other aspect of my life until it consumes me. Maybe it's my family heritage or just my own unique emotional flavor profile, but when I'm upset, *everyone* knows it.

Which was why, when Jones abandoned me for his darkroom yet again after we got home, I flipped through the television channels with an untouched glass of wine, wondering what the best way was to bring up his seeing his ex.

Roofus rolled to his side with a heartfelt groan, and I reached down to scratch his lumpy head. "I hear you, buddy. It's just been one of those days."

I channel surfed for half an hour, but nothing held my interest. Damn it, why wasn't Jones sitting next to me on the couch, rubbing my feet and professing his undying love? Why didn't he know I was upset?

Maybe he did know, and he just didn't want to deal with me. That thought enraged me, and before I was aware of it, I'd pushed myself up off the couch and had taken several steps toward the cellar stairs. Luckily, reason kicked in. The man was working, just like I should be doing. *Take a freaking chill pill, Andy, you nut.* Yes, distraction was what was called for here, not an out-and-out confrontation. I could tear into him later if I was still in the mood.

Grabbing my laptop, I plugged it in beside the pub table and turned it on. The recipe book I'd been transitioning to digital backup was in the bedroom. The task seemed even more crucial since the fire yesterday. No time like the present, and the distraction would do me good. I snagged the book and my glass of wine and settled in to work.

I'd gotten three recipes entered and uploaded to the cloud and was working on the fourth when my phone vibrated.

"Hello?" I asked, not looking at the number.

"Hey, what are you doing?" Donna asked.

Other than fighting not to feel sorry for myself? "Not a heck of a lot. Why?"

"I have rental house for you to look at."

I glanced at the clock. "Now? It's after eight."

"Afraid you'll miss *Diced*?" Donna quipped, naming my favorite cooking competition show. "What are you, ninety? DVR it."

No, but I was comfy. If we went out, I'd have to change into real people clothes. Unless we were going to Walmart, then anything would do. "What about your kids?"

"Got a sitter. Come on. I'll be there in ten minutes. Get your ass into some jeans and a shirt that doesn't have permanent spaghetti sauce stains."

I looked down at myself and grimaced. "All the mystery has gone out of our relationship."

"Good thing I'm in it for the secondhand sex details," Donna said and hung up.

I really didn't want to go out, but if Donna had arranged for a sitter and was already on her way… My gaze slid to the cellar door. Should I tell Jones where I was going? Would he even care? I shook my head, sick of being an insecure idiot.

I went into the bedroom and snagged a black scoop-neck top that was slimming at the same time as it revealed my cleavage, and a clean pair of jeans. My hair was beyond help, so I did a quick French braid and tied it off with a small red silk scarf and a dangly pair of earrings that I hoped detracted from the flyaway curls. It was too cold for the killer heels that would have made the outfit unbeatable, so I settled for motorcycle boots that were surprisingly comfortable.

I coaxed Roofus to go out and do his business in the frigid winter night and then descended into Jones's photography lair. The red light was off, and the door to the darkroom stood open, so I knew he wasn't working with raw film. Clothesline was strung across the room with black-and-white photos pinned up to dry. After a quick peek, I knew those were art focused and not evidence in one of his cases. Good thing. I really didn't want to see portly Mr. Figgs in the raw with his equally stocky secretary. I had to look these people in the eye when they came into the pasta shop, and there was no coming back from that mental picture.

Jones sat at his desk, messing around with one of his photography programs.

"Hey," I said. "Donna's on her way over, so I'll be going out."

He didn't turn away from the screen as he murmured, "Have fun."

That was it? He didn't want to know where we were going or if he could tag along? I'd expected mild curiosity at the very least. The grown-up response would be to tell him I was going out to look at a house and ask if he wanted to come with us. But this was the first real adult relationship I'd ever been in, and let's face facts—I was still immature. Not to mention afraid of being rejected. So I didn't call him on it, on any of it, even though I was hurting inside.

"See ya." I forced a light tone and tromped upstairs to wait for Donna.

"Jones didn't want to come?" she asked when I'd climbed into the car. She still wore her hideous green jacket but had changed into jeans and a red turtleneck sweater.

"He's busy with work," I answered.

Donna's gray eyes narrowed. "You didn't tell him where you were going."

My chin went up. "He didn't ask."

She threw up her hands. "Andy, for crying out loud, you're worse than a teenager. And I have one, so I know what I'm talking about."

"Yeah well, Jones is not my parent, and I can't force him to pay attention to me if he doesn't want to." No, that didn't sound bitter at all. I grimaced but didn't retract my statement.

Donna shook her head but thankfully turned out of the driveway. "You can hear yourself, right? I just want to be sure you're aware that you've hit a new level of neurotic that only insanity-detecting dogs can hear."

Okay, so I was being a bit of a brat, but I had good reason for it. I told her about the conversations I'd overheard with Mr. Tillman and Lizzy and finished with, "What if he's still in love with his ex, and she wants him back, and he's looking for a way out of the situation with me?"

Donna made a face. "Promise me that from now on you'll call me before you go completely off the deep end. Friends don't let friends think alone."

"I'm serious, Donna. He didn't even look at me or kiss me when I said I was going out. I'm telling you, something's off with him."

"Honey, you two just hit that comfortable stage in your relationship. When men get comfortable, they get lazy. If you think this is bad, wait until you two are married. Then it's all about the three S's—sex, sandwiches, sports, not necessarily in that order."

I shivered in revulsion. "That sounds horrible. Why would any sane woman want to get married if that's all there is to it?"

"That's only if you let the man get away with it, which is exactly what you're letting Jones do right now. It's the woman's job to keep the man from being too comfortable and letting it get to that point. You need to light a fire under them periodically. Shake things up. Keep them on edge."

"And how exactly should I do that?"

Donna grinned. "By moving into this rental house, of course."

"No, that's not self-serving *at all*." My tone was dry.

"What can I say? I'm a problem solver."

* * *

"Wow," I said as I looked at the A-frame structure nestled under the pines.

"See, I knew you'd love it. Wait until you get a load of the kitchen. It even makes me want to cook." Donna swung her legs out of the car door and slid to the ground, neon bubble jacket seeming to glow under the floodlights. I followed her up the steps to the small porch where a split-log bench sat overlooking what my ears told me was a small creek.

"You can't see it right now," Donna said as she punched in her Realtor code, "but there's a small arched bridge back there over the water. Very tranquil."

"Why are the owners renting?" I asked as I got my first look at the great room. It was typical A-frame style, with a row of ceiling fans suspended from exposed beams overhead. A massive river-stone fireplace sat front and center between two built-in bookshelves. The L-shaped couch was a deep chocolate color, with oversized ottomans on either end and accented with cream-colored pillows artistically arranged. A Native American woven rug covered the oak floor, giving the grand space a homey feel.

"Death in the family. The mother had cancer, and this was her dream home. Her husband built it for her with his own two hands. He doesn't want to live here anymore but couldn't bear parting with it either, so I suggested renting. Their kids grew up here, and they all want someone who'll take care of it."

The sad story tugged at my heartstrings. This house had known love and loss, just like me. The kitchen was even more glorious. I ran my hand over soapstone countertops, the cherry stained cabinets, the gas stove, and wall oven. It wasn't a Viking like the stove at Lizzy's house, but what it lacked in modern upgrades, it more than made up for in charm. The country-style sink was a chef's fondest dream, with a basin large enough to fill the largest pot with water and a side section for peeling vegetables.

We walked through the master bedroom done up with rich burgundy fabrics. Handwoven rag rugs lay in front of the mirrored dresser and in front of each nightstand. The master bath had a pedestal sink and separate vanity and came equipped with a claw-footed tub and a more modern shower stall, perfect for both lingering and efficiency, depending on one's mood.

The two smaller bedrooms were unfurnished and painted more neutral colors, a light chicory and a sage green. Either would work well for an office, but the green room also had a built-in window seat. Another full bath fit in a tiny nook in between the two.

I went back into the main room and took it all in, trying to smell Italian scents coming from the kitchen with Dean Martin crooning from my iPod and Roofus snoring in front of the fireplace. The vision came all too easily. What I couldn't see here was Jones.

"It's not officially on the market until next week, but it'll get snapped up quick." Donna prodded. "And once the market turns around, they might let it go for a bargain price to the right person."

"I have to talk to Jones about it first." It was one thing to stalk out in a snit, quite another to move out without a real conversation. "Can I bring him back to see it, maybe tomorrow in the daylight?"

"Of course. You're all dolled up, and I've got a sitter. We should go out. You want to head to Judy's? It's karaoke night with dollar shots. I can always call Steve to drive us home later."

I grimaced at the mention of karaoke, but a few shots wouldn't go amiss. I gave one last look to the sweet little house that might soon be my home. I needed a place like this, the security it represented. Maybe Kaylee would like to come visit me here. "That sounds like the best plan I've heard all day."

Classic Greek Chicken Salad With Blue Cheese Dressing

You'll need:
10 oz assorted salad greens
1 cup ripe Greek olives
3 plum tomatoes, cut into wedges
1/2 cup thinly sliced red onion
1/2 medium cucumber, peeled, cut into wedges
1 cooked boneless, skinless chicken breast, cut into strips

Dressing:
1 pint mayonnaise (start with 1/2 and add as needed)
1/4 cup blue cheese, crumbled
1/4 cup white vinegar
2 cloves garlic, minced
Dash of cayenne pepper and Worcestershire
1 cup sour cream
2 teaspoons sugar

Dice veggies and chicken. In separate bowl, mix the dressing until it reaches desired consistency. Toss into salad until all ingredients are evenly coated.

**Andy's note: Blue cheese adds a rich element to any salad, and the tartness combined with the creaminess of the dressing is just dynamite. Salad greens have never been so much fun!

CHAPTER FIVE

———

Judy's Bar and Grill was technically situated outside of the town limits. Located on top of a hill, the bar didn't look like much from the outside. Just another run-of-the-mill, weather-beaten barn, really. But the inside had been completely revamped with colored lights, a gleaming dance floor, and a horseshoe-shaped bar that served the best cocktails this side of Miami Beach, at half the price. When the owner, Judy DuBois, had bought the place a few years back, no one had thought she could make such a modern hot spot a stone's throw from Beaverton, but she'd proven them all wrong. I'd been to the bar a few times and really liked the Cajun woman, both because she was a successful businesswoman and because much like me, the citizens of our small southern town didn't know what to make of her.

"Oh crap," I groused when I spotted the red convertible in the parking lot. It stood out among the dusty pickups and battered sedans driven by the rest of the bar's patrons. And the vanity plate reading Hotstuf demolished any hope I had that it belonged to someone other than Lacey L'Amour. "How did she hear about this place already?"

"She must be plugged in to the town gossip. I know she's all buddy-buddy with Mayor Randal. The two of them were seated together at the chamber of commerce meeting."

Donna had been striding for the door, but I pulled her to a quick stop. "Lacey was at the chamber of commerce meeting? Why didn't you tell me?"

"I just did," Donna pointed out. "She's a new businesswoman after all. Of course she'd be at the meeting. And I didn't know you knew her until just now. What gives?"

"We have an ugly history. She was sleeping with some of the instructors, both male and female, when we were in school together. She never could cook worth spit, so I don't know why she got into the program to begin with. But everyone knew how she always scored top grades. She's all flash and little substance."

Donna whistled low. "Damn, no wonder you're so bitter about her being here."

That wasn't all of it, but I didn't feel like hashing it all out. "Ancient history, but I'd like to steer clear of her, if at all possible."

Unfortunately, that was easier said than done. Seeking out the spotlight was Lacey's forte, and it didn't surprise me to see the French tart up on stage belting out The Divinyls "I Touch Myself." Of course the male population was riveted to her classless performance.

"What'll it be, yous?" Judy, as always, was dressed impeccably in a long-sleeved black dress and a brightly patterned scarf wrapped around her slim waist as a belt. Her perfect white teeth flashed against her flawless ebony skin and ruby-painted lips. Her gold jewelry caught the light as she moved gracefully from table to table. When she reached for an empty glass, I noticed she had little white bird silhouettes painted on her long purple-polished nails.

When Donna had first mentioned coming here, I'd been leaning to the more feminine drinks, something mixed with fruit juice or chocolate and topped with whipped cream, more dessert than drink. My gaze slid to Lacey, and my mouth uttered, "Tequila shooters."

Judy raised an elegant eyebrow as she expertly cut a lemon into wedges. "Rough day, no?"

"And it's not over yet." I nodded and then licked the back of my hand and poured salt on it.

She served me the first drink, and I saluted her with the shot glass. I tipped the glass back and drained it dry.

Dollar shots meant it wasn't the best tequila in the world, but it would take my mind off my multitude of troubles. I winced as I sucked on a lemon wedge.

"I've got the tab." Donna opted for a Barbie shot, which looked like a Creamsicle in a glass.

"No, I can pay my own way." I patted my pockets, checking for cash.

She insisted. "Since I dragged you out tonight."

It was probably a good thing to remember that I was still young and shouldn't be tucked away at five every evening. I wondered if Jones missed me yet. Or if he even remembered I'd left.

"I really liked that little house," I confessed two shots later.

"But?" Donna quirked an eyebrow.

"No buts. It was perfect." I turned my fourth shot glass upside down on the tray Judy provided. "Lizzy's house is perfect too."

"Except that it's *Lizzy's* house," Donna murmured.

"Exactly." I blinked at her. "No one understands me like you do, you know?"

"If you tell me you love me, I'm going to cut your inebriated hide off."

I giggled at her word choice. "You're funny."

She just rolled her eyes.

Since Donna didn't seem interested in my newfound insight, I swiveled in my chair to survey the rest of the room. Lacey's song had ended, and someone new had taken her place onstage, singing some god-awful auto-tuned piece of garbage. I scanned the room and spotted my nemesis seated at a nearby table, surrounded by men.

Including my man.

"Is that Jones?" Donna asked. "What the hell is he doing with the French tart?"

Good damn question.

Lacey laughed and flirted as though she didn't have a care in the world, until her eyes met mine. Then a smug satisfaction slid over her congenial mask. Jones hadn't spotted me yet, the rat.

"So let me get this straight. He can't leave the damn darkroom to talk to me, yet here he is hanging out with my bitter rival. Does that seem right to you?" I was impressed with how calmly I was taking this.

"There has to be an explanation for this," Donna said a minute too late.

I slid off my stool and made for my mark like a trollop-seeking missile.

"Andy?" Donna sounded panicked. "Where are you going?"

But my target was locked. Lacey's phony smile slid back into place as I approached.

"Andrea?" Jones looked up and caught sight of me. To his credit, he didn't appear guilty of doing anything more than talking to Lacey. "What are you doing here?"

"What am I doing here? This is my town. I live here. The better question is, what is she doing here, with you?" I didn't sound drunk, just belligerent. Good, Lacey needed to understand that I wasn't going to go down without a fight.

She dipped her chin and fluttered her eyelashes for her bevy of admirers. "It's a free country, is it, no?"

"No, I mean yes, it is. But that's not my question. Why are you here, in Beaverton?"

"Settle down, Little Bit," Rudy Flannigan grumbled. He was one of Kyle's high school chums. "No need to go gettin' your bloomers in a bunch."

I narrowed my eyes at the hated high school nickname, which always came out sounding like the guys called me "Little Shit." "Mind your own business, Rudy, before I go call your wife and tell her you're out drinking and carousing. Where does she think you are right now anyhow? Working late at the office?" The last part I tagged on for my boyfriend's benefit.

A chair scraped along the floor as Jones got to his feet. "Andrea, let's talk about this outside." He reached for me, but I stepped back, stumbling on an uneven floorboard.

"I am in the middle of a conversation, Malcolm."

Lacey rolled her eyes. "Come now, Andee. Let's, how you say, bury the ax?"

"It's *hatchet*," Winston Marsh corrected helpfully. He had the worst case of halitosis I'd ever encountered, and Lacey actually coughed as he breathed on her.

"Maybe we should go." Donna tugged at my other elbow, trying to pry me away from the gathering throng.

"There's no hatchet. I just want to know what you're doing here in my hometown." Jerking my arm out of Donna's grip, I leaned down to get in Lacey's face. I guess I didn't know my own strength though, because Donna stumbled and would have gone down, except she fell against the back of a nearby patron. He, in turn, dropped his drink over the head of the man sitting behind Lacey, who came up swinging.

Directly at Jones.

"Fight!" Someone yelled a second before the free-for-all started. Chairs scraped against the wooden floor. The sound of angry shouts and breaking glass drowned out the guy singing "Why Don't We Get Drunk" (and screw).

"See what you've done!" Lacey shoved me. "You must always cause trouble."

"Me?" Righteous indignation made me shove her back.

She made a grab for my hair, but I was scrappy, and I ducked out of her hold and sank my shoulder into her stomach. She let out a satisfying *oof* but managed to grab hold of my shirt. It ripped. I staggered, and we went down in a tangle of flailing limbs.

A sudden report from a shotgun overpowered the noise. Judy was on the bar, the double barrels of a sawed-off pointed at the hole in the roof above my head. Anger flashed in her eyes, and the emotion was directed at me. "Take your bad juju up out of my place, yous. Before I call da law."

"Too late!" another male voice called and was drowned out by wailing sirens. "Five-o."

The bar patrons scattered like roaches.

I scanned the remaining faces but saw no sight of Jones. "Malcolm?" I called out.

Lacey scrambled away from me, her hair wild, dress rumpled, eyes ablaze. "You are completely insane!" she panted.

The sheriff strode in, followed by half a dozen deputies.

"What happened?" Kyle was at my side, helping me to my feet.

I didn't answer him, too busy looking at the destruction around me. "Donna? Where are you?"

"Here," she rasped. She'd crawled under a nearby table to keep out of the fray. Her blue eyes were round, but she appeared unhurt.

"You okay?" I asked to makes sure. "Have you seen Jones?"

"I'll live," she muttered.

"Will someone tell me what the hell is going on here?" Kyle yelled.

"She attacked me!" Lacey wailed. The running mascara added to her victim's air.

I lifted my chin in defiance. "What a crock! You shoved me, remember?"

Kyle turned to Judy. "You want to press charges?"

Judy's eyes narrowed, but she shook her head. "No, as long as they agree to pay for the damages."

I nodded, but Lacey wasn't satisfied with that. Thrusting a finger at me, she spat, "She assaulted me! You must arrest her!"

Kyle put his hands on his hips, his expression grim. "I'm taking you both in for disturbing the peace. Maybe some time in jail will cool those hot heads."

He couldn't be serious. "Kyle, you know I wouldn't have just gone off and hit her." Even if she'd deserved it. I'd only been defending myself and staking my claim on Jones. Wasn't my fault if I was better at it than Lacey.

He moved in closer and lowered his voice. "What I know is that you smell like a distillery and were caught up in a bar brawl. You need time to dry out. Now come along peaceably so I don't have to arrest you. I don't want word of this getting back to your grandfather. Or to Kaylee's mom."

My shoulders slumped as the alcohol-induced fog lifted. He was right. By morning the entire town would hear that Andy Buckland had been drinking and mixing it up at Judy's. It would be bad for my reputation both professionally and on a personal level if there was an official arrest to boot. With his hand wrapped around my arm, Kyle led me out of the bar, Donna trailing in our wake.

"Donna, I'm going to call your husband to come pick you up," Kyle said. "If you've been drinking, don't get behind the wheel."

"I won't," Donna was quick to reassure him. "Andy, do you want me to call your grandfather?"

"No." I sucked in a deep lungful of frosty night air to help clear my head. "But next time when I say I don't want to go out, do me a favor and listen."

* * *

The drunk tank at the county jail smelled of urine and bile and other foul odors I didn't want to think about. I sat with my back to the wall, drew my knees up, and rested my head in my hands. Noises echoed off the painted cinderblock walls. Somewhere out front a television blared a late-night infomercial at ear-splitting decibels. Someone was snoring like a bear with a head cold in the next cell over. Someone on the other end of the hall was crying. The dull murmur of sober voices and the angry shouts of the inebriated all echoed in a depressing cacophony. The florescent lights overhead hummed and made my eyes hurt. I lowered my lids and tried not to feel too sorry for myself.

On the plus side, at least Lacey wasn't anywhere in sight. Either someone had bailed her out or Kyle had been wise enough to keep the two of us apart. What was it about her that got under my skin and gave me a rash?

Time dragged by like a hunter towing a ten-point buck, but eventually footsteps came down the hall. I shielded my eyes and looked up. "Aw, crap."

"Lovely seeing you too, Andrea." Jones's expression gave nothing away. "Although I must say you've looked better."

"Where the hell did you go?"

"He was there?" Kyle had come up behind him.

Frigging fantastic. They already had me at a disadvantage, what with my being incarcerated and all, but I didn't want Jones literally looking down on me while he was figuratively looking down on me. I rose, and the room spun slightly. Damn it, I didn't think I was still drunk, but then my stomach rolled as though it had gone out to sea without me.

Jones shouted something as I slid back down to my seated position, and a moment later he and Kyle were by my side.

"Andrea, look at me," Jones prompted, peeling my eyelids up.

I tried to swat his hands away and failed miserably. "I'm fine, just buzzed."

"Did you hit your head?" The man was relentless.

Had I? I couldn't remember and told him so.

"She seemed all right when I brought her in," Kyle told him. "Just drunk and pissed off."

"She needs medical attention." Jones's energy shifted, and his voice grew lower, more sinister. "You left her in here by herself with a possible head injury for three hours, Sheriff?"

"I didn't know she was hurt!" Kyle put his hands up as though warning Jones off.

"Call an ambulance," Jones barked.

"No," I snapped, aware enough to know that I didn't need an ambulance so much as a glass of water. "You can take me to the hospital, but no ambulance."

I was, of course, ignored and was wheeled out of my jail cell on a stretcher.

"I didn't know," Kyle repeated to the EMTs, to his deputies, to anyone who would listen. I couldn't be sure, but I thought he looked ready to cry. "I didn't know she'd hit her head. Will she be all right?"

"I'll be fine," I reassured him, though I'm not sure why I bothered. He had tossed my carcass in jail and called Jones, when he knew I didn't want that.

For his part, Jones stayed silent, gripping my hand as I was loaded into the ambulance. I closed my eyes so the motion from the vehicle wouldn't make me lose my lunch. Luckily, the community hospital wasn't far, and I managed to keep everything down.

I was examined and told I had a slight concussion, which accounted for the headache more than the tequila did. After being hooked up to a banana bag and told not to sleep for more than an hour at a time for the next twenty-four hours, I was left face-to-face with one very pissed-off boyfriend.

"What were you doing there?" I asked him.

"Working," Jones said. "Or at least I was until you decided to intervene."

"Working?" It was probably the head injury, but that made no sense. "You were working when I left."

He sighed. "I was on a case, Andrea. You know I don't frequent bars unless I have a reason."

"And how come you left without me?"

"I didn't leave. I hid until after the sheriff took you away so I could offer to pay for the damages to the bar. One of us had to stay free to post bail." He ran a hand through his hair, looking exhausted. "This has been an expensive night. Probably more trouble than the case is worth."

Shame burned through me. Jones wasn't a barfly, and he didn't hook up with random women. He was committed to me and to our relationship. So why hadn't I trusted him?

Because he'd been with Lacey, and seeing it had made me nuts.

"I can explain," I began, but he shook his head.

Threading his fingers through mine, he murmured, "Later. When you're up to your fighting weight."

I blew out a breath, relieved that if he was planning on dumping me, at least he wasn't going to break up with my sorry carcass in the ER. I felt pathetic enough. I didn't need the old heave-ho while lying on a gurney in ripped and dirty clothes, fresh from county lockup.

There was a commotion out front, lots of feet moving at a brisk clip, and the high, excited murmur of voices. Jones frowned, dark eyebrows meeting above his sharp blade of a nose.

I struggled until I made it upright. "What's going on out there?" It was a hospital after all, but most of the emergencies in Beaverton were of the drunk and disorderly type, with the occasional car accident or heart attack thrown in. Whatever had happened sent a massive amount of people into the emergency room at once, long after last call.

"I'm not certain." Jones let go of my hand and moved toward the privacy curtain. He pulled it back about a foot. From my position, I couldn't see anything, though the voices were drawing closer.

"Third-degree burns..." someone said.

Curiosity blotted out the intense pain in my head, and I slid off the gurney in an ungraceful heap just as Jones strode out into the hallway, disappearing quickly in the commotion.

"Malcolm?" I called just as he shouted, "Eugene!"

Pops was here? I shoved aside the curtain to face the chaos. There were people everywhere, gurneys rolling by, and medical staff cutting off clothing. I scanned frantically for Pops but didn't have the advantage of Jones's height.

Then he was back, dragging Pops in his wake. For his part, my grandfather looked singed around the edges, his clothing covered with what looked and smelled like ash. I threw myself at him, and he hugged me tightly.

"What happened?" I asked. "Why are there so many people here? And where's Aunt Cecily?"

"Sshh, Andy girl. She's fine." He gestured down the hallway, toward the waiting area. "She's sitting with Joe Humphries. It seems Ruth didn't make it out."

A cold chill skittered through me, and I shivered, which only made the dull ache in my head throb. "Out of where? Pops, what happened?"

My grandfather met my gaze, his expression grave. "There was another fire. This time at the seniors' facility. And now there's a body count."

Antipasto Platter

Options (mix and match to your tastes):

Jarred marinated artichoke hearts
Water crackers
Camembert cheese
Sliced tomatoes marinated in Italian dressing
Havarti dill cheese
Thinly sliced Genoa salami
Fresh crusty Italian bread/baguette
Prosciutto
Chunks of fresh cantaloupe or honeydew
Jarred roasted red and yellow peppers
Roasted red pepper or garlic hummus
Pita bread
Toasted rosemary focaccia
Sardines
Olives, black and green
Capers
Sweet pickles
Pepperoni
Smoked turkey breast
Roasted pine nuts/almonds/cashews
Dried or fresh figs/dates in season
Green tomato relish
Cold shrimp
Grilled deli vegetables
Marinated fresh buffalo mozzarella

**Andy's note: I always follow the two-by-two rule—2 meats, 2 cheeses, 2 grains, and 2 veggies/fruit. Mix and match to see what you'll come up with. Play with in-season delicacies, or do regional themes. The sky's the limit! Try a milder meat like smoked turkey combined with Genoa salami, or fresh figs with marinated veggies. Color is the name of the game. Remember, this is just your opening act, so save room for the main event!

CHAPTER SIX

———

"Thank you for letting them come home with us," I said to Jones as I eased myself down on the white couch. Pops and Aunt Cecily had taken the master suite, the only one of the three bedrooms that actually had a bed in it.

He shrugged as he crouched beside me. "They're your family. And it's not like either of us will be doing much sleeping over the next twenty-two hours."

My grimace had nothing to do with pain. "Still, you shouldn't have to stay up the entire time."

He gave me a dark-blue look. "Andrea, someone has to check in on you."

I could tell from his tone that he meant more than just the concussion. "Would you shut the curtains, please? The sea of white is making my head throb."

Jones glowered at me but then rose and moved toward the windows. I sighed in relief as dimness filled the space, and snuggled under the red afghan Lizzy had given her brother for Christmas.

"Try to rest. I'll wake you in an hour." He moved quietly through the room toward the kitchen. I heard the scrape of the pantry door, then water running in the sink. Some more shuffling and a few moments later, the enticing scent of coffee.

Though I was sore and exhausted, I couldn't sleep, seeing the mad press in the emergency room. Pops telling us that there had been another fire and that this time, people had died. Was it arson again or just an accident? And why was I focusing on that instead of my own personal multitude of issues?

I cracked an eyelid. Rochelle. This all stemmed back to me finding out about Jones meeting with his ex. That he wouldn't make plans with me to move forward with our lives. I told the man everything and was getting a little tired of his man-of-mystery shtick. We'd been together for almost a year, and yet I still didn't know much more than I had in the beginning.

Slowly, I sat, waiting for the wave of nausea to pass by. When it finally did, I got to my feet, slung the blanket around my shoulders like a shroud, and shuffled into the kitchen to face the music.

Jones was staring into his coffee mug, seemingly lost in thought. I cleared my throat, and his eyes shot up. "Andrea? What's wrong? Can I get you anything?"

He was already on his feet, a look of medical speculation in his eye.

"I can't sleep." I moved to the fridge and extracted a bottle of water. Even though the IV full of fluids had kept me from shriveling up like a grape left in the sun, my throat had gone dry.

I settled in across from him at the breakfast nook and opened my water.

"Would you like some tea?" he asked as though I were a stranger stopping by instead of the woman he'd been living with for nine months.

I met and held his gaze. "What I'd like is some honesty between us."

Jones frowned, the lines creasing his handsome face, making him even more attractive. "What do you mean?"

Physically I was in no condition for this conversation, and emotionally I wasn't much better. Was there any way to admit to your current flame that you'd spied on him without looking like a crazy stalker in the making? Probably not, so I just went for it. "First of all, I know I acted like a lunatic last night, and I'm sorry."

He sat beside me. "All right. Can you tell me why you acted like a lunatic, as you so succinctly phrased it?"

I loved when he used words like succinctly, or at least I usually did. At the moment though, I was too busy gathering my courage. "I know you met up with your ex."

"Do you now." Jones raised a brow. "And may I ask how you came by this knowledge?"

I frowned, and even that small working of muscles made my headache worse. "It's not important."

Jones set down the mug he'd been holding and moved toward me. "What happened to honesty? You don't think the fact that you're spying on me is important?"

"I wasn't spying."

He crossed his arms over his chest.

I blew out a sigh. "Okay, I was sort of spying."

He didn't smile, but I could tell from the glint in his eyes that he wanted to. Good thing somebody was enjoying this conversation. He simply nodded and murmured, "Go on."

"The important thing is that I felt the need to spy because you haven't been telling me important stuff."

One jet eyebrow went up. "And what sort of 'stuff' would you like me to tell you, Andrea?"

Normally I loved the way he said my name, his New Zealand accent buttering the syllables so they seared me to a perfect temperature. But his tone had turned frigid.

Damn it, I was no good at this adult relationship crap. Jones was usually so easy going. He'd been a rock over the past several months, supporting me unconditionally, being there when I needed him. Sure, we'd squabbled a bit, but this was different. There was some sort of chasm between us, filled with all sorts of hidden secrets.

My head pounded, and I sank onto a barstool. It took all my willpower to look into his vivid blue eyes. "I'm sorry. I know I'm acting crazy, but I don't know what to do to fix this."

He took a step closer, close enough to touch me. I wished he would, but he didn't. Instead he spoke softly. "Tell me what's really going on."

For no real reason, that made me angry. "You know something? I tell you everything. Every dirty little detail, no matter how stupid or insignificant, or how much it could affect someone else. You've helped me clean out my family's home, met my ex and my daughter. I share everything with you, and you just shut me out."

"You know I can't talk about my clients," he began, but I cut him off.

"I know that. It's not just about work. You skulk down into your darkroom and leave me up here to my own devices all the time. And that's a disaster in the making, because then I have time to drive myself crazy speculating at why you're hiding down there. I really don't want to be one of those needy girlfriends, and I'm trying to support you, but it's more than that, and you know it. You dodge me every time I bring up moving out, and I feel as if you're avoiding me."

He blinked, clearly surprised I was so upset. His mouth opened and then closed again. He shook his head and ran a hand through his hair. "I don't know what to say."

He looked so lost, so completely out of his depth, that I reached for his hand. "You've been sidestepping any talk about what happens next."

He ran a hand through his hair and then down his stubble-covered chin. "Because I don't know, Andrea. I don't know what comes next. And I don't know what topics are open for discussion."

"What do you mean?"

He gave me an exasperated look. "You get upset when I talk about Lizzy or when I talk about my father or my ex. You've been high strung ever since Christmas."

I read between the lines. "You mean since Kaylee came to town."

He didn't nod. He didn't need to, because all of a sudden, the picture clicked into focus.

If my head didn't hurt like the devil, I would have thunked it against the quartz countertop. "You haven't wanted to upset me, so you've been keeping it all to yourself."

He smiled faintly. "I'm no better at this relationship business than you are, Andrea."

I'd forgotten that. The only real long-term relationship he'd had before me was with Rochelle, and that had been a soul-shredding disaster. *So here comes Andy and her big old bag of crazy triggers. The poor man must feel like he was walking on eggshells with me.* I blew out an enormous sigh, mingled with regret and relief. "Jones, I'm one-quarter Italian. I get as worked up over a hangnail as I do the quarterly reports. Passion and showmanship—it's the Rossetti way. I thought you liked that about me."

"I do," he insisted, and his eyes were intense. "I love that I always know what you're feeling. I simply don't want to overload you when you're already wound so tightly."

I squeezed his hand. He had such beautifully masculine hands, strength and elegance all at once. "See, that's one of the benefits of having a passionate nature. I have these mini-eruptions all the time, so I'm not gonna pull a Krakatoa on you. I can handle more stress than your average crazypants. What I can't handle is you dodging me or keeping things from me for my own good. Got it?"

He smiled, then reached out to steady me as I listed too far to the right. "You're about to fall off that stool. How about I promise we talk after you're fully recovered?"

I made a face, partly from my throbbing cranium and partly from his avoidance. "Malcolm…"

His hands were warm on my arm. "I'm not dodging—I'm choosing my moment."

Okay, well, I was in pain and having a hard time holding a thought. Still, one side of my family tree was Scotts-Irish ornery, and the other was related to Aunt Cecily. I didn't know the meaning of the word quit. "I can handle it now."

Jones grinned down at me. "I know you can, but I can't. Let me tend to you. Twenty-four hours, and then we'll talk. "

I gave him my best Evil-Eye glare, which only made his grin spread. I really must have looked as though I was about to face-plant onto Lizzy's gorgeous tile floor. "Have it your way, then."

Jones escorted me to the couch, helped ease me into the most comfortable position I could manage, and then covered me with a black-and-white blanket.

"Thank you," he said softly, as though allowing him to care for me was a huge inconvenience on my part.

"Anytime," I mumbled as I drifted into a light doze.

* * *

It was a miserable twenty-four hours. The headache proved relentless, and every time I managed to escape into sleep, someone was shaking me awake. Jones took the first eight hours, but his hovering drove me nuts, so after I insisted I was well looked after, he left to follow up on one of his cases. I worried about him driving, as he was operating on zero sleep, but he promised he wasn't going far.

At the fourteen-hour mark I gave up on the mini-naps and escaped into the master bath for a long soak in the tub and almost drowned when I fell asleep, cocooned in warm water. I surfaced, sputtering and swearing, completely waterlogged and as uppity as a wet cat.

"Everything all right, Andy girl?" Pops knocked on the bathroom door.

"Yes," I called, sounding testy even in monosyllables.

"Do you need me to get you anything?" Pops was still there, obviously not taking the hint. "Or maybe do anything for you?"

"No, thank you," I called. The light hurt my eyes, and I covered them with my hands, blocking out the gleaming white bathroom.

A pause and then, "You sure 'bout that?"

I took a deep breath, inhaling the scent of garlic and oregano drifting under the crack in the door to mix with the aroma of lavender bubble bath. Aunt Cecily had taken over the kitchen. As much as I loved her cooking, at the moment with my head splitting like a ripe melon, the thought of food made me want to gag. I closed my eyes, feeling that drowning sensation all over again, only this time I was suffocating from the crush of well-meaning relations.

Then I recalled the tragedy of the retirement home fire. Tending to me was a good distraction for my older relatives, even if they were driving me up the freaking wall. "Be out in a few, Pops," I called.

"I'm gonna walk Roofus. Call Cecily if you need anything."

I breathed a sigh of relief as his footsteps shuffled off to go pester the dog. Roofus was only getting lazier as he aged, and he detested the cold, so Pops had his work cut out for him. After climbing from the tub, I dried off and swathed myself in Jones's black fleece robe. I pulled the stopper on the tub and then opened the window to let the arctic air break up the cloying scents in the room.

"Come on, boy," I heard Pops say from the other side of the house. He clapped then whistled. "Don't you want to go out?"

I wondered how Roofus would have responded if he could talk. "Kiss off, old timer," maybe. Or more succinct, "No thanks, but if you want to, go nuts." Or maybe if, like me, he would have endured it because that's what you did for family

I stood there as long as I could stand it, concussed and feeling both sick and grateful at the same time. Grateful that I had family who cared enough to smother me with devotion. If I had real people clothes on, I would have slithered right out of the window and run screaming into the purpling twilight.

The flash of headlights as a vehicle crested the hill burned into my brain like acid. I hissed like a vampire caught by a random shaft of sunlight and ducked back into the shadows. Who the heck was that? My heart leapt as I thought of the arsonist. Would he toss a Molotov cocktail through the window?

Breaks sounded, and then a car door slammed. My heart raced, and I stood frozen to the spot.

"Hey there, Miz Lizzy," Pops called out in greeting, and I breathed a sigh of relief, cursing my overactive imagination.

"Hi there, Mr. Buckland." Jones's sister was sweet as cannoli filling to pretty much anyone who wasn't me. Her saccharine tone made my eye twitch, which made my head hurt all the more. "I'm so sorry to hear about what happened at your building."

Since I'd recently sworn off eavesdropping, I shut the window and shuffled into the bedroom. Aunt Cecily had made up the bed with precise hospital corners, the kind that were nice to look at but made sleep impossible, unless you were used to being swaddled in a straitjacket.

Jones still hadn't returned from his latest job. I hoped Lizzy wouldn't stick around too long waiting for him, as I didn't want to be trapped in the bedroom all night.

"Of frigging course she showed up," I grumbled to myself. Because I was already feeling like crap, Lizzy had to come rub my nose in it. Not that she was actively *doing* anything to me at the moment, but then again, her presence had a habit of getting my dander up, as Nana used to say.

"You girls have always rubbed each other the wrong way," Nana had told me one day when I'd been complaining to her about how Lizzy had superglued my locker shut. "Some people are oil and water together and just shouldn't mix."

"Like Pops and Aunt Cecily," I'd said.

Nana had rolled her eyes heavenward. "Those two are a whole different kettle of fish."

I smiled at the memory, then frowned as I wondered if Nana had seen the spark between her older sister and her husband of forty years even then. I sure as hell hadn't known their bickering was anything other than two stubborn people who were forced together on a regular basis. In reality, their sniping had been based in their mutual attraction, a thought that still made my lip curl up in revulsion.

Someone knocked on the bedroom door. "Andy?"

"Yeah?" I called out, then frowned when Lizzy pushed open the door. Technically this was her bedroom, the one she would share with my baby daddy whenever the hell they got around to tying the knot. The fact that I was hanging out in my bathrobe only added another level of awkwardness to the mix.

Lizzy entered the room and shut the door behind her, though she didn't come any closer. "How are you feeling?"

"Like crap on toast," I griped. Pulling punches wasn't my style. "What's up?"

"I wanted to talk to you about my dad."

"Oh?" I said, surprised. "Why?"

She shook her head and lowered her voice until it was barely audible. "Not here. Will you be at the pasta shop tomorrow?"

"Yeah," I said slowly. Was she trying to set me up for something? Damn it, I couldn't think. My thoughts were too insubstantial. We were adults now, and the childhood pranks and resentment were behind us. Well, mostly. "Lizzy, is everything all right? With your dad, I mean?"

I hoped Mr. Tillman hadn't received any bad news. God, how would Jones cope if his estranged father had been diagnosed with a terminal illness? My former nemesis looked more discomposed than I'd ever seen her, her eyes darting to the window, back literally against the wall. Either she was a great actress, or she was seriously freaked out. Not a good sign.

"No." She spoke softly, and her eyes filled. "I think my dad might be the arsonist."

Parmesan Pasta Salad

You'll need:
8 oz corkscrew pasta, cooked until al dente
10 oz fresh spinach, washed, dried, and torn into small
pieces
8 oz mozzarella cheese, cubed
8 oz ham, cubed
4 oz green chilies, chopped and drained

For the Parmesan dressing:
1 egg
1 cup extra virgin olive oil
1/2 cup grated Parmesan cheese
1 teaspoon pepper
1/4 teaspoon cloves
1/4 cup white wine vinegar
1 teaspoon salt
2 minced garlic cloves

Place egg in blender, and blend 5 seconds.

With blender running slowly, add extra virgin olive oil until thickened. Add and blend until smooth. Mix with remaining dressing ingredients, then toss with salad and chill. Sprinkle with additional Parmesan cheese, and serve.

**Andy's note: A friend of mine from culinary school grew up with this dish in her family's restaurant, and it's a crowd pleaser. For the record, she didn't like Lacey L'Amour either.

CHAPTER SEVEN

———

"Lizzy thinks her father might be setting the fires?" Donna screeched.

"Sssh," I shushed her, glad I'd had the forethought to talk to her in the car, where we couldn't be overheard. My head still hurt, though it didn't feel about to split open like an overripe melon as much as it had the day before. The incredulous note in her voice was like a fork scraping over bone china though. "Yes, and you can't tell Steven. Lizzy doesn't want anyone to know."

"Are you sure she isn't just messing with you?" Donna raised a brow. "I mean, why tell you and not tell her fiancé or her brother, who could, you know, do something about it?"

I'd asked Lizzy the very same questions and repeated what she'd told me to Donna. "Kyle's the sheriff. He'd investigate, and if he found something linking Mr. Tillman to the fires, he'd have to act on it. Just like if you told Steven something of a criminal nature, especially if people died because of it."

Donna nodded as though accepting the inherent wisdom in that reasoning. "She still could have told her brother though."

I shifted in my seat to look at her more closely. "When I mentioned that to her, she shut me down quick. I've been mulling over the why of it all night. The only thing I could come up with was that she doesn't want to turn Jones against his father for good. If he found out his father was an arsonist, he just might turn his back on the man forever."

Donna shook her head. "It still doesn't make sense though, Andy. Lizzy doesn't even like you, so why would she trust you with such a huge secret?"

"There's no one else. She doesn't have any friends she could trust with this sort of thing—they'd all go blabbing it around town. Even though Lizzy and I aren't besties, she knows me. I would do anything to protect Jones. If news that his father is a suspected arsonist spreads around town, it'll ruin the whole family's reputation."

"Not like it could take another blow," Donna agreed. "So is that the only reason?"

"Well that, and she knows I'd believe her."

Donna raised a brow. "And do you?"

I considered it for a moment. "It makes sense. I told you about how we found him in the woods at Christmas, right? All drunk and crazy, wielding a shotgun. I barely recognized him. He was a far cry from a respectable business man."

Donna snorted. "Sounds like half the population of the town, if you ask me."

"This is serious. What if he really is setting these fires? What do I do?"

"Does she have any proof?" Donna drummed her fingers on the steering wheel.

"Not that she mentioned, but Pops and Aunt Cecily were loitering outside the door, so she didn't really get into it. She's coming by the pasta shop in a little bit to talk to me."

Donna's even, white teeth sank into her lower lip. "If she asks you to do something crazy, promise you'll call me first."

I rolled my eyes and then wished I hadn't. "So you can do it with me? Seriously, Donna, we're turning into Beaverton's own modern-day Lucy and Ethel."

She pointed an accusing pink-polished fingernail at me. "Don't look at me—you're the one who started a bar fight."

"Well, you're the one who took me out drinking. You know I'm banned from Judy's for life? What kind of an example is that to set for my kid?" Never mind where would I go when I needed a stiff drink?

"Do as I say, not as I do," Donna quipped. "Seriously though, don't let Lizzy get you in over your head."

I nodded and then regretted it when the residual ache in my cranium gave a noticeable pang. "Trust me, Donna. I've got it handled. I'll call you later."

I slid out of her car and waved as she drove off. The morning was clear and crisp. Across the street I saw Lacey L'Amour fussing with a grand-opening banner in her front window. When she saw me, she stuck her pert little nose in the air and flounced away. I shrugged and headed into my own restaurant, trusting that the people of Beaverton would see right through all her phony glitz and she'd be out of business in a month.

"Good morning, Andy." Mimi greeted me with a huge smile and a stack of receipts. "Would you like to go over the sales from yesterday?"

"A little later. Thanks for handling the place all alone yesterday. I hope it wasn't too much for you."

"Not a problem. Business was sort of slow." Mimi's smile was a little too bright. It was the kind of expression someone wore when she had bad news and thought delivering it in a positive way would lessen the impact. For the record, that never worked.

I blew out a sigh. "Okay, Mimi, you might as well tell me what happened."

She cringed. "The health inspector stopped in."

"Theo?" Theodor Randolph, our county health inspector, was as old as the hills. "Did he give us a score? What was it?"

She winced. "An 89.9."

My eyes rounded in horror. "He gave us a B? The Bowtie Angel has never once gotten a B. Not in fifty-two years." When word of this got out, I'd be the subject of gossip for months. Never mind what Aunt Cecily would do. Not even a month into running the pasta shop on my own, and I'd already tarnished her pristine sanitation record. "What went wrong?"

Mimi wrung her hands. "I'm sorry. He caught me at a bad moment. The walk-in was open, and the temperature was up too high. Not dangerous or anything. We didn't lose any inventory. I don't know what happened. I swear I'd shut and latched it, but the latch was broken, and it was hanging open. I had to prop a chair against it to keep it shut. Plus, the trash bag broke when I took it out of the can, so I was in the middle of cleaning up garbage when he showed up. He said he understood, that those things happened, but he still penalized us for it."

"That's a lot of crappy luck all at once." I hung up my coat and purse and sidled back to the walk-in refrigerator and bent down to examine the handle. It looked fine to me, just as it had the last time I'd used it. I moved the ladder-back chair Mimi had propped against it, and sure enough, the door swung open. "Son of a gun, it's busted, all right. I'll run to the hardware store and get a padlock to keep in place until we can get it repaired. No idea how that could have happened?"

Mimi shook her head. "It was fine in the morning, caught and held as always."

"And no one else was back here? Did we get any deliveries?" I swore on my best spaghetti pot that if Druggie Don had brought over tomatoes while he was high and busted my walk-in without saying anything, I'd take it out of his hash-smoking hide.

Mimi's forehead creased as she thought back. "No deliveries. Kaylee came in after school and did some dishes. Oh, and that French lady stopped by."

I'd been reaching for my apron but froze midmotion. "French lady?"

Mimi smiled. "Yes, Lacey L'Amour. She offered me a job in her restaurant, as a pastry chef. I declined of course." She said this last in a rush and stared worriedly at me.

Damn, damn, damn. Bypassing Mimi, I strode for the pantry, took down the box of garbage bags, and took the next one out. "That sabotaging, sous-chef-stealing skank."

"What?" Mimi had followed me in. "What's wrong."

I showed her the small slit someone had cut in the next trash bag, and the one after that. "Mimi, did you leave her alone back here? Tell me everything that she said and did, word for word."

"No." Then Mimi scowled, the expression so dark on her delicate features. "She said she wanted to make sure your grandfather and aunt were all right after the fire. I told her that yes, they were fine and staying with you for now. I had to bring some fresh pasta out front, and she said she'd let herself out."

Which she had, but only after she'd submarined my restaurant. I wondered if she'd known about the health inspection. Probably. Theo was a gossipmonger who thought way too much of his own importance, and if he'd been in town to inspect her froufrou place, he'd have mentioned he was going to pop in to the Bowtie Angel next.

I pushed up my sleeves and squared my shoulders. "This," I told Mimi, "means war."

* * *

Kaylee arrived again after school. "Hey, I heard about your bar brawl. Pretty boss there."

I was in the middle of a pan of meatballs I'd been preparing for a football party order, but I turned away for a split second to look at her. She looked so much like a younger version of me, though there was a good bit of Kyle in her too. "It wasn't exactly a brawl."

She shrugged as though she didn't give a fig one way or the other. "What can I do?"

I put the pan of meatballs in the oven to keep warm and then turned to face her. "Want to learn my crowd-pleasing Sweet 'N Tangy meatball recipe?"

She made a derisive noise. "Whatever."

Every time she said that word was like someone took a meat skewer to my left ventricle. Still, I wasn't about to quit on her yet. Teenagers were tough, and I had yet to find a gap that couldn't be bridged by quality food.

I clapped my hands and rubbed them together. "Okay, here's what we'll need."

She made an incredulous face as I rattled off the ingredients for my secret sauce, but went to the pantry and collected the assorted items. Soon I had her whisking a bubbling pot of gook on the stovetop while I retrieved the meatballs.

"The meatballs are actually the most time-consuming part, so if you want to make this without all the work, use the frozen kind."

One pierced eyebrow lifted. "You're a professional chef, and you're telling me to use prepackaged food?"

I shrugged. "Not always. Obviously, I wouldn't do that for the business, but if you want to make a fast hot dish and don't have the time, it's an option. Jones loves them either way."

"He's hot." Kaylee grinned at me.

I grinned back. "Yeah, he is. And the accent just makes him hotter."

She looked away, and I saw her frown. I touched her shoulder and asked, "What's wrong?"

She shrugged me off. "Nothing."

Damn, and I thought we'd been bonding over my boyfriend's supersexiness. "Kaylee—"

Before I could continue, she slammed her whisk down and stomped off to the bathroom. Mimi looked up from where she was preparing tortellini and offered me a faint smile.

"What did I say?" I asked her.

Mimi shrugged. "I do not know."

"Was she like this yesterday?" I asked, half afraid of the answer.

Mimi spooned more cheese mixture into the dough. "No, she was quite helpful."

So it was me. I took the sauce off the heat and covered it. The meatballs could wait. My daughter shouldn't have to.

I followed her into the restroom. The first two stalls were open, but I saw her pink-and-black high-tops under the third. "Kaylee, what's wrong?"

"Go away," she sniffled.

I leaned against the wall. "Not happening, kid."

"I'm not your kid," she mumbled in a resentful tone.

She was, but telling her so didn't seem wise. I had a sudden thought—was this how Jones felt with me, worried that every little thing would set me off? I hoped not, because the habit was getting old, fast. "Fine, you're not my kid, but you're still *a* kid. Let's pretend I'm just an average part-time employer, and then you can tell me why you stormed out of my kitchen when we were in the middle of something."

There was silence, followed by a sniffle. Then the squeal of the stall door as she poked her head out and glared at me. "I don't like you."

I gave her a tight smile, ignoring the pain in my heart. "Noted."

She let out a puff of air. "How can you just take that? I'm mean to you, so why would you want to be around me?"

Because I'm a glutton for punishment. Thankfully, I didn't say that out loud. "Believe it or not, we have a lot in common."

She gave me a condescending look that only a teenage girl could pull off. It was a perfect blend of "Yeah right" and "You wish, loser."

"We do," I insisted. "We have lots of people in common. Aunt Cecily, Pops, Kyle, Lizzy, Jones, Mimi. Even Roofus. That's all common ground."

She appeared to grudgingly give in to my logic and mumbled, "What else?"

"This place." I waved a hand around.

"A bathroom?" she sneered.

"No, smartass, the Bowtie Angel. Cooking is in our blood. Why else would you have come here yesterday to do dishes when no one was making you?"

"Because I want to get paid."

I didn't buy it for a minute. "Admit it—you like being here."

Slowly, she nodded. "I do."

"I always did too. It's part of our family legacy. Lot of calories came out of that kitchen, and with any luck, there will be truckloads more for years to come. Then there's our taste in men."

She actually blushed at that, and I grinned. "Yeah, admit it. I've got great taste in men. First your dad and then Jones. Man, I bagged the two hottest bachelors in the county." I mock-buffed my nails on my apron.

She wrinkled her pert little nose. I sent up a silent prayer that she would never be moved to pierce it. "Ew, don't say things like that about my dad."

I wondered what took Kyle off limits but made Jones fair game. Probably the whole blood-relation thing. This was North Carolina, but still…ick. "You have to admit I have stellar taste in men."

She bit her lip and looked down.

I felt as though were on the verge of something and thought maybe a heaping dose of honesty might add to our connection. "I know I have no right to call myself your mother, because I wasn't there for you the way your mom was. I'm not looking to replace her. But I think with time you'll realize you have room in your life for both of us. She knows that. That's why she moved here, for you to get to know your roots. We both want what's best for you, and that isn't going to change. It's fine if you're mad at me, if you don't like me. Because I'll like you, no matter what. Got it?"

She nodded, and I turned to leave her alone to digest my words for a few. Eventually she'd come out, attitude firmly in place, distain oozing from every pore. I'd been the same way at her age. My disdain had been for Beaverton and my own mother, who'd been a total letdown and had eventually taken the coward's way out, ending her own pain and leaving me to cope. At least Kaylee wouldn't have to deal with that.

I returned to the kitchen and washed my hands, thinking about my daughter. Her extra-crunchy exterior hid her soft and tender heart, an organ that was already badly bruised. It was scary how much we had in common. Lord, was she my daughter or my clone?

After finishing the meatballs, I headed out into the dining area. The midafternoon lull had settled, and I took the time to wipe down tables and chairs as well as remove the lukewarm pasta dishes from the display case. I made the mistake of looking out the big plate-glass window and seeing Lacey L'Amour strolling arm in arm with none other than the good sheriff. She'd attached herself to him like a burr, holding on to his arm as he escorted her to her car. Man, if Lizzy saw that, I wouldn't know who to root for in the knock-down drag-out kerfuffle that would ensue.

I frowned. Speaking of Lizzy, where the heck was she? Considering the bomb she'd dropped on me the night before, I would have thought she'd actually show up at the pasta shop to talk.

Unless I'd imagined the entire thing. Did concussions cause hallucinations?

I dug my cell phone out of my pocket and had dialed Jones to ask him if he'd seen his sister the night before, when someone tapped me on the shoulder.

"Speak of the devil," I said as I stood on tiptoe to kiss the handsome man who was offering me a bouquet of red roses. "I was just about to call you. What are these for?"

He handed me the flowers, thirteen in all. "You told me that one rose means I love you, and a dozen means I screwed up. I thought it was fitting that I get you thirteen so they say both at once."

I grinned up at him. "You really do listen to me. That's so cool. Most of the time I don't even listen to me. But we discussed this yesterday. You have nothing to be sorry for, right?"

I expected him to agree, and a wave of dizziness hit me when he didn't.

Jones's expression was grim when he murmured, "We need to talk."

I set the flowers down on a nearby table. "About what?"

"My ex."

I sat down.

Sweet 'N Tangy Meatballs

You'll need:
1 tablespoon olive oil
1 small red onion, diced
1 small red bell pepper, cut into chunks
1 10 oz jar marinara sauce
1 8 oz can pineapple chunks
2 tablespoons apricot jam
1 package 20 oz frozen, fully-cooked, cocktail-sized meatballs, thawed

Heat olive oil. Cook onion and red pepper, stirring occasionally, 4 minutes. Remove from pan and set aside. Stir marinara, jam, and 1 tablespoon of reserved pineapple juice together. Bring to a boil over medium-high heat. Add meatballs. Reduce and simmer for 10 minutes, stirring occasionally so sauce doesn't stick. Stir in pineapple, and heat through. Add cooked veggies, and serve.

**Andy's note: I know, I know. A *real* chef doesn't use frozen meatballs. You don't have to for this recipe. But let's face it, sometimes speed trumps hours slaving over a hot stove prepping meatballs that are going to get smothered in sauce—and I swear, your guests won't know the difference. Especially if you serve them up over some tri-colored linguini!

CHAPTER EIGHT

———

"What about her?" I asked, wishing I hadn't stirred this particular pot. Dread coiled in my gut. Why oh why could I never just leave things alone?

Jones sat across from me, his hands flat on the table between us. We were far enough away that Francine O'Reilly and Tommy Gibbons, the only current customers, couldn't overhear us. "You know that my marriage was never legally binding."

I nodded, not taking my eyes off him. "So you said."

"Which I didn't know at the time. I was completely naïve. Even though I followed cheating spouses for a living, it never once occurred to me that Rochelle had an entire life separate from me. I was her dirty little secret." His tone was bitter

My throat went dry. Jones had said the same thing about his mother, how she'd been just another mistress in a long line of them for his father. How it must have devastated him to find out that the woman he loved viewed him in the same dismissive light as his father had perceived his mother. "I'm sure that must have hurt."

"It did. The thing that I didn't mention was that before we got…involved, Rochelle was also my business partner, the other PI in my business."

"Okay." I drew the word out. "Not sure where you're going with this."

He took a deep breath and looked me square in the eye. "She's here investigating you."

My eyes went round, and I squeaked, "Me?"

"Flavor TV hired her to dig into your background after I quit."

I sucked in a sharp breath. "I can't believe they're still coming after me."

Jones shook his head. "They aren't. After the network declared bankruptcy, they had to get rid of her."

"But you said she was here investigating me. If not Flavor TV, then who is she working for?"

Jones shook his head. "She wouldn't tell me. Whoever it is has to have money though. Rochelle doesn't come cheap."

Frickin' chicken fricassee. "I thought this was all over."

Jones's intense blue eyes were steady, his expression grim as he murmured, "There's more."

I didn't like the sound of that. "She found something?" I guessed.

Jones didn't say anything, but his gaze moved to the pasta bar, where Kaylee was stacking plates.

I swore long and low under my breath. "Oh no. Please tell me this is a joke."

"I'm sorry," he said, putting a hand over mine.

I snatched my hand away, setting it back. "How long have you known?"

A muscle jumped in his jaw. "A week."

"A *week*?" My heart shriveled up and descended down to the vicinity of my naval. "And you didn't bother to tell me what was going on?"

His gaze pleaded with me for understanding. "Andrea, I was trying to stop it."

My gaze landed on the roses. He did indeed screw up. Epically, colossally, monumentally. There weren't enough adverbs in the English language to weigh how badly he'd screwed up. If it had been just about me, I could have taken it.

But Kaylee...

A fierce wave of protectiveness washed through me, powerful and all-consuming. "I finally had a moment with her, Jones. A solid bonding moment. But if news gets spread around town about who she is and what she's doing here, it will ruin *everything*. I can't let that happen, not now, not to her." My head swam as all the possible ramifications hit me one on top of the other, like a badly plated dish ready to topple.

As far as the town of Beaverton knew, Kaylee and her mom were just newcomers to the area. Only a handful of people knew she was my daughter. "Oh god, have you told Kyle about this yet? Or Lizzy? Their relationship is already hanging by a thread."

"I wanted to speak with you first. So we could decide what to do."

"Why now?" I said coldly. "Why all of a sudden, when you've been sitting on this for over a week?"

"I tried to talk Rochelle out of it," he pleaded. "I tried to buy her off."

"Buy her off? With what?"

He looked down, seemingly unable to meet my gaze.

I gritted my teeth. "I'm imagining the worst here, Jones. You better tell me all of it."

"I offered her money."

"What money?" As far as I knew, Jones was living hand to mouth.

"Not cash. But I owned my co-op in New York. I offered to sign it over to her."

"I take it she didn't agree?"

He snorted. "She said it wasn't about the money—it was about her business integrity."

I bit back a slew of curses. No wonder he hadn't wanted to talk about moving in with me. He'd been scurrying around to rebury the dirt his ex had dug up. My hands shook, and I clenched them into fists. In the back, someone had turned on the radio. I could hear Mimi and Kaylee chattering away happily.

The kid had been through too much already. I couldn't let this ghost from my boyfriend's past do further damage.

"Okay, then. I want to hire you. To find out who Rochelle is working for. If I find out who, I can maybe figure something else out. Some way to encourage them to keep her findings under wraps."

Jones frowned. "You don't need to hire me. I'll do whatever I can to help."

He reached for me again, but I bolted from the table. "No, I want to keep this strictly professional. And I'm moving out."

He blanched. "Andrea—"

"It's the right thing to do." I said it with as much conviction as I could muster. "Aunt Cecily and Pops need a place to stay, and I don't need the distraction of a relationship right now."

"Don't do this," he said quietly. "Don't shut me out."

I almost sniped that I was only following his example. That he'd shut me out first, and Kaylee was the one who'd pay for it if we couldn't fix this. But I couldn't get involved in an emotional public spat for the second time in a week, especially not in my place of business. My reputation was already a disaster—I didn't mean to give the town gossips any more fat to chew. "I'll be by after work to get my stuff and pick up Roofus."

"So that's it then?" Jones stared at me for a full minute. He didn't telegraph his emotions at all, but I knew him well. He'd been afraid that this was a deal breaker, which was why he'd kept the information from me for as long as he could. I understood the why of it, but if I couldn't trust him, I couldn't hope to have any kind of a future with him.

"I won't accept this." He said it quietly but firmly. His stubble-covered chin was set in a stubborn angle. "I will find out who hired Rochelle, and I'll fix this. Fix us."

I wanted to believe him, badly. He'd been my emotional crutch for months, and I didn't know what I'd do without him. That was the trouble with crutches though—you fell when they got yanked away. My head shook back and forth. "I can't trust you."

"You can," he insisted as he rose from his seat and towered over me. "And you will again. I won't lose you."

He pulled me close, and though I tried to push away, his grip remained firm. My back arched, and he slanted his lips over mine, stealing the kiss I refused to give.

I held out for all of ten seconds before I melted against him, leaning on him, into him. His heat seeped into me the way it always did, warming my cold places, thawing the permafrost that settled on my heart.

Outside there was a wolf whistle and a few jeers from passersby. I pushed him away, eyes bulging.

"This isn't over." He let go and turned away, exiting through the gathered crowd. Applause followed him to his SUV.

My body swayed, and I felt as though someone had scooped all my insides out, sautéed them in garlic butter, and stuffed them back in willy-nilly. Nothing fit the way it had before. Everything had turned all shriveled and gooey.

I dug out my cell phone and called Donna. "I want the A-frame. And I want to move in as soon as possible."

Being the stellar friend that she was, she asked, "How does tonight sound?"

"Perfect," I said, picking up my roses and bringing them outside to the Dumpster.

* * *

"It will do," Aunt Cecily said as she set her purse down on the kitchen counter. "Plenty of room to make the pasta."

Pops was busy poking through the fully furnished living room. "This is a bit much for the two of us."

"The three of us," I corrected as I set down the box I was carrying. "Don't forget—I'm living here too."

Pops eyeballed me. "That all you got?"

I nodded. Sadly, my worldly possessions fit in the backseat of Mustang Sally, which had barely made it up the icy driveway. Four boxes marked Kitchen and one marked Clothes, plus one smelly old hound dog. My life had turned into a bad country song.

With my laptop and purse, that was six trips to make the move official. I'd stop by the storage unit and grab a vase and a few other tidbits from the Grove Street house to round it all out tomorrow.

Jones hadn't been home when I'd gone there to pick up my relatives and possessions. Something had torn in my chest when I'd shut and locked the door, leaving my key under the mat. It was over. The best relationship of my life had come to a screeching halt. Part of me couldn't believe it, like it was some kind of dream that I'd wake up from any minute.

"I think it is good." Aunt Cecily nodded with approval. "Woman should not live with a man and give him the pasta for free before they are wed."

I rolled my eyes. Talk about your pot and your kettle scenario.

Aunt Cecily caught the gesture and said, "I was not living with Eugene. We just had the intercourse."

"Ew," I said, pretty sure I never wanted to have "the intercourse" again after that announcement. Now I knew how Kaylee had felt earlier when I'd talked about my love life. Queasy and embarrassed all at once. "And you're still not married."

"We are old, and we are family," Aunt Cecily said as though that made it any better. "Do as I say, not as I do."

Arguing with her was an exercise in futility. I took my sad little box of clothes back to the master bedroom and locked the door.

The room was dark and cool but not frigidly cold. I put down my box and opened the lid. It took all of two minutes to hang every article of clothing I owned on a hanger. Thirtysomething and moving in with my grandfather and great-aunt. A daughter who disdained me. Incapable of an adult relationship with a man, and not like I had many prospects for future dates either. Between my crazy work hours and being banned from the only decent bar in the county, my future dating life looked dimmer than a burnt-out light bulb. The dating pool of Beaverton was remarkably shallow, especially with two of my ex's lurking around every corner.

I sat down on the bed, blinking back tears. Well, didn't this just bite the big ol' hairy Italian sausage? I didn't want to date anyone but Jones, and he'd gone and screwed that all up. The big sexy jerk.

Someone tapped on my window, and I let out a startled shriek.

"Psst, Andy!" a female voice called from the azalea bushes.

What the hell? I rose and moved over to the window. The shade had been down, and I had to tug it several times to get it to retract. It snapped up with a *thwack*, and I stared down at Lizzy Tillman's half-frozen form.

I opened the window. "What are you doing here?" After my last conversation with Jones, I'd forgotten all about her and her wild theory.

She was in full ski regalia. Powder-blue jacket and ivory mittens, with a matching ear band. Skintight black ski pants. Hastily removed baby-blue poles and skis stuck out of the bush almost obscenely. "I didn't want anyone else to see me. Will you let me in? It's colder than a witch's britches out here."

I bit back the retort that if she didn't want anyone to see, her she shouldn't have skied over the pastel rainbow to get here. All in favor of shutting the window again as soon as possible, I held out a hand and hoisted her up. "You could have come to the door, you know. It's just Pops and Aunt Cecily here, and trust me, they know how to keep a secret."

Lizzy whipped the cover off the bed and swaddled herself in it. Her pale face was almost translucent. I could see the blue of veins snaking beneath the surface of her skin, but her eyes were bright, her cheeks flushed from more than windburn. "I don't want anyone to know I was here."

I frowned. "I just moved in. How did you know I'd be here?"

"The whole town is talking about your breakup with my brother."

"They are?" I blinked. Even for Beaverton, that was some fast work.

Lizzy nodded. "I made a few calls and found out which house had been rented today."

Cursed small town. "Is this about your dad?" I asked.

She nodded. "You know that little shack in the woods where he goes to imbibe?"

"Sort of." If imbibe meant getting out-of-control plastered. Lizzy had to learn to call a spade a spade. The man had pulled a shotgun on Jones and me when we'd been looking for a Christmas tree, for crying out loud. "What about it?"

Lizzy shivered and pulled the blanket more tightly around herself. "After he left for his business trip, I went there, looking for clues. And you'll never guess what I found there."

I was in no mood to guess and told her so.

"Gasoline cans." Lizzy's expression was grim. "Lots of them."

An uneasy feeling took root in my gut. "That doesn't prove he's the arsonist. There could be any number of reasons he's got a bunch of gas cans. Besides, he doesn't have a motive."

"Yes, he does," Lizzy insisted. She withdrew something from her coat pocket. "You see there? That's the jury list from my mom's lawyer. Both Mrs. Bradford and Freddy Harris sat on the jury during her trial last fall. I bet he blames them for her conviction."

I took the paper from her and stared down at it. "Freddy Harris?"

"Owns the assisted living home," Lizzy said. "Or what's left of it."

Dread snaked inside me. "Lizzy, this is serious. You have to tell Kyle."

"I can't," she hissed. "Don't you get it? People died in the last fire. If I tell Kyle and he finds evidence to tie my dad to the arsons, he'll have no choice but to arrest him."

I threw my hands in the air. "Well, what do you expect me to do about it? If he is going after people who are behind your mother's conviction, he's not going to want to talk reasonably to me. And if he is doing this? You can't let him just keep it up."

"I know." She looked down at the floor. "It's just…well, there's got to be something I can do to help. I don't want to lose my father too. "

I watched her struggle with her emotions for a minute and, despite myself, felt sympathy toward her. Through no fault of her own, her entire life had been turned upside down over the last year. I could *so* relate, something I never thought possible with the high-strung, devious diva version of Lizzy Tillman I'd known in high school

I made a face as realization hit of what had to happen next. "Okay, so no involving Kyle. And you still don't want to tell Jones?"

Lizzy bit her lip. "I'm afraid he'll leave if I do." She frowned. "Did your moving out have anything to do with this?"

"No," I told her, unwilling to elaborate. "So no Kyle and no Jones. There's only one person left for us to call."

Lizzy frowned. "Who?"

I let out a breath. This was going to suck. "Your bigamist sister-in-law."

Caprese Salad

You'll need:
1 (8 oz) ball buffalo mozzarella
1 pint fresh grape tomatoes
9 whole basil leaves
1 tablespoon basil-infused extra virgin olive oil

Wash and drain tomatoes, and set aside to dry. Cube mozzarella, and add to a bowl. Tear basil leaves, and add to bowl. Add tomatoes, and toss with oil.

**Andy's note: Fresh ingredients are the key to this simple and fast recipe, so don't skimp on quality.

CHAPTER NINE

———

Rochelle Harrison was a total knockout. She possessed an effortless kind of beauty, the sort of woman who looked gorgeous with no makeup and her hair pulled back in a ponytail. She was tall and lean, with supermodel-esque cheekbones, and her white sweater and black slacks combo fit her like a second skin. Without even trying, she made every other female around her aware of the snag in her own black sweater, and the cheap fabric of her black broomstick skirt, and the fact that her black snow boots were neither designer nor fashionable. At least I hadn't spilled spaghetti sauce on myself yet that day, but only because I'd just come from a funeral.

The three elderly people who had died in the last fire were all put to rest, even though their killer hadn't been brought to justice. With any luck, our visit here would help change that.

If Rochelle was surprised to find Lizzy and me at her door, she hid it under a terrific poker face. "Ms. Buckland. Ms. Tillman. What can I do for you?"

"We want to hire you," Lizzy announced point-blank. "To find the arsonist."

My unlikely companion also wore black, some designer label that allowed her to look good while in mourning. Maybe it was the monochrome dress code, but this was the first time I'd seen a real resemblance between her and her half brother. Something in her eyes, combined with a determined set of her chin. I had no idea she could be that ornery. She'd even given me a run for my money when we'd argued in the car.

Lizzy had agreed that if Rochelle unearthed solid evidence to prove her father was setting fire to buildings all around town, she'd turn whatever we found over to the proper authorities. Of course she must be hoping Rochelle Harrison would discover that someone else was the firebug so her father could be let off the hook. Personally, I didn't really care who was behind it. I just wanted the fiend brought to justice.

Rochelle opened the door to her motel room wider and gestured for us to come in. I felt her eyes on me, curiosity coming off of her in waves. I had a pretty solid grip on what was going through her head, because the same sort of gale-force thoughts gusted through mine. Technically, it hadn't been necessary for me to come with Lizzy to hire Rochelle, but I'd insisted. Though I told myself I only wanted to find out who was paying her to keep tabs on me, really I just wanted a look at the woman Malcolm Jones had loved enough to marry. And who'd broken his heart.

Funny, she didn't look like demon spawn.

"So you want me to find an arsonist?" she asked, gesturing toward the clunky vinyl chairs. There were only two, so she sat on the hideous floral bedspread. The woman was way too elegant for her shabby surroundings. Unfortunately for her, Beaverton didn't have another lodging facility. Most people who came to town stayed with their relations or bought a house and settled down. Long-term guests were rare and, I'd often thought, gluttons for punishment.

I nodded. "My grandfather and great-aunt were residents in the assisted living facility that burned down. Three of their friends died. We just came from their funeral."

"I'm sorry." Rochelle's dark eyebrows drew down. "But why come to me? You have your own licensed PI at the ready."

Lizzy cleared her throat and lifted her pointed chin. "Jones is busy with his photography." We had a heated debate over telling her the things we'd found out about Lizzy's father. I'd wanted to tell her everything and give her a place to start, while Lizzy refused to divulge any of the information she'd dug up on her dad. In the end, we'd opted to let the PI start from scratch and see what she discovered on her own. If she cleared Mr. Tillman, so much the better, and Jones never needed to know we were here.

"I see," Rochelle murmured, her expression neutral. She frowned, looked down my less-than-svelte figure, and then shook it off. "Okay." She rubbed her hands over her thighs. "If this has anything to do with your wanting to keep me off of your case, I can assure you that I'm done with my investigation. I've already booked my flight back to New York."

I liked that she assumed Jones had been honest with me. Clearly she knew his character. Though she was beautiful, there really wasn't anything overtly seductive about her. She wasn't an obvious sort of ho-bag like Lacey L'Amour. Rochelle maintained a reserved demeanor. I couldn't tell if that was for my benefit or Lizzy's, or if that was just her natural state.

Unfortunately, my overly active imagination could easily picture her with Jones. The two of them cool and polished, attractive like marble statues. His black knight to her white queen, like yin-yang bookends, each the perfect match for the other.

So why the hell had he been into a hot mess like me? I felt sort of itchy and uncomfortable all over, like I'd been rolling around in wet sand.

"So will you take the job?" Lizzy asked.

Rochelle's topaz eyes fixed on me. "As much as I'd like to help, I can't mix cases. There's a severe conflict of interest here."

"One thing has nothing to do with the other," I said. Unless the arsonist was also the person who was digging into my past and threatening Kaylee. Maybe if I got lucky, it would turn out to be Lacey, and that would be three birds with one stone.

But Rochelle shook her head. "I'm sorry. I can't help you."

One thing about Lizzy, she wasn't above using emotional blackmail to get her way. "Look, Rochelle. I don't like you. You broke my brother's heart. So believe me when I say that if I had any other option, I'd take my business elsewhere. But I don't. You owe this to me, to Malcolm, and to our family for what you did."

Rochelle looked away, but not before I saw the regret on her face. Was that because she was sorry she'd hurt the Tillman family or because she missed Jones? Did she want him back even now? Was that why she'd decided to dig up some dirt on me, maybe to edge me out and get back under his skin? If so, her plan was working, but somehow I didn't think so. She didn't look at me as though I was the competition, the way Lacey did, or with obvious dislike, the way Lizzy always had. Rochelle looked at me with a mixture of curiosity and sympathy.

No, I decided in that moment, she hadn't come to win Jones back. My gut told me that although she still had affection for him, she wasn't here to seduce my man. I relaxed a little as relief coursed through me. Then I recalled that he was no longer my man, and flinched. Rochelle wasn't the only woman in the room who'd hurt Jones.

Maybe I could make it up to him by getting Rochelle on board to investigate the arsons and, with any luck, clear his father. Though I had no hope it would bring us back together, it felt like the right thing to do.

"If it helps," I said to Rochelle, "you're not really working for me. You'll be working for Lizzy. I'm really not involved at all, only here for moral support."

That did seem to help, because Rochelle nodded slowly. "Okay then, I'll see what I can do."

Though I could tell it galled her, Lizzy shook Rochelle's hand and then slid her a business card with her name and cell phone number. "Call me the second you find anything."

Rochelle looked down at the card and murmured, "I will."

Satisfied she's gotten her way, Lizzy exited the room without a backward glance, assuming I'd be trailing her like a water skier in her wake. I wasn't nearly so sanguine.

Rochelle raised one elegant eyebrow in my direction. "Is there something else?"

Was there? I cleared my throat, unsure of what to say but knowing I had to say something. "Did you love him?"

She held my gaze for a moment and then uttered a quiet, "Yes."

I believed her. "Then why didn't you tell him you were married? Why not get divorced?"

She would have been well within her rights to tell me to mind my own beeswax. That's probably what I would have done in her situation. Rochelle took a different approach. "If you want the whole story, I'll give it to you. I've been trying to tell him for a week now, but he doesn't want to hear it. But I have a meeting I need to get to. Meet me later, say for dinner?"

Was I really going to have dinner with my ex-boyfriend's former wife? The woman who was probably on her way to hand over all the gory details that would ruin my daughter's newfound stability?

Though I'd only just met Rochelle, I thought I understood her. She did her job to the best of her ability and took pride in her work, the same way I did, the same way Jones did. Plus, curiosity gnawed a giant hole through me. Besides, it wasn't like I had anything better scheduled.

"Okay. But not in Beaverton." The last thing I wanted was for it to get around town that I was hanging out with Rochelle. I doubted Kaylee would ever forgive me if she found out I'd talked to the PI who might be helping some unknown person to ruin her life.

"There's a diner two towns over. You know it?"

I did. Their main food was a total grease fest, but they had excellent Kentucky pie. "What time?"

"Any time after six."

"Make it seven." Pops and Aunt Cecily would be busy until late, sharing food and stories with their friends. They wouldn't even notice if I had other plans for dinner

I nodded and then took my leave, wondering if I'd lost my last marble.

* * *

After the funeral, I'd decided to leave Pops's town car at the Bowtie Angel and ride with Lizzy, a fact I'd been sorely regretting. She'd grilled me over what I'd said to Rochelle in private, and she drove so slowly I could have walked back to the pasta shop faster. "I told you—it wasn't about the case."

"Was it about Malcolm?" she peppered me.

I cast her a level look. "What do you think?"

She glanced into the rearview mirror and then frowned. "I think we're being followed."

When someone announces that you are being followed, the natural impulse is to turn around and see who or what is doing the following. I checked the urge and asked her, "What kind of car is it?"

"I'm not a car person," she griped.

I didn't bother to stop my eye roll. "What color is it? Is it an SUV or sedan?"

"It looks like Jones's car," she said. "All big and dark."

An SUV then. "Can you see the driver?"

"The windows are tinted." Lizzy turned off onto Main Street. "What should I do?"

I thought about it for a second. "Drop me off at the Bowtie Angel."

"What will that do?" She braked for an upcoming turn.

"We'll see if they follow you or me. If they stick with you, drive right to the sheriff's office and make like you were heading to visit Kyle anyway. If they park, circle the block and try to get the license plate. Then call Kyle and tell him what's going on. He'll find out who it is."

She gave me a look of grudging respect. "You're kinda good at this."

I shrugged. "I've picked up a few things from your brother."

Lizzy pulled up in front of the Bowtie Angel. I shivered as a gust of wind hit me, yanking the door out of my grip. I'd be so glad when this damn cold finally let up. My entire body was sore. I felt like a partially frozen piece of meat, as though I could never get warm all the way through.

After hanging up my coat in the kitchen, I peered out the window beside the back door. Lizzy pulled back into traffic— then Mrs. Jaeger's gold Lexus went by. No sign of an SUV.

I pulled the business card Lizzy had given me earlier from my back pocket, wondering why she always seemed to have one to hand out. It was a plain white card with her name and number etched in silver calligraphy. There was no job title, since being a buttinsky wasn't an actual profession. Maybe they were like social cards. I'd have to ask Jones.

Then I winced and remembered I wasn't in any position to ask Jones anything. Shoot, when was that going to sink in? He'd become such an ingrained part of my life that coming to terms with never seeing him again was getting harder, not easier.

If Rochelle discovered that Mr. Tillman was indeed behind the arsons, would Jones leave town? What if I never saw him again?

"Eye on the prize, Andy," I muttered to myself. Lizzy. I had to text Lizzy and let her know the SUV had stayed with me. My fingers were stiff, aching from the cold, and I dropped the phone. It slid under the workstation. "Frick."

"Is everything all right, Andy?" Mimi pushed her way in from the front room. We'd delayed opening again because of the funerals, but since Mimi lived over the pasta shop, she'd offered to get things going. The air was spiced with tomatoes, garlic, and oregano.

"Yeah, just dropped my stupid cell."

She gave me a puzzled look. "You sure? You look a little pale."

I pasted on a bright smile. "Just thinking about the new menu. Are you looking forward to getting back to pastries again?"

Mimi grinned. "I can't wait. When are we going to launch it?"

Changing up a long-standing menu wasn't something that happened overnight. There were supply issues, cook-time issues, freezer-space issues. Some current menu items had to be chopped or changed, and I was having trouble picking which ones to cull. They were all classics, dishes Aunt Cecily and my grandmother had implemented with love and care over decades. Deciding what to leave behind was like *Sophie's Choice*, the pasta edition.

Essentially we were launching a new restaurant at the same time as we tried to run the old one. Tough stuff, but if I was going to compete with Lacey L'Amour across the freaking street, I had to make some damn decisions already.

"I'm thinking Valentine's Day. You up for that?"

Mimi nodded. "Of course. Oh, and Malcolm Jones called."

I blinked. "Today? He called today?"

She nodded. "This morning. Did you hurt your hands?"

I'd been distracted, wondering why Jones would have called the pasta shop instead of just phoning my cell, and answered absently, "No, why?"

"You keep rubbing them."

"It's just the cold. Makes me feel kind of stiff all over. Did Jones leave a message?"

"He said he'd call back."

Curiouser and curiouser. "Okay then. Do you need any help up here before I make the rounds out front?"

Mimi shook her head. "I've got it. And we have a group waiting at the door."

"I'll go open up." After checking my cell one more time, I slid it into my back pocket and pasted on my game face. There were several people waiting outside. Some had come to the funerals, others just stopping in for a to-go container of spaghetti and meatballs on their lunch hour. I served for almost an hour. As owner and head chef, I had to ensure that everyone who walked through the door of the Bowtie Angel would have the best dining experience possible and hopefully let us feed them again.

"Where's Eugene?" Ursula Mulvaney asked as I dropped off her bowtie chicken and pesto. "I thought sure he would be here after the funeral."

"Oh, he and Aunt Cecily offered to help host the gathering at the seniors' center this afternoon."

Ursula looked down at her plate and then fluffed her frosted gray hair. "Can I get this to go?"

"Sure." I whisked the plate over to the counter where our Styrofoam take-out containers were stacked, smiling to myself. Ursula had the hots for my grandfather and conveniently forgot that he was taken. And she wasn't the only one. Eligible bachelors weren't exactly thick on the ground for the seniors in Beaverton, and there were a lot of lonely hearts hoping that because Pops and Aunt Cecily hadn't made anything official yet, there was still hope my grandfather was up for grabs.

I smiled and served and listened to about as much gossip as I could handle. Several people offered me condolences about Jones, as though it had been his funeral earlier that morning. My happy face was starting to crack around the edges. Though I'd trained myself to deal with being in the limelight, it didn't come naturally to me. I was an introvert by nature and had to overcome my own personality quirks to be a successful business owner. But add on the looks of pity that I was single yet again, and I was on the ragged edge.

"Hey, Little Bit," Mike Jefferies of Mike's Garage called out.

He sat with a group of guys we'd both known since high school. Mike knew full well I despised that nickname. He was just needling me. It proved how far I'd come that I was still smiling instead of handing him his man parts on a platter. "How's your mom doing?"

"She can complain and does. Mostly as how I'm a good-for-nothin' son who won't settle down and give her grandkids already. How's the 'Stang?"

"Snug as a bug in a rug and garaged for the winter." I sighed, missing my vintage wheels. The town car got me where I needed to go, but every time I parked, it was like docking an ocean liner.

"Heard about you moving out on Jones," Derek Gibbs said. "Tough break. Does that mean you're back on the market?"

"Nope. I'm focusing on my career." Something Derek wouldn't know about, since he'd been on unemployment since high school.

"Will your career keep you warm at night?" Derek slung an arm around my waist and pulled me in close. He smelled like a combination distillery and locker room.

I tried to pry myself loose, my temper rising. We didn't serve alcohol in the Bowtie Angel, but that didn't stop idiots from coming in drunk and causing trouble. "I've got a dog. Let go of me."

Mike looked worried, and he reached across the table, trying to help free me. "Come on, man. Let her go."

Derek opened his mouth to slur some other nonsense, when he was yanked up by the collar. He was so startled that he let go of me, and I backed away quickly.

Oh no. I thought. No, no, no, no-no. "Malcolm..." I began.

Jones wasn't listening. His eyes glittered with deadly intent as he dragged Derek out of the booth. The tables had all gone quiet—all conversation ground to a halt. "Apologize to the lady."

"She ain't no lady." Derek obviously had less sense than I thought. "Getcher hands offa me."

"The lady is with me." Jones's tone was low and deadly.

"That ain't what I heard." Either Derek was too drunk or too stupid to recognize the threat.

"From now on, you treat her with respect, or you find somewhere else to eat." He let go of Derek, who slumped to the floor.

Jones turned to face me, gripping me by the arm. "Come with me."

He looked terrible, beard stubble coating his usually perfectly shaven jaw, blue eyes ringed with dark circles as though he hadn't slept, the whites bloodshot. He was a man on the ragged edge, and a pang went through me as I realized I'd helped put him there.

Still, I wasn't about to let him push me around in my own place of business, in front of half the town. "Let go of me this instant, Malcolm Jones."

To his credit, he did, but not before a bullhorn blared. All heads whipped toward the plate-glass window.

Outside the window, lights flashed. Cripes, was that the entire Beaverton police force out there?

"Malcolm Jones." Kyle spoke through the bullhorn, decked out in full sheriff's regalia. "Come out with your hands up. You are under arrest."

Baked Cauliflower

You'll need:
1 head of cauliflower, cut into equal-sized florets
1 1/2 cups Panko bread crumbs
1/3 cup grated Parmesan cheese
1 teaspoon dried oregano
Pinch of red pepper flakes
salt and pepper
3 eggs, beaten

Preheat oven to 400 degrees, and baste a foil-lined baking sheet with olive oil.

In a shallow bowl, toss together the crumbs, cheese, oregano, pepper flakes, salt and pepper.

Place the eggs in another bowl, and first dip the florets in the egg mixture, then roll in the crumb mixture until coated.

Place the cauliflower pieces on the prepared baking sheet, and continue until all of the pieces are breaded. Baste the top of the cauliflower florets with some olive oil, then bake for about 40 minutes or until golden brown and tender-crisp.

**Andy's note: This dish is even more engaging if you use orange or purple cauliflower. A delicious and colorful surprise. Some surprises are better than others.

CHAPTER TEN

———

"What are the charges?" I pounced when Kyle finally entered his office. He'd been puffed up with his arrest and had put a decent amount of distance between the two of us, knowing I'd deflate his ego faster than he could spit. I'd left the Bowtie Angel and driven down to the station only to be ushered into his office to wait for news on Jones. I had been twiddling my thumbs for over an hour and was fit to be tied by the time he walked in. "You can't arrest him just because you don't like him."

Kyle narrowed his gaze on me. "Give me a little credit, Andy. I would have thought you were glad to have him out of your hair. I heard the two of you broke up finally. The whole town is speculating that you found out what Jones had been up to, and that's why you moved out."

"This town needs a hobby," I grumped. "And just because we broke up doesn't mean I want to see him behind bars."

"Did you know that he was the one following you?" Kyle asked. "That's stalking, in my book."

"Um, no." I blinked. Lizzy really was a car idiot. She'd said the SUV that had been tailing us looked *like* Jones's SUV, not that it *was* Jones's SUV. "Besides, it's not stalking unless Lizzy or I press charges. I haven't. Are you going to sit there with a straight face and tell me that Lizzy's pressing charges against her brother?"

I really hoped that wasn't the case anyway. Which Kyle confirmed when he grunted noncommittally.

Time to pull out the big guns. "Are you going to answer my question, or am I going to have to get a lawyer on your case?"

"Bigamy," he said. "It's a criminal offense in North Carolina."

I frowned. "Jones isn't a bigamist. It was his wife that committed bigamy."

"I can't get the wife—she's not a resident of the state. Conspiracy to commit bigamy then."

I huffed out a breath. "What the hell is your major malfunction, Kyle? You may be a moron, but you've always been a good cop."

"Gee, thanks." His tone was dry. Then he glared. "Why do you think I'm a moron?"

I stood and leaned over his desk. "I saw you sniffing around Lacey L'Amour. And I'll have you know that's a double betrayal, to Lizzy and to me."

Kyle scowled. "To you?"

I thumped a hand against my breastbone. "In case it's slipped your mind, I'm the mother of your child. You can*not* flirt with my professional competition in full view of the town, including our daughter, and expect me to be okay with that. Especially on the day said competition has sabotaged my business in front of a health inspector. Do you know how much it'll cost me for a new freezer door? I should take it out of her hide. So, is a little flipping loyalty too much to ask you for?"

Kyle blinked. "Are you saying I can't eat at the new restaurant?"

"Oh, you can," I said, my tone deceptively mild. "But who knows what'll happen if you do."

Kyle stared at me. "That's threatening an officer of the law, Ms. Buckland."

"No threats, Sheriff. She's a gawd-awful cook. She'll probably give the whole town salmonella."

Kyle's eyebrows went up. "Women who live in glass houses..."

I gave him my best squinty-eyed death glare. "We've gotten off the subject. You need to drop the charges against Jones. You and I both know he hasn't done anything wrong."

"Nothing that you know of," he said. "That doesn't mean he's not a criminal. Even you have to admit that things have been crazy around here since he showed up."

I stared at him, unable to believe his dislike of Jones would go so far. "Kyle, I swear, you better release him or..." I stumbled, at a loss as to what to say next.

"Or what?" he taunted.

At that moment, I resolved to say anything that would wipe that smug look off his puss. "Or I'll go to the district attorney. I'm sure she'll be very interested to know how you're using your authority. They may even try you on abuse of power."

He scanned me head to toe, as if wondering if I was serious. I wasn't, but he didn't need to know that.

"Fine, I'll release Jones. As long as he gets an annulment in the next thirty days. Otherwise, I'm coming after him again."

I rose, slinging my purse over my shoulder. "And you owe Jones an apology. You humiliated him in front of half of Beaverton."

"Don't hold your breath on that one, Little Bit."

I bared my teeth in his general direction. It wasn't a smile.

"Want to tell me what happened between the two of you?"

"We broke up. I moved out." The *Reader's Digest* version of events was all he was getting out of me.

Kyle's eyes narrowed. "Witnesses said he was causing a ruckus in the pasta shop."

"It wasn't him. It was your good buddy Derek who showed up drunk for the third time this month. Jones was only—" I clamped my lips together.

"Only what?" Kyle asked.

I shook my head fervently. No way was I handing Kyle any more ammo. I'd deal with Jones and his outburst myself.

He blew out a sigh. "Have it your way. But I'm telling you, Andy, he is up to something."

I waited in the parking lot for Jones to be released. No doubt tongues were wagging all over town that my ex-boyfriend had been arrested in my pasta shop by my other ex-boyfriend. I rubbed my stiff hands together. I really hoped I could talk Rochelle into burying what she found out about Kaylee. The poor kid didn't need the crazy that came with her parents and their significant others.

It was almost an hour later when Jones left the police station. As I was driving Pops's town car, he didn't spot me until I opened the door and rose.

"Andrea." He said my name in the way that made me melt.

"Get in. I'll give you a ride back to your car."

He climbed in. I backed carefully out of the parking lot, not saying a word.

"Where are we going?" Jones frowned as I drove past the Bowtie Angel and took Main Street out of town.

"Somewhere where we can talk."

He raised an eyebrow. "You mean somewhere you can dump my body if you don't like what I have to say?"

The man knew me so well it was scary.

I took the highway about five miles out of town, to the big meadow by the manmade lake. In mild weather, there would be health nuts walking the nature trail during the day and teenagers necking by the lake at night. But the frigid cold turned the great outdoors into a ghost town. In essence, it was the best place I could think of to have some privacy for the upcoming conversation.

I debated leaving the car running so we'd have heat but opted to shut it off instead before turning to Jones. The biting cold would help me keep my anger on a razor's edge as warmth and Jones in close proximity made me logy.

"I can explain—" he began, but I cut him off.

"You'll get your chance. First, I want to know how long you've been tailing me." It galled me a little that Lizzy had picked up the tail before I had. Of course, she'd been driving, but I was irritated that I hadn't spotted him myself.

"Just since the motel. And for the record, it wasn't you I was watching."

Damn it—that meant I'd overlooked him in the parking lot too. "So you were staking out Rochelle? Why?"

He gave me a look of pure exasperation. "I told you yesterday. I intend to find out who she's meeting with so we could find out why they want information on you."

I frowned. "So why follow me and Lizzy and not Rochelle?"

He swallowed and looked away. "I wanted to make sure you were safe. There's an arsonist running around town. I knew you were at the funeral this morning and that you'd be safe enough there. But when you showed up at the motel, I had a bad feeling."

So he'd followed me to make sure I was safe. How could I not love this half-crazy man?

"You look terrible, by the way. Almost as bad as I feel."

His gaze turned assessing. "Are you all right, Andrea?"

I hadn't slept the night before from missing him, but no way would I tell him that. "There's been a lot going on, and I'm not thinking clearly."

His eyes narrowed, and my temper snapped. "Get that look off your face right now, Malcolm Jones, or so help me, I'll—"

He kissed me. The bastard just leaned right over the seat and kissed the stuffing out of me. It was a good thing I'd shut the heat off, because I would have melted to a puddle of Italian spiced goo under the onslaught.

His hands worked on my jacket while mine were busy working the fastening on his black pants.

"This doesn't get you off the hook," I gasped as he kissed his way down the side of my neck. "I'm still furious with you."

"I know," he mumbled as he dragged me over the gearshift and onto his lap. "Take it out on me."

"As long as we've got that straight," I breathed before giving myself up to the moment.

* * *

"I hope there aren't any cameras around here." I sighed, totally blissed out and uncaring if we had been caught on film in flagrante delicto.

Jones had his face buried in my hair. I heard him mumble something incomprehensible and asked, "What was that?"

"I hope there are cameras so there's proof that this really happened." He brushed my hair out of my face. "Andrea, I'm sorry about earlier."

I pushed against his chest, so I could look him in the eye. "Which part? When you made a scene in my place of business, or when you got yourself arrested for bigamy, and I had to go blackmail Kyle out of pressing charges."

He grimaced. "All of it. Mostly for how I acted at the pasta shop. I'm not sure what came over me. I just saw that cretin with his hands all over you, and I snapped."

My teeth sank into my lower lip.

He looked me up and down, his sharp blue gaze assessing. "You're pleased that I was jealous."

"No," I fibbed.

He gave me a *get real* look.

"Maybe," I said. "Okay, but you have to understand that no one's ever been jealous over me before."

He blew out a breath. "Well, you better get used to it."

God, what was wrong with me that I loved his possessive streak? Jealousy was so not sexy. Except on Malcolm Jones.

"Seriously though, you have to trust that I can handle myself at work. I've known most of those guys since they were in diapers. A little flirting is normal, but they won't take it too far, if not for my crazy jealous boyfriend, then because they're scared witless that Aunt Cecily will put The Eye on them."

"Boyfriend?" he asked, hope lighting his face. "Does that mean we're back together?"

What woman could resist him? One stronger than me. "Well, I certainly can't leave you unattended now, can I? Look at the mess you got yourself into in less than twenty-four hours."

He kissed me again, a long, lingering kiss full of thanksgiving. "Will you move back in with me?"

"To Lizzy's place?" That would just plop us back into the hot water where we'd started.

His brows drew down as he studied my face. "What's wrong? I thought you loved that house."

Now that we were no longer pressed skin to skin, I'd grown chilled. Needing both heat and distance, I scrambled back to the driver's side and turned over the engine. "I do."

His brows drew down. "I don't see the problem, Andrea."

"It's not about the house. Malcolm, we haven't solved anything. We're sort of drifting back together, but there's no real plan here."

"A plan?" His countenance turned darker, almost foreboding. "Where's this coming from? A month ago you were half-hysterical because you thought I was going to ask you marry me."

Not my finest moment. "I know. I'm commitment-phobic. But that's the thing—I'm not talking about commitment here. I'm talking about stability."

"What's the difference?"

Only a man would ask that question. "Stability is knowing you're not going to yank the rug out from under me at a moment's notice, like you did yesterday. It's knowing that you're not going to bury yourself in work at every opportunity and leave me to my own neurotic devices. It's understanding that while I may not be in a place where I want commitment now, I won't ever get there if you keep these huge secrets from me."

I was shouting by the end of it, my hands flailing in grandiose gestures that, if left unchecked, could very well put an eye out. Jones grabbed both my hands in his and brought them to his lips. He kissed them softly. "Are you done?"

"You know very well that I can't talk without using my hands."

He grinned. "All right. So if you're not going to move back in with me, then can we look for a place together?"

A week ago I would have jumped at the chance. But I liked my little A-frame, and having Pops and Aunt Cecily under the same roof with me helped remind me of who I was, a Buckland. "I think we should live apart for a little while."

He looked ready to protest but then shook it off. "I suppose I deserve this." His accent, usually so crisp, sort of drawled the words, adding an air of defeat.

I patted his cheek. "It's not a punishment, love. I will miss you. But everything just sort of happened over this last year, what with Pops selling the Victorian. I should have been looking for my own place then, but you made it so easy to just fit me into your life. It was convenient for both of us. And that scares me a little. I don't want us to get to the point where we're taking each other for granted."

He nodded and then let out a breath. "If that's what you want. Will you invite me to your new house? Maybe for dinner tonight?"

"Shoot, I can't tonight. I've got a date with your ex."

Jones blinked. "Come again?"

"Rochelle wanted to talk to me."

"What about?" Jones looked wary.

I blinked, surprised he would have to ask. "You, of course. What else do you think we have in common?"

He grimaced as though in pain. "Andrea—"

I held up a hand. "Believe it or not, I like her."

His jaw dropped. "You *like* her? Are you serious? I ask you to like my sister, but you don't, and now you're making friends with my ex, the bigamist?"

"Making friends is overstating it a little. And actually, Lizzy and I are making progress."

Jones opened his mouth, a retort at the ready, and then paused as though something had occurred to him. I'd promised Lizzy that I wouldn't tell Jones why she felt the need to involve herself in the arson investigation. I wasn't about to lie to him either.

I took a deep breath and cringed a little as I spoke. "Okay, you're not going to like this, and it's going to sound hypocritical as all get-out, but...I can't tell you."

He stared at me for a full minute. "So I'm just supposed to sit around and do nothing?"

Silly man, I'd never endorse doing nothing. "Of course not. I want you to keep tailing Rochelle. Oh, and get a freaking annulment already, because a Facebook status of 'It's complicated' is just not going to fly anymore. Kyle's serious, Malcolm. He wants you behind bars or run out of town. Don't give him an excuse."

My phone rang, and though I was tempted to let it go to voice mail, I needed to let Mimi know where I was. I'd abandoned her too much lately, and with Lacey L'Amour mincing about, the Bowtie Angel needed all hands on deck.

Unfortunately, it wasn't Mimi on the other end of the phone. It was Donna.

"Andy, oh my god. Where are you?"

"I'm on my way back to the pasta shop. What's going on?"

"Kaylee's missing."

Braciole

You'll need:
1/2 cup dried Italian-seasoned bread crumbs
1 garlic clove, minced
2/3 cup grated Pecorino Romano
1/3 cup grated provolone
2 tablespoons chopped fresh Italian parsley leaves
4 tablespoons olive oil
Salt and freshly ground black pepper
1 (1 1/2-pound) flank steak
1 cup dry white wine
3 1/4 cups Tasty Tomato Sauce (recipe below)
2 tablespoons extra light olive oil
1 large onion, sliced
1 carton mushrooms, sliced
2 cloves garlic, minced
2 8 oz cans salt-free tomato sauce
1 6 oz can salt-free tomato paste
1 teaspoon dried oregano
1/2 teaspoon dried basil
Half-and-half, as needed

Sauté onion, garlic, and mushrooms in oil until brown. Stir in tomato and herbs. Cover and simmer at least 1 hour, stirring occasionally. If sauce tastes too acidic, add half-and-half, 1 tablespoon at a time, to round out the flavor.

Pour half the tomato sauce into the bowl of a food processor. Process until smooth. Continue with remaining tomato sauce.

If not using all the sauce, allow it to cool completely and then pour 1- to 2-cup portions into plastic freezer bags. Freeze for up to 6 months.

Lay the flank steak flat on the work surface. Sprinkle the bread crumb mixture over the steak to cover the top evenly.

Starting at 1 short end, roll up the steak as for a jelly roll, to enclose the filling completely. Using butcher's twine, tie the steak roll to secure. Sprinkle the braciole with salt and pepper.

Preheat oven to 350 degrees. Heat the remaining 2 tablespoons of oil in a heavy large ovenproof skillet over medium heat. Add the braciole, and cook until browned on all sides, about 8 minutes. Add the wine to the pan, and bring to a boil. Stir in the marinara sauce. Cover partially with foil, and bake until the meat is almost tender, turning the braciole and basting with the sauce every 30 minutes. After 1 hour, uncover and continue baking until the meat is tender, about 30 minutes longer. The total cooking time should be about 1 1/2 hours.

Remove the braciole from the sauce. Using a large sharp knife, cut the braciole crosswise and diagonally into 1/2-inch-thick slices. Transfer the slices to plates. Spoon the sauce over, and serve with pasta cooked al dente.

**Andy's note: Braciole takes some work, but it's one of those make it and then leave it dishes. You have plenty of time to clean up before your dinner guests arrive. Your house will smell divine, so pour yourself a glass of wine to visit with your guests before serving them a stupendous meal.

CHAPTER ELEVEN

"What do you mean, missing?" Jones asked as we sped back into town. His knuckles had turned white where they grasped the overhead handle. "Andrea, slow down. A tank corners better than this car."

My foot stayed firmly planted on the accelerator. Senior citizens in motorized carts passed Jones when he was behind the wheel. No way was I about to take driving advice from him. "According to Donna, Kaylee's mom called the pasta shop looking for her. She never came home after school, and she had a dentist appointment. But when Mimi said Kaylee was a no-show, her mom got really worried."

"Do we know if she was at school today?" I could tell Jones was making a mental list of whom we needed to call.

"Donna didn't know. Usually the school calls when kids are missing during attendance. It's not as easy to ditch as it used to be, back in my day."

I'd been heading to the pasta shop but changed my mind, driving back to the sheriff's office. Thoughts of skipping school had made me think of Kyle. With luck, Kaylee would be with him. If not, at least he had more resources to tap that would help us get a bead on her.

"Stay in the car," I told Jones as we took the sharp left into visitor parking.

"You're not going to make it." Jones gripped the handle as if his perfectly good seat belt wouldn't keep him in place. I loved the man, but he could be such a wuss.

I curb-checked a wee bit but otherwise pulled into the parking lot with nary a scratch.

"Stay in the car," I repeated, giving him my best *no nonsense will be tolerated* look. "I mean it, Jones. Waving you under Kyle's nose is not a good plan, especially if I have to tell him his daughter is missing."

He glowered at me "I've never seen a town car balance on two wheels before."

I looked at him. "You didn't see it this time either."

"The sensation is unforgettable." He unbuckled his seat belt. "Give me the keys. I'm driving from here on out."

It seemed a minor concession, so I handed them over. "Just don't go anywhere without me. The last thing we need is you getting arrested for grand theft auto."

The dispatcher today was Millie Barnes, and she waved when she saw me. She'd been a few years behind me in high school, a quiet girl with a lisp and really bad acne. In the years since I'd left Beaverton, she'd taken speech lessons and had invested in a skin care regime though, because now she was a knockout. "Back again so soon, Andy?"

"You know me, Millie. Can't get enough of this place. Must be the fluorescent lighting. Is Kyle still here?"

She shook her head. "He had to head over to the courthouse. Alfred Hennessey is being arraigned for a DUI. Again. Ran over Nelly Bateman's prized cherry blossom tree. They know it was him too, because he ripped his gas tank open in the collision. Deputies followed the gas leak all the way back to his house like a trail of bread crumbs and found him passed out in the front seat with a bottle of Johnny Walker in his lap. I'm keeping my fingers crossed he loses his license for good this time."

"It's amazing Al hasn't killed anyone yet." It was a long shot, mostly because Kyle would have insisted that Kaylee call her mom or me and tell us about her change of plans, but I shifted my weight and asked anyway. "I don't suppose you saw the girl who works at my pasta shop with him, did you? Maybe following him for a school project or something? She's short, about five three, with short dark hair and blue eyes. Usually wearing pink and black?"

As expected, Millie shook her head. "Can't say that I did. Want me to text him to make sure?"

I waved her off, even as my worry increased. "It's not a big deal. I'll track her down myself. But I'd appreciate a heads up if she does show up here, okay?"

"No problem, Andy. Say hi to your granddad for me. And Cecily too, o-of course." She tagged on the last bit with the faintest hint of her old stutter.

I smiled to myself. She'd said my aunt's name with the same trepidation that people used for the IRS. As though mentioning the name would bring the wrath of an audit to their very doorstep.

I returned to the car and faced Jones. "Home, Jeeves." My heart wasn't really in the joke. The last twenty-four hours had been an emotional roller coaster, and I was hitting the end of my badly frayed rope.

He ignored my pithy remark but did start the engine. "Do you want to stop by the school? Or perhaps go to see Kaylee's mother?"

I shook my head and dug my phone out, pulling up Kyle's contact info. I typed in a quick text. *Call me the second you get out of court. –A*

With that done, I turned to face Jones. "I want to keep looking for her, but I've abandoned Mimi for too many days in a row. What should I do?"

"Finding people is my job, Andrea. Trust me to do it. It's better you go to work. Be where she expects you to be, and call me if you get any word from her. Do you have anything else for me to go on? Does she have a boyfriend?"

I shook my head. "Not that she told me about. We're not exactly besties."

"I'll check with her mother, as well as Eugene and Cecily."

"I'll grill Mimi too and get in touch with Donna again. She can get you a listing of vacant properties, just in case she's being a teenaged idiot and breaking in to drink and get high." The thought enraged me, but not as much as the one that came in on its heels.

Kaylee with some older kids taking advantage of her. Or an actual vagrant, like Pops always claimed were passing through the area. A serial killer, or a pedophile. There were so many bad things that could happen to kids.

I worried my lower lip. "Are you going to check with Rochelle?"

He nodded once. "It's a reasonable place to start, since we know she was digging into Kaylee's background."

"God help her if she'd turned information about my daughter over to some child-molesting scumbag with a grudge against me. I'll have her guts for garters."

"Speaking of grudges..." Jones said as he backed into a free space in front of the pasta shop. He wasn't looking at the Bowtie Angel though. He was staring across the street at Lacey's hideous banner.

I frowned. "You think she's in there? Why would she go to Lacey's place?"

"You said it yourself—you're not exactly besties." The word delivered in his crisp accent made me snort, but I sobered immediately when he continued. "Put yourself in her shoes. You're trying to irritate your long-lost biological mother. What better way than to go hang out with her hated competition?"

Damn, that made sense, if the word could be used for a petty, self-absorbed teenager's actions.

I got out of the car and was halfway across the street when Jones grabbed my arm. "Andy, you can't go in there."

I stared at him. "Give me one good reason why not."

"I'll give you two. One, it's what Lacey wants, for you to storm into her place and make a big scene. It'll look as though you're threatened by her restaurant. And two, because it's what Kaylee *doesn't* want, for you to call attention to your relationship with her."

"I hate it when you're right," I grumped.

He kissed me quickly. "Good thing it doesn't happen often. I'll go in, check around, and report back on the double."

It took every ounce of willpower I could muster to go inside the Bowtie Angel. Once there, I washed my hands, poked my head out front to let Mimi know I was there, and then attacked the sink full of dishes with a vengeance. The warm water made my cold hands hurt worse, the joints stiff and slow to respond. I knew I'd pay for it later with chapped and cracked skin too, but I didn't care.

A timer went off, and I shut off the water to check the oven just as Jones entered through the back door. I barely stopped myself from snagging the lasagna out bare handed as I asked, "Well?"

He handed me two potholders and wisely waited for me to set the dish down before saying, "She's there."

I cursed long and loud, even as I let out a breath of relief. "What are they doing?"

Jones watched my face carefully. "Cooking."

I staggered as though someone had skewered me. It felt as though they had, right through the heart. "She's cooking with that no-talent hack instead of me. Did you get pictures?"

He shot me an incredulous look. "Of course I didn't take any photographs. I was only there for two minutes."

"What was your cover story then?"

"That Kaylee's mother was looking for her,"

I sucked in a sharp breath, the skewer moving to pierce both my lungs.

"And that she'd called here, wondering where she was. That's it."

"Oh," I said and then sagged onto a nearby stool. That mother, right.

Jones, good man that he was, put his arms around me. "It'll be all right, Andrea."

How I wished I could believe that.

* * *

To make up for all the time I'd taken off that day, I let Mimi go early. I filled the yawning space inside myself the way I always did, with food. I cooked and cleaned, scoured and scrubbed, swept and mopped. And I made plans, mental lists of all the things I needed to get done to launch the new menu. It was nearly six when I remembered the dinner plans I'd made with Rochelle. Since I thought it would be a tad awkward to call Jones and ask for his ex's number, I called Lizzy instead.

Of course, Lizzy being Lizzy, she did nothing to make the task easier. "Why do you want Rochelle's number?"

"Um…" I was too emotionally and physically drained to make up a plausible excuse. "Well, you see we were going to meet up for dinner—"

"You were going to discuss the case without me?" Lizzy screeched.

I jerked my head away from the phone. Damn, that tone was like a dog whistle for humans. "No, it wasn't about the case."

"Well, I don't see what else you could possibly have to talk to Rochelle about." Lizzy sniffed.

"She wants to talk to me about your brother."

"You don't need to talk about him. You two broke up." She sounded so pleased about that fact that I didn't dare correct her. Not while I wanted something from her anyway. Besides, it was kind of cute that she was looking out for her big brother. If by cute, I meant verging on a psychotic break.

"We're forming a Malcolm Jones lonely hearts club. Just give me the damn number, Lizzy, or I swear I will call Kyle and tell him about the time we were camping out by the lake and you put sugar in my gas tank."

"How'd you know that was me?" she hissed.

"I didn't, but I do now. And I've got your confession on tape," I fibbed.

She huffed out an indignant breath. "Fine, I'll text you the number. You two deserve each other."

"Nice way to talk to the woman who has gone out of her way to help you. And by the way, it's just so darn sweet of you to lend your fiancé to escort Lacey L'Amour around town. The two of them looked oh so chummy."

She sucked in a sharp breath, and I nodded in satisfaction. Served Kyle right for arresting Jones. The way I saw it, he'd brought his fiancée's wrath on himself for escorting my competition around town. Sure, it was petty and vindictive to blurt out the facts in my best *well bless your heart* tone, but my motives were pure. Lizzy deserved to know that Kyle had been sniffing around Lacey so she could put a stop to it. It's how I would have wanted to be treated had it been my fiancée, though the needling was my own selfish indulgence.

Lizzy hung up without saying good-bye, and a minute later my cell dinged with a text. After dialing Rochelle's number, I waited for three rings before her voice mail picked up.

"Hi, this is Andy Buckland. I'm not feeling so hot, so I won't be meeting up with you tonight. Hope you get this before you make the drive."

I thought about offering to reschedule, but I decided against it and simply said good-bye. That done, I took one last glance around to make sure the place was squared away. Mimi had gone to the movies and dinner with a friend, but she had her own key. I locked the pasta shop, set the new alarm, and climbed into the town car. The cavernous interior of the car took forever to warm up, and I was halfway home before I realized I was headed to the wrong house. Stupid autopilot had taken me toward the Tillman property and Jones's place. I thought about turning around but figured it'd be easier to stay with Jones for the night. We'd had a rocky patch, and a little quiet time together without ex's or extended family would do us both some good.

I'd just rounded the bend where the house came in sight when I met an SUV coming the opposite direction. I rolled down the window as Jones pulled up beside me.

"Hey," I said, feeling stupid for dropping by unannounced after the hard line I'd taken earlier. "I was in the neighborhood and thought I'd drop by. Are you heading out on a case?"

Jones shook his head. "No. Actually, I was just heading out to see your new place."

"Really?" The cold air coming in the open window dispelled the little bit of heat that had gathered in the vehicle, and I shivered.

Jones grinned, a roguish smile. "Cecily invited me to dinner, and I was planning to stick around until you got home. What happened to your dinner plans?"

"I decided I'd had enough drama for one day." Freezing and too tired to drive, I asked, "Do you mind if I leave the town car here? I'm beat."

One dark eyebrow rose. "You want to ride with me?"

"Yeah, I figured I could squeeze in a full eight hours of sleep by the time we get there."

He laughed. "Go park the car, wiseass."

I did and then hustled back to the SUV, which was about ten degrees warmer and climbing. Combined with the lingering kiss I received, I was doubly glad to have cancelled on Rochelle.

We'd barely made it another forty feet when a new set of headlights appeared around the bend.

"Now who's that?" Jones frowned. "I don't recognize the car. Do you?"

Since I was the resident car expert, I squinted into the gloom. "It's too dark to get an accurate make or model, but judging from the headlights, it's a sedan, and not a high-end one, so not Lizzy's Audi. More likely a domestic model."

Jones put the SUV in park and waited while the other vehicle pulled up by his side. He swore, something he rarely did in my presence, when he saw who was behind the wheel. "What the devil is she doing here?"

I frowned as Rochelle got out of her rental—a 2009 Chevy Impala, was I good or what—and saw her heading toward us. Jones gripped the steering wheel so hard his knuckles turned white. A stab of irrational jealousy went through me. I wanted to urge him to go, to just drive away, leaving his past in our dust, but had learned from firsthand experience that running never solved anything.

"Malcolm." She gave him a small smile and then turned to me. "I got your message. I'm sorry to just show up like this, but I really need to speak to you. To both of you."

"We have nothing to discuss," Jones said, his accent even sharper than usual. If the air outside didn't freeze her, his tone would do the trick.

"I'll tell you who's been investigating Andy," she said. "Please, it's important."

Jones and I exchanged a speaking glance. He shook his head slightly, indicating that no, he hadn't been able to find out who she was working for. It surprised me that she'd betray her professional confidence. She really must want this audience with us.

I nodded once, and Jones unlocked the doors and said, "Get in."

Vegetarian Chickpea Pasta

You'll need:
1 tablespoon basil-infused olive oil
3 cloves garlic, chopped
7 cups vegetable broth
1/2 teaspoon crushed red pepper
1 pound angel-hair pasta, cooked al dente
1 15.5 oz can chickpeas, drained and rinsed
1 cup flat-leaf parsley, chopped
1/2 cup grated Parmesan
1/2 cup toasted pine nuts for topping

Heat the oil in a large saucepan over medium-high heat. Stir in the garlic, and cook for 1 minute. Add the broth, crushed red pepper, and 3/4 teaspoon sea salt. Bring to a boil. Add the pasta, and cook, stirring, until the broth is nearly absorbed and the pasta is al dente, about 6 minutes. Stir in the chickpeas and parsley. Divide among individual bowls, and top with Parmesan.

**Andy's note: Beans are such a great source of protein but require a little extra zip, and the toasted pine nut topping adds a delicious crunch to this vegetarian dish.

CHAPTER TWELVE

———

"All right. Tell us what's so important." Jones turned in his seat to glare at Rochelle. The man could pull off frosty distain like no one else, but the glower he sent his sort of ex-wife chilled me to the bone. I made a mental note to never do anything that would put me on the receiving end of that look.

Though Rochelle didn't squirm under the scrutiny, she appeared distinctly uncomfortable, unable to hold that piercing blue gaze. "First of all, I feel as though I owe you an explanation. About my husband."

One of Jones's eyebrows lifted. Though he didn't say it, I could almost hear him murmur a droll, "A little late for that?" He didn't respond but simply waited for her to continue. Out of the three people enduring this awkward moment, I was the one squirming like a two-year-old who had to tinkle. I'd been cast in the role of a voyeur, and I felt slightly perverse but still intently curious. From what little he'd told me of his relationship with Rochelle, Jones had been informed by a mutual friend about her deception. He'd left without confronting her, ignoring all of her attempts at further communication. He'd put off the annulment, but that was such a guy thing to do, not make waves until it became an issue. Well, thanks to Kyle, it was now officially an issue we needed to tackle.

My guess—as a purely neutral observer, of course— was that Rochelle had tracked him down hoping for closure. Maybe even a shot at redemption. She sat there as though waiting for some signal from him. How had this gone in her head? Did she imagine he would rant and rave? If so, she didn't know Malcolm Jones, at least not the way I did.

Though he was never overly demonstrative, his stillness told me he was angry, so angry that we could have fried an egg on his raging temper. He hadn't talked much about his brief marriage, but I knew he'd been humiliated by it. I hadn't pushed him to share more information about that time in his life, a fact I was regretting now because I had no idea how he was going to react. He'd been a great support for me as I dealt with Kaylee. And now he was facing off against his own personal demon for the two of us. Only his steely control and need to help me kept him from walking away again.

But at what personal cost?

I threaded my fingers through his in a silent show of support. His head jerked my way, surprise clear in his eyes. I offered him a small smile of encouragement. He blinked, clearly unsure. My heart ached for him. He'd endured so much on his own, never having a stable support network, anyone to lean on when push came to shove. That was different now. I might not want to live with him in his sister's house at the moment, but I did want to offer support when and where I could. Trust went two ways, and he needed to know he could count on me.

Our eyes locked, and he blew out a slow breath, then nodded.

"We're listening." I turned my smile on Rochelle. Though Jones had painted her as some sort of money-grubbing villainess, I didn't see that in her at all. She may not have had the most integrity in the world, but she was a decent person who was trying to do the right thing. I respected that.

To give her credit, she didn't pussyfoot around the issue, just cut straight to the heart of the matter. "Paul was the love of my life. He meant the world to me. He was an artist, always temperamental. I thought that was just part of the package." Her expression turned sad, her eyes downcast.

Jones had fallen back into that eerie stillness, though his knuckles whitened as he gripped my hand. The conversation had to be killing him, hearing that Rochelle considered another man the love of her life, and I squeezed back, silently communicating that he was mine and we'd get through this together. I braced myself, knowing this story was about to take a dark turn, and not just because of her use of the past tense.

"We'd been married about a year when he told me he'd been diagnosed as a paranoid schizophrenic. At first I thought I could live with it, with him. He was still Paul, and I actually admired him more because I knew how hard he fought his illness. But then he went off his meds."

Emotion clogged my throat, and I was glad we weren't hearing this sad tale over an appetizer in a restaurant. A thumb stroked over my knuckles, as if Jones was checking to make sure I would be able to hold myself together. I squeezed back to reassure him that no, I was not about to blubber like an emotional idiot and add another layer of awkward to the moment.

Rochelle continued. "It was sort of a roller coaster after that. The doctors played around with different drugs, but nothing stabilized him, not really. He'd get depressed or angry, with no external cause. Be unable to separate reality from his hallucinations. I really thought I could handle it, did my best to get him home care. But when he attacked me, I knew I was fooling myself. If the day nurse hadn't been there to give him a sedative, he'd have cut my throat. He needed more help and supervision than I could ever give him."

She stopped, took a deep breath, and looked up at Jones. "He's in a group home, in upstate New York. Most of the time when I go there, he isn't lucid, doesn't recognize me. Paul's gone in all but body and name."

"I know," Jones said quietly.

He did? That was news to me.

Rochelle's jaw dropped. Apparently, she hadn't known either. "How long have you known?" she asked.

Jones cleared his throat. "Since the day I moved out. I'm a private investigator— it's what I do. What I should have done before we went through with that sham of a wedding." There was no malice in his tone. He sounded completely detached, as though reciting a particularly uninspired scene for the community theater.

Rochelle shook her head, unable to accept his words. "You never said anything."

Jones looked at me, and I made a go-on gesture with my free hand.

He cleared his throat, his accent thicker than usual. "I'm sorry for what you both went through. Are still going through. But it didn't change anything between us, then or now."

Rochelle shook her head. "You wouldn't even take my calls. All this time you knew?" If anything, she was the one who sounded pissed off. Having been on the receiving end of one of Jones's digging expeditions without warning, I could so relate.

"There was nothing to talk about. It was over the second you made the choice to intentionally deceive me." That steely glint was back in his gaze. "I know you aren't here to try and win me back. So why go after my girlfriend?"

Rochelle still hadn't recovered from the thought that Jones had known all along about her first husband. Her cheeks were flushed from more than the cold, and she looked from him to me.

"He doesn't talk about it." I shrugged. "So I had no clue."

Rochelle let out a humorless laugh and then shook her head. "Sounds familiar."

"I know, right? He's not much of a sharer."

"Tell me about it."

Jones wore a slightly horrified expression, as if we were about to start trading tales of our sexual escapades with him. I rolled my eyes and then for his benefit added, "Anyway, we're working through it. And I am also very sorry about your husband. Er, the other one. Now, please tell us who hired you."

Rochelle looked from me to Jones and then back. She nodded slowly, struggling to compose herself. "His name is Griffin, Jacob Griffin. He called me soon after Flavor TV dropped the investigation."

Who? I frowned at the unfamiliar name. "What do you know about him?"

"Nothing, other than that name. I sent my reports to a PO box in Atlanta. I've never spoken to him, so for all I know, it could be a woman using a man's name."

So it could still be Lacey L'Amour.

Jones frowned at her. "It's not like you to take on a job for someone you'd never met."

Rochelle shrugged. "I'd already done a good chunk of the work. Flavor TV had no basis for a lawsuit, and they didn't care what I did with the information I'd gathered. No matter what you think, this wasn't personal. The place where Paul is housed is expensive. I needed the income."

I couldn't blame her. Well, I *could*, but I wouldn't. Though I wasn't happy to be the subject of yet another investigation, she'd only been doing her job. "Did you tell Mr. Griffin about Kaylee?"

She bit her lip, then shook her head. "No. It might end up costing me the job, but from what I've found out about her, the kid already had a rough life. I don't know what my employer wants the information for, but I wanted to keep her clear of it if I could."

I blew out a breath that seemed to start somewhere around my kneecaps. "Thank you. You don't know how important that is to her. And to me."

She looked at me, and this time, her smile was genuine. "Actually, I think I do."

Though I knew the answer, I asked anyway. "So, you'll be staying in town awhile?"

She nodded, glancing from me to Jones, as if wondering if I'd told him about Lizzy's case. I gave a slight shake of my head to communicate that no, not yet, and she closed her eyes and pinched the bridge of her nose as if she had a headache.

"I should be going." She fixed me with a hard stare and then turned to Jones. "Thanks for hearing me out."

We watched her walk back across the driveway to her rental.

"Andrea." Jones watched her even though he spoke to me in a mild tone. "What aren't you telling me?"

"I told you, it isn't my secret to tell." And hadn't I just witnessed firsthand how well that had worked out for him and Rochelle? Damn Lizzy, and her snooping, straight to the fiery gates of hell.

He turned the engine over and put the SUV into gear. "I thought we were working through it."

"Rome wasn't built in a day," I murmured. Between the exhaustion of the day's work and the relief that Rochelle was going to keep Kaylee's identity to herself, I was drooping with fatigue. "Come on. We're late for dinner."

* * *

"You are late," Aunt Cecily said in a menacing tone when we walked in the door to my rental. It had taken my great-aunt no time at all to make herself at home. Between the smells of cooking Italian spices, and Pops's football game blaring from the television, and Roofus snoring on the rug, the place felt like home.

Or maybe that was just because Jones was with me.

He leaned down and kissed Aunt Cecily on her papery cheek. "She was being stubborn, as usual. Had practically chained herself to the stove."

Aunt Cecily nodded with approval. Her work ethic was of the "I'll rest when I'm dead" variety. "I will go in to work with you tomorrow. Make sure you aren't ruining the pasta shop."

Audible gulp. "Um, Aunt Cecily, tomorrow really isn't a good time—"

She set the piping hot casserole dish down on a hot pad. "Tomorrow. After the Mass. You must go to Mass more. And confession. And then we will make the pasta. Go now and wash for dinner."

Having been given his marching orders, Jones loped off to the second bathroom. I washed up at the kitchen sink and tried to think of a way to get my rigid great-aunt on board with my new recipes. Oh man, she was going to fillet me like a flounder when she saw that B from the health department.

"Hey there, Andy girl." Pops kissed my forehead in the same way as he'd done since I was little. "What's new?"

I shrugged. "Not too much. Hey, Pops, do you know someone named Jacob Griffin?"

Pops knew everyone who'd lived in the town of Beaverton since before I was born. If anyone in town knew the man, it would be my grandfather.

He'd been bent over the refrigerator, extracting a wine bottle from the door. He froze midmotion.

"Pops?" I asked, frowning. "Are you all right?"

"My back," he gasped, still hunched over. "Damned arthritis."

I was by his side in a moment, calling for Jones to come help. "Where do you want to go, Pops? The couch?"

He shook his head slowly. "I'll never be able to get back up. The table."

"You sure?"

He nodded and then winced. "It'll pass in a bit. Don't feel much like eating, but at least I can sit with my family."

Jones moved to his other side, and together we guided Pops to the table. He winced with every step and grimaced as we helped ease him down onto the chair, Aunt Cecily looking on the entire time.

"You go to doctor," she declared. "Tomorrow."

"Ain't nothing the doctor can do for me." Pops had brought his ornery streak to the fore. "I'm old. They don't got a way to fix old."

"It's called death," Aunt Cecily said. "Permanent fix. *Testardo capra vecchia!*"

Jones held out a chair for me and whispered, "What did she call him?"

"A stubborn old goat," I whispered back, and then louder, "and you really should go, Pops. Just have Doc Harrison take a look. Maybe he can give you something for the pain. I can drive you."

He was taking deep breaths, inhaling and exhaling in a steady rhythm. "You're busy at the pasta shop."

"I can make time." I just had to stop wasting hours sleeping and possibly develop time travel. "This is important."

"I would be happy to drive you, Eugene," Jones offered out of nowhere.

All three of us looked at him.

He stared back, unflinchingly. "I've got some business in town. It wouldn't be out of my way."

Pops looked at me, raising one bushy eyebrow. I shrugged, at a loss for words.

"It is done then. Malcolm will drive you to Doctor Harrison, and I will go to the pasta shop with Andy after Mass."

"Aunt Cecily, you know I don't go to daily Mass." I barely made it on Ash Wednesday and Palm Sunday.

"You will go to Mass." Aunt Cecily had spoken, and so would it be.

God help us.

"I'll get the wine." I pushed back out of the chair. "Malcolm, a hand?"

The kitchen was open but far enough away that we could exchange a private word.

"What was that?" Jones asked as I took down the wineglasses.

"Oh, nothing, other than when I left this morning, Pops and Aunt Cecily were under the impression we were broken up. And here you are at dinner, offering to drive my grandfather to the doctor."

He frowned. "But Cecily invited me for dinner."

"Of course she did. She knows you're a prize and thinks I'm an idiot for moving out. She busted out eggplant parm for you. It's the Italian woman's equivalent of a siren song."

"Maybe she wants me for herself then," Jones teased.

"You know nothing." I did my best Aunt Cecily impression, brandishing the corkscrew. "The Rossetti women must ensure the next generation is married with many fat babies who will one day make the pasta."

Jones barked out a laugh. "Okay, so then why is my being here a problem?"

"It isn't a problem. They're just surprised you've come around so quickly, and possibly that I managed to fix our relationship myself without the cholesterol bomb for life support. Fricking hell," I grumped, exasperated with the situation and the damn cork, which wasn't budging from the desperately needed merlot.

"Allow me." Jones plucked the bottle from my hands and expertly divested the bottle of the cork.

I scowled up at him. "Show-off."

"It's a ride into town," Jones mumbled as he poured the wine. "Not a commitment."

"Taking my grandfather to the doctor—equivalent of taking a bullet for me, and you know it," I hissed.

He offered me a glass, which I took. He didn't let go though, only waited until I lifted my gaze to his face. "I'd do that too."

I melted on the spot. "I don't think I deserve you."

He cupped my chin with his forefinger and brushed a soft kiss across my lips. "We deserve each other."

"My eggplant, it gets cold," Aunt Cecily called. "You, come, sit, eat."

I turned, wine fortification in hand. "And just what did we do to deserve her?"

Jones laughed. "We'll do that later."

Eggplant Parmesan

You'll need:
2 eggplants cut into 1/2-inch-thick disks
 Salt and freshly ground black pepper to taste
1/2 cup Egg Beaters
4 cups Panko bread crumbs
1/2 cup grated Parmesan cheese
2 tablespoons all-purpose flour, sifted
1 cup olive oil for frying
1/2 cup prepared tomato sauce
1/4 cup fresh mozzarella, cut into small cubes
1/4 cup chopped fresh basil
1/2 cup grated provolone cheese
1/4 cup grated Parmesan cheese
1 tablespoon olive oil

Preheat oven to 450 degrees.

Pour Egg Beaters in a shallow bowl, and set aside. Mix bread crumbs and 1/2 cup Parmesan in a separate bowl. Set aside. Place flour in a sifter or strainer; sprinkle over eggplant, evenly coating both sides. Dip flour-coated meat in egg product. Transfer to bread crumb mixture, pressing the crumbs into both sides. Repeat for each slice.

Heat 1 cup olive oil in a large skillet on medium-high heat until it begins to simmer. Cook eggplant until golden, about 2 minutes on each side. Place in a baking dish, and top each with about 1/3 cup of tomato sauce. Layer each with equal amounts of mozzarella cheese, fresh basil, and provolone cheese. Sprinkle 1 to 2 tablespoons of Parmesan cheese on top, and drizzle with 1 tablespoon olive oil.

Bake in the preheated oven until cheese is browned and bubbly, and eggplant is cooked through, approximately 40 minutes. Serve with al dente pasta.

**Andy's note: This may seem like a lot of work for a vegetable, but believe me, it's worth doing right. Just like you want evenly cooked chicken in chicken parm, or veal in veal parm, the eggplant is the star of the show. It's important to cut your eggplant disks into proper thickness so they cook evenly for a consistent texture throughout.

CHAPTER THIRTEEN

———

After eight o'clock Mass, in which I prayed that Aunt Cecily wouldn't kill me for changing her tried-and-true menu, I drove us to the Bowtie Angel. She frowned at the grand opening banner for Lacey's restaurant. "What is this?"

"That's Lacey L'Amour's new restaurant. French food." I tried to not sound bitter.

"French." She spat on the ground, a wordless gesture letting everyone around us know what she thought of the concept. Or perhaps the French in general. With Aunt Cecily, who could tell?

"Yes, well, it'll be opening tomorrow. Fine dining, cloth napkins, all very different from us." Well, at least the way we were now. I was hoping Aunt Cecily would see the need to spiff the place up a bit, now that we weren't the only ethnic game in town.

Aunt Cecily gave the restaurant one last glare and then shuffled into the pasta shop. I said a silent Hail Mary and followed her, still trying to figure out what to say and possibly where to hide.

Mimi met us in the kitchen. She hugged Aunt Cecily and then beamed at me. "Good news, the health inspector agreed to come in and—"

I'd been busy making a slicing motion across my throat, but my keen-eared great-aunt had picked up on the key word.

"The health inspector?" she repeated. Slowly she rounded on me in a terrifying way.

"He was sick," I lied. As far as lies went, it was a crappy one.

"From our food?" Her steely eyes narrowed.

"No!" I practically shouted. This was becoming ridiculous. I needed to get a grip. Surely she wouldn't give me The Eye. Not her own flesh and blood. Who else would make the pasta?

"It was my fault," Mimi said before I could compound things further.

Aunt Cecily pivoted toward her. "Your fault?"

Mimi and I exchanged horrified glances. "Yeah, Mimi has a cold, and she gave it to the health inspector. By accident of course, at the post office, not through the food."

Mimi sneezed unconvincingly and whispered, "I called him to apologize."

Aunt Cecily looked between the two of us and muttered something in Italian too low for me to pick up. Probably for the best. "Come then. We must make the pasta."

When she moved to the office, I scurried over to Mimi. "Sorry, she sprung herself on us at the last minute. So, what did Theo say?"

"He agreed to take another look and average the two grades. Of course, he didn't say when he'd be back around, so it could be at any time." Her gaze followed after Aunt Cecily. "Do you still want me to bake today?"

I nodded. "Yeah. I was hoping to ease her into this slowly, so slowly that she wouldn't notice. But maybe it's better to spring it all on her at once."

"Like a surprise party?" Mimi asked.

I tried to picture Aunt Cecily at a surprise party, all the color and energy and happy people around her small, dark, and glowering form, and winced. "Sort of."

The back door opened, and Kaylee came in. "Hey."

I looked to the clock. "Shouldn't you be in school?"

She shook her head. "Teacher conference day. Is it all right that I'm here?"

"Of course," I said, still miffed that she'd blown us off yesterday to hang out at Lacey's, but not wanting to make a big deal out of it.

She looked around. "What can I do?"

"Come, you will make the pasta." Aunt Cecily had appeared like a small Sicilian apparition to spirit Kaylee away.

"But I thought…" I began. I was the one who always made the pasta with her, had been since I was eight years old.

Aunt Cecily waved me off. "You can do the vegetables and the gravy."

I blinked, confused. Was I really being demoted to chief veggie prepper and bottle washer in my own pasta shop?

I opened my mouth to say something, but as I watched Aunt Cecily instruct Kaylee on what she needed to get from the pantry, I resigned myself to the situation. So what if I'd wanted to be the one to teach my biological daughter how to make pasta? I'd learned from the best, so she might as well go to the source. Aunt Cecily was getting up there in years. Was it really right of me to cheat Kaylee out of the firsthand experience?

Plus, I couldn't afford to be sentimental—I had a business to run.

I did the veggie prep, which included chopping arugula, fresh spinach, sweet bell peppers, mushrooms, and green onions for the new house salad. Aunt Cecily glared at the combination but said nothing.

With the gravy simmering on a low heat, I scurried back to the office to make a few phone calls. The first was to Jones. "Well, my morning's been a slow-motion train wreck. How about you?"

He laughed. "Your grandfather gave me a strong talking to about not letting the good ones get away. Then he refused to go into the doctor's office, claiming he was feeling just fine. I told him you'd break up with me for good if I didn't follow through on my promise, so he went in."

I grinned, clearly able to envision the scene. "You have a dark and devious mind, Malcolm Jones. I find that incredibly sexy."

"I try to use my powers for good instead of evil," he quipped. "What's been going on there?"

I summed up my morning and then confessed, "I'm actually hiding in the office, as the three of them don't seem to want me anywhere underfoot."

"Andrea, you need to tell Kaylee how you feel about what she did yesterday. And tell your aunt that you wanted to teach Kaylee how to make pasta."

I blew out a sigh. "If I read her the riot act, she'll leave. Then Aunt Cecily will glower at me, and I'll be right back where I started. There's been enough conflict around here lately."

Jones sighed. "You're trying to build a relationship with Kaylee, right? Think about what you and I have been going through. Wouldn't everything have been so much easier if we'd been up-front with each other? I know you, love. You can only keep things bottled up for so long."

"When did you get so smart?" I asked him bitterly.

"Oxford, remember?" There was a smile in his voice.

"And so modest too. All right, but if this goes sideways, I'm blaming you."

"I would expect nothing less. Now I need to go get an annulment before your baby daddy arrests me again."

"That sounds wrong on so many levels." I said good-bye to him and then rose from the desk. It was time for me to stop hiding and start taking charge. The Bowtie Angel didn't belong to Aunt Cecily anymore, and while I still respected her as my elder and a chef, she was no longer the boss of me.

Well, not officially anyway.

"Aunt Cecily," I began as I strode down the hall, wearing my determination like a badge.

I paused outside the restroom door, sucked back a deep breath—and a hand clamped over my mouth. I shrieked, but it was too muffled for anyone to hear. Another hand snagged me around the neck and tugged me into the bathroom.

The door shut in front of me, closing me in with my assailant. I'd been too stunned to move immediately, but as my adrenaline kicked in, I struggled with all my strength, flailing wildly in my attempts to free myself and recall my self-defense training. I'd taken a course when I'd lived in Atlanta, and remembered to go for the soft parts. I drove one elbow back. It connected with my attacker's stomach with a meaty thud.

There was a woof of expelled air, but the hands didn't let go. I sank my nails into the wrist holding me still.

"Calm down, Little Bit," a familiar voice wheezed. "It's just me."

I ceased my struggles as realization dawned. The hand left my mouth, and he spun me to face him. Jeez-a-lou. "Kyle?

What the hell?" I shoved him, irate that he'd manhandled and scared the marinara right out of me.

There were small crescents dug into his wrist, a few of them oozing blood. "I wanted to talk to you without your boyfriend around."

"So you abduct me in my pasta shop with our daughter twenty feet away? What exactly is your damage?" I shoved him again for good measure.

"Take it easy." He held his hands up in a defensive position. "And no, I didn't abduct you. You're still here, aren't you?"

"Doesn't change the fact that you scared the crap out of me. You ever heard of a phone? Send me a text, and ask me to meet you," I huffed. "And just what is so important that you want to hide it from Jones?"

"Because he talks to Lizzy, and I don't want Lizzy to know I talked to you."

And around and around we go. "Kyle, I really don't want to get in the middle of you and Lizzy and your issues. I have more than enough of my own."

"Oh no? Then why did you feel the need to tell her I was escorting Lacey L'Amour around town?"

I opened my mouth to respond, but he cut me off. "Don't even try to deny it was you that told her."

My hands went automatically to my hips. "I won't. It was me. I thought she ought to know. If Jones had been mincing about with that strumpet, I'd want someone to tell me. Lacey is bad news."

Kyle scowled at me. "Some folks said the same about you when you came back to town. At least Lacey didn't poison an entire live studio audience."

"If I kick you in the shins, would that be considered assaulting an officer of the law?" I asked sweetly.

He glowered at me. "Anyway, mind your own business."

I fisted my hands on my hips and lifted my chin. "I'll have you know that Lacey lured our daughter into her lair yesterday."

Kyle actually rolled his eyes at me. "You make it sound like she's a witch who lives in a gingerbread cottage and eats children. If you must know, I asked Kaylee to go there yesterday."

"What?" I blinked, stunned by his admission. "Why would you do that?"

"To cover our asses?"

I poked him in the chest. "If you don't start making sense, I will have to beat it into you, sheriff or no." Something dawned on me. "Hey, why aren't you in uniform?"

"Because I'm not officially on duty. I took the day off so I could bring Lizzy to visit her mom. She's under a lot of stress, and I would consider it a huge favor if you would stop getting her so worked up."

"The problem with that, Kyle, is that Lizzy gets herself worked up. She's an instant stress machine. Just add air. I just can't stop myself from needling her when she's three seconds from detonation." I barely refrained from asking him if he knew his fiancé spent her nights lurking around the woods and hiding in the bushes. And he was calling me a drama queen?

"Well try," Kyle said dryly. "I'll talk to you later."

"Can't wait." He was gone before I realized that he'd never told me why he'd wanted Kaylee to go to Lacey's place. What had I ever seen in that man? I pushed out of the bathroom and headed back to the office, having all I could handle of personal conflict for a spell.

* * *

"Is Jones gonna be stopping in again tonight?" Pops asked. "I was gonna show him my target shooting trophies."

I'd just settled myself on the couch, glass of Chardonnay in hand and aching feet up on the coffee table. "I don't know, Pops. He's got a lot of work to do on his photographs for the show this summer, plus his regular work."

"Man's got to eat," Pops grumbled

"I know, but if he comes over for dinner, he'll end up spending the night. Besides, I sent him home with a care package from the pasta shop when he stopped by to see me earlier. Trust me. I won't let him starve."

Pops made a disparaging noise, probably at the carrying on of the younger generation.

I took my grandfather's hand and squeezed lightly. "I'm glad you like him, Pops."

"Who says I do?" he harrumphed.

"Well, you let him take you to the doctor. You've never let anyone but me or Nana do that, so I know you trust him. Speaking of which, what did the doctor say?"

Pops shrugged and looked away. "Same as I thought. There ain't nothing he can do. This dag-burned cold just makes it all that much worse."

I squeezed his hand again and made a mental note to check up on homeopathic arthritis remedies. "Where's Aunt Cecily?"

Pops smiled. "Taking a nap. She wouldn't tell you to save her life, but she ain't as young as she used to be. Spending a whole day on her feet in the pasta shop plum tuckered her out."

"Her and me both." I sighed and leaned my head back against the couch cushion.

"You all right, Andy girl?"

"Just tired, I think. The last few days have been an emotional roller coaster. Want me to grill a steak for dinner?"

Pops smacked his lips. "Sounds right tasty."

I got up and retrieved a steak from the freezer. Normally speaking, I would marinate a steak for a few days to infuse flavors, but I'd just got a new gadget that vacuum sealed the meat and spices to supposedly the same effect. Aunt Cecily considered most modern gizmos the work of the devil, so I'd been waiting until she was otherwise occupied to use it.

After setting the meat to defrost in the microwave, I took my grill pan out from under the stove and turned on the left burners. The meat dinged, and I transferred it along with a few cloves of peeled garlic, Worcestershire sauce, Kosher salt, and freshly ground black pepper. I'd just hit the vacuum sealer and started peeling potatoes when my phone rang. Distracted by the promise of dinner, I didn't bother to look at the number. "Hello?"

Silence.

I repeated my greeting, wondering if it was one of those stupid automatic phone solicitations that had a delayed start. Still nothing, though I thought I heard someone breathing. Not a cyborg wondering about my personal purchasing power then. Probably a teenager crank calling me.

"Last chance, and then I'm hanging up." I didn't have time for adolescent pranks.

"Andy?" It was a woman's voice, though not one I recognized right away. She didn't sound right, a little reedy as though she stood a distance from the phone.

"Yeah? Who is this?"

"No!" Her voice was filled with panic. "Please, don't—"

A shot boomed across the line. I dropped my vacuum-sealed steak.

"This will be your only warning." It was a digitized voice. "Back off now, or you're next."

"Who are you?" I whispered, clutching the phone in a white-knuckled grip.

The only response was a sudden click as the line went dead.

Steak Pizzaiola

You'll need:
4 tablespoons olive oil, plus more if needed
2 cloves garlic, minced
3 large tomatoes, peeled and chopped
3 sprigs plus 1/2 teaspoon chopped fresh oregano
3/4 teaspoon salt
1/2 teaspoon freshly ground black pepper
1 1/2 pounds sirloin steak, about 1 inch thick

In a large saucepan, heat 2 tablespoons of the oil over medium heat. Add the garlic, and cook, stirring, for 1 minute. Add the tomatoes, oregano sprigs, 1/2 teaspoon of the salt, and 1/4 teaspoon of the pepper. Reduce the heat, and simmer partially covered until the sauce thickens, about 15 minutes.

In a large frying pan, heat the remaining 2 tablespoons oil over moderate heat. Season the steak with the remaining 1/4 teaspoon salt and 1/4 teaspoon pepper. Cook the steak for 5 minutes. Turn, and cook until done to your taste, about 5 minutes longer for medium rare. Remove the steak, and let rest in a warm spot for 5 minutes. Cut the steak diagonally into thin slices, and top with the warm tomato sauce and the chopped fresh oregano.

**Andy's note: For a juicy steak, be sure to let red meat rest to finish cooking before you slice into it.

CHAPTER FOURTEEN

———

"I don't know who she was," I repeated for the third time to Jones. "I didn't recognize her voice."

Bless the man—he'd rushed over the second I'd called him. A good thing too, as I was barely hanging on to my sanity. Pops hovered over the two of us like an anxious bumblebee, but he let Jones do all the talking.

"You're sure it was a gunshot you heard?" Jones said.

I shook my head. "I have no idea, but that's what it sounded like."

Though he hid it well, I could sense his frustration. "Love, you need to give me something more to go on. Start from the beginning."

"I was in the kitchen when my cell rang. I said 'hello' twice, then threatened to hang up. That's when I heard the woman say my name."

"Did she have an accent?" he asked.

I shook my head. "She didn't say much, and it wasn't a strong accent if she did. Not like you or Pops or Aunt Cecily."

"Did she sound young or old?" he probed.

"She just sounded scared. Malcolm, she was terrified. And he just..." My throat clogged with tears, and I chocked on a sob. "He killed her."

"Shouldn't we call the police or something?" Pops asked. "Death threats are illegal, ain't they? Never mind committing a murder."

Jones shook his head. "He told Andy to back off, but the threat was nonspecific. He didn't clarify what he wanted. For all we know, they're watching the house to see how Andy reacts. The best thing we can do now is try to identify either the victim or the murderer and decide how to proceed from there."

"How can we though?" I asked. "I'm telling you, I really wasn't paying attention, and everything happened so fast. How can we find out anything with so little to go on?"

"Where's your phone?"

I pointed. "In the kitchen."

Jones got up from the sofa and went into the kitchen. He came back holding my phone out to me. "Did you recognize the number? Or even the area code?"

I shrank away from the thing as though it were poisonous. "It was blocked."

Jones pocketed the cell and then handed me his phone. "Let me hang on to it. I have a friend who might be able to trace the call. Use mine for the time being." He headed for the door.

"Wait," I said, the numbness finally wearing off. "You're leaving?"

His gaze went from me to Pops and then back. "Yes."

That threw me. I thought for sure he'd want to guard me like a Rottweiler, not leaving my side until the creep had been brought to justice. But now he was just walking away as though it were any other night and I hadn't just been ear witness to a possible murder.

I moved closer, tripping over the afghan I'd tossed to the floor. "You can't just leave me."

Pops cleared his throat. "I better wake Cecily. Tell her what's amiss."

"Come outside with me," Jones whispered.

The idea of leaving the sanctuary of the house terrified me, but I wanted to understand why he felt the need to leave. I grabbed my parka off the coat tree and, not bothering to zip it, followed him out into the cool night.

I'd expected to have it out with him on the front stoop, that if he had some grisly detail to divulge, he didn't want to bring up in front of Pops. Instead, he led me to his SUV and opened the door for me.

I blinked in surprise. "You're not planning to abduct me, are you?"

He shook his head. "No, I simply want you to be warm while we talk."

Okay then. I climbed in the vehicle and waited while he circumnavigated it and started the engine. He turned to me and then said, "All right. I need to know what you've been keeping from me."

I frowned. "Who says there's just one thing?"

He gave me a level stare. "Andrea, I know you. Even your feud with Lacey L'Amour isn't going to end in bloodshed. And while I respect the fact that it's not your secret to tell, I do need to know everything if I'm going to be of any use. So start with the reason why you and my sister went to see Rochelle yesterday."

I swallowed hard. On the one hand, I didn't want to break my promise to Lizzy. We'd established a weird sort of truce, and though I would never admit it out loud, I kind of liked having her on my side for a change. But if I didn't tell Jones and he ended up hurt or worse because I hadn't been up-front with him, I'd never forgive myself.

Decided, I blew out a sigh. "All right, but you have got to promise me that you aren't going to let on to anyone you know this. To anyone, Malcolm."

"If it helps me catch the killer, I'll need to use the information," he warned. "Whatever it is."

I stared at him a moment. "Fine then. But at least promise me that if you do find out who made that phone call, you'll take it to the police. To Kyle."

That, apparently, he could live with, because he nodded. "I promise."

There was no good way to phrase it, so I just came out with the blunt truth. "Lizzy thinks your dad might be the arsonist. We went to Rochelle and hired her to investigate the fires, hoping to prove it wasn't him."

Jones didn't even twitch. "Why would she suspect our father was behind the fires?"

"She said she found gasoline containers at his place in the woods. You know, where he goes to get loaded? And both of the buildings where the fires occurred were owned by jury members in her mother's trial."

Jones looked away. A muscle jumped in his jaw. "Did you tell Rochelle about what she discovered?"

I shifted in my seat. "No. I convinced Lizzy not to. She didn't want it to be him, so we figured if Rochelle started from square one, maybe she could find something else."

His gaze remained locked on the small A-frame, but something about the way he was staring at the house made me think he wasn't seeing it. "And why didn't you come to me? Or tell Kyle?"

I shifted, uncomfortable with his tense manner. "Well, we didn't tell Kyle, because then he'd have to do something about it. You know, all publically and whatnot. Lizzy didn't want to bring that down on her father's head."

Jones nodded, seemingly lost in thought. "I could have looked into it discreetly. That had to be better than bringing in an outsider."

"I wanted to, believe me. I did. But Lizzy was afraid it would put the final nail in the coffin of your relationship with your dad. I agreed because I didn't want to hurt you."

He rounded on me so fast I actually leaned back. His temper flared to life. I'd thought him cold and distant before. Keeping to the theme of the week, I was wrong again. He wasn't cold. He was enraged, and it took all of his control to subdue that emotion. It burst from him like an exploding firework. "So instead, you involve my ex in my family affairs and yourself and my sister in an arson case. You're both in needless danger. Do you really think that's a better option, Andrea?"

I flinched. "Malcolm—"

But he'd turned away again.

"I really am sorry," I whispered. The words were hollow and changed nothing.

He simply nodded. "Is there anything else?"

Even though he sat right next to me, it felt as if we were miles apart. "No."

"I'll call you when I find out anything about the phone call." He spoke low and calmly, but I'd seen under the mask. I knew how his rage seethed.

Though I wanted to say something, words wouldn't fix this. He needed time to wrap his head around the idea that maybe his father was an arsonist-murderer. And that his girlfriend was in a killer's crosshairs.

Again.

"I'm going to fix this." I repeated the same words to him that he'd spoken to me when I'd shut him down. "I promise, Malcolm. I'll do whatever it takes to make this right."

He nodded. Feeling like utter garbage, I slithered out of the SUV and stood back, watching him drive off.

* * *

The following day, Aunt Cecily and Pops invited themselves to the pasta shop. Aunt Cecily had been as maternal as I'd ever seen her, making me tea and not calling either me or Pops any unfortunate names. She'd cooked my steak, forced me to sit at the table and eat. If my vacuum-sealing gizmo added additional flavor, I couldn't tell, as everything tasted like rubber. Though it'd been a struggle, I'd forced myself to swallow a few bites before retiring to my room with Jones's cell phone to call every woman I knew and make sure she was still breathing.

I'd called Kaylee's mom first, to check on her and my daughter, and been able to take my first deep breath when I heard their voices. Donna had been fine, although she'd wanted to come over the second I told her what had happened. I'd begged off, having been smothered enough for one night, and proceeded down the list. Mimi hadn't picked up, which had sent me into a near panic, until she texted me a few seconds later to tell me she was out of minutes for the month. I'd cursed a blue streak at cellular providers worldwide and then made the hardest call of all.

The good news was that no one had shot Lizzy. The bad news was that after she'd heard that I'd spilled the beans to Jones, Lizzy wanted to shoot *me*. So much for forward progress in our relationship. Both physically and emotionally spent, I told her to get in line, turned the phone off, and crawled into bed.

Lacey glared at me from her front stoop. I gave her a subtle one-fingered salute and checked her name off possible victims of a homicidal firebug. She sucked canal water backward, but I wasn't about to wish that fate on her.

Mimi greeted us as we tromped in the door. "The new delivery service called," she whispered to me as Pops helped Aunt Cecily with her coat. "They'll be here at nine."

Either my priorities had been straightened out or I didn't have enough energy to get worked up over Aunt Cecily finding out about the new menu items, because I just nodded.

"Is everything all right, Andy?" Mimi asked.

I shook my head. "Honestly, no, but I really don't want to get into it."

Aunt Cecily overheard this last statement and added, "She is fighting with her man again. Young people are foolish and hot tempered. They get mad—they get glad. They get married, then they learn a thing or two about fighting."

Mimi's eyes were the size of duck eggs.

I made a face at the Sicilian Dr. Ruth and her tough love and then trudged off to the kitchen. Actually, I felt grateful that Aunt Cecily had intervened. The last thing I wanted was to make Mimi feel unsafe at the pasta shop. And until Jones got back to me with whatever he'd found out about my disturbing phone call, I wouldn't know if the threat to my life was real.

It had occurred to me sometime over my mostly sleepless night that the entire phone call could have been staged to do exactly what it was doing—scare the wits out of me. Maybe there had been no murder at all, and it was just an elaborate prank. After all, wouldn't a real killer have been more specific about what exactly he wanted me to back off from? Jones and I had both assumed the arson investigation, but it could very well have been something else entirely. And if it was a hoax, I'd bet my best wooden spoon that Lacey L'Amour had something to do with it.

The morning passed in a flurry of hectic activity. Aunt Cecily's eyes narrowed when she spotted the new delivery guy, but at least she didn't curse him in rapid-fire Italian. She and Pops left around noon to run errands and check on some of their friends who were staying with family in town while the assisted living apartments were rebuilt.

The lunch rush kept us hopping until about two thirty. As the midafternoon lull set in, I turned to Mimi. "You can take off early again if you want."

"You sure?" she asked.

"Yes, I'm waiting for Jones." And hoped to get in a private moment if he did show up. Though I still didn't know what to say, the last thing we needed was an audience.

Mimi untied her apron. "All right. There's a new market a few towns over that I wanted to try. Do you want anything?"

"See if they sell sanity. I misplaced my supply."

Mimi grinned. "I'll see what I can do."

She left, and I wiped down the kitchen, did the few lingering dishes, and then headed out front to clean up. I'd just finished wiping down the tables when Theodore Randolph arrived. Theo Randolph was a large lumbering man with a shiny pink scalp, which he covered with an old-fashioned straw boater's hat. He was paler than I was in the dead of winter, and his polyester checked suit did nothing to flatter his rotund stature. His piggy black eyes roamed across the room, checking for hidden grime.

"Andy." The health inspector extended his beefy hand, and I shook it. Theo was something of an old-fashioned dandy. He had soft, almost effeminate skin, as white and puffy as a marshmallow. The contact never failed to make my own flesh crawl.

I discreetly wiped my palm on the seat of my jeans and forced a genial expression onto my face. "Thank you so much for coming back, Theo. I think you'll see we have everything in A-plus order this time." Mimi and I had scrubbed like madwomen every chance we got.

Theo tut-tutted me. "I must say, I was very surprised, Andy. First B for the Bowtie Angel in the twenty-odd years since I took over as county health inspector."

"It was really just bad timing. I had a concussion." I rubbed my forehead, hoping for a little sympathy.

Compassion wasn't on his to-do list. "Yes." He drawled the word in a disapproving tone. "From starting a bar fight, I heard. Really, Andy, what would your grandmother say?"

I bared my teeth in what I hoped passed for a smile. "It's been a rough month. Would you like to see the kitchen?"

I held open the door so he could see the gleaming pots and pans and the brand new door to the walk-in tightly shut.

"Hmmm." Still not overtly impressed, Theo extracted a digital thermometer that looked more like a radar speedometer gun. He pointed it at a vat of bubbling sauce, then a platter of raw veggies. He looked like a wannabe vegetable cop determined to meet this quarter's quotas of tickets. Take that, eggplant!

Though he gave it his all, all my food was refrigerated well within the health code temperature standards. He narrowed his eyes on me as he poked at a jar of pickled tomato relish. "Who made this?"

"I did." Under his watchful gaze, I washed my hands and put on a pair of gloves for good measure.

"Did you sterilize the jars?" he asked.

"Of course." Only because I made it with Nana a few years before she'd died. The relish wasn't for sale. I just kept it around because it reminded me of her. Admittedly, it was a weird sort of tribute, but better than Pops's suggestion of putting her cremated remains next to the flour and salt on the shelf.

Theo checked my grease traps and then did a bacteria meter swab on the tops and undersides of our food prep station. I glanced over his shoulder and smiled at the 0.0 reading.

"Well, everything seems on the up-and-up." The health inspector sniffed delicately. "I'll just check the walk-in and be on my way."

No, atta girl, Andy, good job, or any other indication that I was rocking the culinary casbah. That was fine. I didn't need his praise. What I needed was the A-plus score to bring my B to an A-minus so I could maintain the family legacy. And so Aunt Cecily wouldn't put The Eye on me.

Not wanting to hover, I turned my back on Theo and started peeling the pile of potatoes I'd left out to make gnocchi. Jones had never had my gnocchi before, and I planned on bringing him some, along with an apology for last night. And if that didn't win him over, at least he couldn't curse me out with his mouth full.

There was a clatter from the walk-in as if Theo had dropped his clipboard. "Is everything all right in there?"

No answer.

Frowning, I set my peeler aside and circumnavigated the prep station. The health inspector's hefty back blocked most of the walk-in, and he stood stock still, his posture ramrod straight. "Theo? What's wrong?"

He pointed, and I looked down. All thoughts of the inspection left my head as I saw the sexy high-heeled black boots sticking out from under a giant sack of flour. Familiar boots.

I moved around Theo, praying I was wrong. That couldn't be Rochelle in my walk-in. It couldn't, no way.

It was though. Jones's ex lay sprawled, her wrists bound and a hole gaping in the middle of her frozen forehead.

Cheesy Gnocchi

You'll need:
5 pounds of potatoes
5 cups all-purpose flour, plus 1 cup for working dough
1 cup ricotta
3 cups fresh grated Parmesan
2 eggs
1 tablespoon sea salt
1 teaspoon white pepper

Prepare potatoes as you would for mashed potatoes. Use a ricer for a more even consistency. Set aside to cool and drain. Pour 5 cups of flour on a clean dry work surface. Make a well in the center, and add the potato mash. Break eggs in a bowl with cheeses and salt, and mix. Add to the center of the potato. Slowly incorporate flour by mounding over potato and egg mixture. Use only what flour is absorbed by the potato mixture. You may have some left over.

Knead dough, adding flour if necessary to hold its shape. Cut dough into 10 equally sized pieces 4 inches long. Roll each piece, one at a time, into thin rope and cut into 1 1/2-inch pieces with a dough cutter or flat-edged knife. Cook within 45 minutes in salted boiling water for approximately 5 minutes or until gnocchi floats to the top of the pot. Toss, and serve with your favorite sauce.

**Andy's note: Be sure you don't overwork the dough. Tough dough means tough gnocchi. If you cheat and buy pre-made gnocchi, I promise I won't tell a soul.

CHAPTER FIFTEEN

———

Kyle was the first to respond to my 9-1-1 call. He was through the door within two minutes, ushering Theo and me out of the kitchen to preserve the integrity of the crime scene.

Dear sweet baby Jesus, my walk-in was a crime scene! "I feel dizzy," I murmured to no one in particular.

"Sit down." Kyle urged me into a booth. "Where's Mimi?"

The question took several moments to register and even longer for me to respond. Rochelle was dead in my walk-in. Dead. I'd talk to her less than forty-eight hours ago, and she was dead. "I let her go early."

"Anybody else here? Eugene or Cecily?"

I shook my head.

"How about Jones?"

"I haven't seen him since last night." Oh god, the phone call. That had been Rochelle's scream over the phone. There was no way I couldn't tell Kyle about that, not after finding Rochelle's body.

My final warning.

The room started to spin. I blinked, then put my head between my knees, trying to slow my racing pulse.

When I looked up again, more uniformed men and women filled the room, some in khaki and others in blue. The Bowtie Angel was technically within the city limits of Beaverton, so the city police had picked up the case. But between the arsonist and now a murder, Police Chief Leroy Fontaine was probably glad for the assist from the sheriff's office.

Kyle had turned away to talk to one of the city police officers, and I stared unseeingly out the window. A crowd had gathered in front of the pasta shop for the second time that week, drawn like flies to a cow pie. And that's just what my business was becoming, a cow pie.

How had it happened? I knew for an absolute fact that Rochelle had not been inside the walk-in that morning. She had to have been dumped there—no, *planted* there—for me to find. And it had to have been done sometime in the last hour, sometime since Mimi had left. Jones was right—the killer had been watching me, waiting for his chance to deliver the final part of his grisly message.

"Malcolm Jones," Kyle said to a deputy I didn't recognize. She was stall and stocky with close-cropped blonde hair and an expression that looked as though she ate nails for breakfast. She nodded as Kyle uttered, "Find him."

"I'm on it." The blonde bruiser nodded and turned away.

Good, I wanted Jones here with me, to feel his strong arms around me, his heat seeping into me, especially because I couldn't shake off the chill of the walk-in.

The phone in my pocket started vibrating like it meant business. I ignored it, staring back out the window, trying desperately to make sense of it all.

Who had killed Rochelle? Had it been the arsonist? Or was more than one sociopath lurking around Beaverton?

"Come with me." Kyle put a hand under my elbow and urged me to my feet.

"Where are we going?" I asked, still dazed.

"To my office."

"I thought you were getting Jones? Shouldn't we wait for him here?" The phone went off again.

Kyle gave me a patient look. "Andy, that's his ex in there."

"Yeah, and…"

"Most homicides involving women are committed by their husbands or boyfriends. Jones is wanted for questioning."

I blinked as reality snapped back into focus with a vengeance. "You can't be serious."

But he was—I could see it from the set of his jaw. "Let me put you out in the car."

Like I was an unruly dog? "Don't forget to crack a window," I snapped.

He ignored my venom, ushering me out the front door. I heard people calling my name, but the roar of voices was too much for me to process.

Kyle opened the rear door of his official vehicle, a tan-and-black mini-SUV. It was much less roomy than Jones's luxury model, but it had been equipped with the standard mesh cage separating the backseat from the front. I got in without any further protesting, resolved to give him an earful once we had a little more privacy. He shut the door and then circled around to the front.

"Hey!" I heard one voice call out. My heart deflated as I saw Kaylee push her way through the crowd. I didn't want her to witness her father carting her mother off to the station, even if it was only to answer questions.

Kyle pulled our daughter aside, pulling her close so their conversation wasn't overheard. I could see the thin, mousy form of her adoptive mother right behind her, big brown eyes filled with worry. Dear god, her adoptive mother was probably mentally packing up their rental, preparing to take Kaylee away from Beaverton as quickly as possible. I wouldn't blame her if she did.

The phone buzzed for the third time. Whoever was calling me was insistent. Though it took something resembling an amateur contortionist's act, I managed to get the phone out of my back pocket. It wasn't until I was looking down at the unfamiliar display that I remembered. Jones had my phone, and I had his.

My thoughts were moving at the speed of light. Should I give the phone to Kyle? Well, I had to. They would trace it eventually and find out that I had it. But I didn't have to tell them that Jones had my cell.

Though it might be interfering with a police investigation or obstruction of justice, I made up my mind then and there that—no, I would not help Kyle haul Jones in for questioning, at least not yet. Kyle had an agenda when it came to my boyfriend, and he couldn't be trusted as an unbiased investigator. I'd promised to buy Jones time to look into the phone call, and so help me, that was exactly what I intended to do.

Outside the vehicle, Kaylee's expression hardened. She cast a look of disgust at Kyle and then at the car, presumably at me. I wanted to give her a hug and tell her everything would be all right, the way Nana had done for me after my mother's death.

Kyle said something else and turned away. Kaylee rolled her eyes, and I smiled a little in spite of the circumstances. That was such a "me" gesture, especially when dealing with Kyle.

The sheriff climbed behind the wheel.

"Hey, I forgot to mention, Jones doesn't have his phone. I have it."

"What?" Kyle had turned the engine over, but he twisted in his seat to look at me. "Why do you have his phone?"

"He left it at the house last night. We had a bit of a falling out, and he took off without it." That was almost the truth, if one didn't look too closely at it. Or ask any follow-up questions.

Lucky for me, Kyle didn't. He swore and then reached for the radio. I kept my yap shut as he related what I'd told him to someone at the other end. Operation protect Jones was officially underway.

Now I had to figure out exactly what I could and couldn't say to Kyle that would skirt the line between messing with a murder investigation and protecting the man I loved.

I leaned back against the seat and shut my eyes. Some days it just didn't pay to get out of bed.

* * *

"Kyle, what were you doing in town today?"

"What?" Kyle sat across from me in his office. He'd paused to draw breath between his rapid-fire questions, most of which I hadn't really answered. My inquiry wasn't just a stall tactic however. At the time I'd been too distracted after finding Rochelle's body and whatnot, but he had shown up fast.

"You arrived at the pasta shop only a few minutes after I made the call. It takes fifteen minutes to drive from here to Main

Street, and that's the way I drive. So you must have already been in town. What were you doing there?"

It wasn't just my imagination—the good sheriff looked distinctly uncomfortable. He cleared his throat and then drawled, "I'm the one asking the questions here, Andy."

"Did you have court?" I pressed. How long would it take the city police to show up here looking for the witness who'd found the body?

Well, another body.

"Yes, that was it. I had court." Kyle nodded and cleared his throat again. Classic nervous tell.

Liar, liar, badge on fire. But why bother lying? If he was patrolling or having lunch with members of the city council, he would have just said so. The fact that he felt the need to lie only proved he was doing something sneaky. Something he didn't want me to know about.

It clicked into place. "For the love of grief, Kyle, please tell me you weren't with Lacey L'Amour again."

A hot flush crept up from his collar. "That isn't relevant to—"

I slammed my hands down on the metal desk. "You were, you rat. Are you screwing around on Lizzy?"

"Keep your voice down," he hissed, gaze sliding to the closed door.

"That isn't a no, Sheriff Landers. What the hell is wrong with you, sniffing around that tramp?"

My powers of deduction had thrown him completely for a loop. "You don't even like Lizzy."

"Well, I don't dislike her as much as I used to. And besides, it isn't about me. It's about you."

"You don't know me," Kyle said. "Not anymore."

"Bull. I know you better than you want to admit. You haven't changed that much, no matter that you wear a badge now instead of a letterman jacket. Some guys are like that, but you've always been the Dudley Do-Right type."

He made a face at that, obviously insulted. "Dudley Do-Right? Really?"

"You aren't a cheater, so what the hell is your game?"

He glanced down. "You don't understand."

I reached out and touched his hand. "Then tell me the truth. Why are you hanging around that faux French slag?"

"Because you don't like her."

That made about as much sense as a screen door on a submarine. "What?"

Kyle rubbed a hand over his face. "Lizzy has been distant lately. She's distracted, never wants to talk about anything with me or go out to dinner. Half the time, she doesn't return my calls or text messages. I know the past year has been hard on her, what with her mother and then Kaylee showing up. She's gone through some major life changes. I thought if I gave her some space to deal, she'd get used to everything. It's getting worse though, not better. Sometimes I go days without seeing her. It's almost like she's avoiding me."

Because she *had* been avoiding him, and I knew exactly why. Lizzy was worried her father might be the arsonist, and she didn't want to reveal her suspicions to Kyle. But Lizzy didn't multitask well, so her solution was to shut Kyle out while waiting for the news.

"I'm sorry for you guys."

Kyle gave me a level look.

I huffed out a breath. "Well, I am, whether you believe me or not. But still, what does that have to do with me despising Lacey?"

"Promise not to laugh?" he asked.

"I don't make promises I can't keep," I told him.

He leaned back in his chair. "Fine then. I knew you were the only one in town who'd tell Lizzy about me being with another woman."

"Kyle, this is Beaverton we're talking about. Gossip is an accepted form of currency."

"People talk," he agreed. "But they don't want to get involved. You though, you'd meddle."

"I don't meddle," I huffed. Then after thinking about it for another moment, I corrected, "Well, I don't always meddle."

"Only when it matters to you. I knew you'd take the news back to Lizzy, but I had to make sure you noticed first. Any other woman in town I was polite too wouldn't even register, but you've been watching that woman like a hawk. I knew if I spent some time talking to her, you'd tell Lizzy, or at least tell Jones, and he would tell Lizzy."

"So when you snuck into the Bowtie Angel and asked me to butt out, you really wanted me to butt in some more? How'd you know it would work?"

Kyle raised a brow. "Because you're the most contrary woman alive. I tell you it's day, you'd tell me it was night."

"That is the most ridiculous plan I've ever heard." I paused and then asked, "So did it work? Did you make Lizzy jealous?"

He shook his head slowly. "Not jealous enough. She was rip-roaring mad after you called her, but then she went right back into hibernation. What should I do, Andy?"

My plan had worked better than I'd hoped. Kyle was so focused on his romantic disaster that he'd completely forgotten about the murder investigation or the fact that Jones was wanted for questioning.

I took a deep breath and then said, "Tell her how you feel?"

Kyle's blond eyebrows drew together in a sandy line of confusion. "What?"

"Don't keep secrets from her. Come clean, and tell her exactly what you've been doing and why."

He went pale beneath his tan. "Um, she'll kill me."

"I can't believe I'm saying this, but give her some credit. You're right. She's had a lot of stuff to deal with over the past year. How is she about you spending time with Kaylee?"

"She's been better than I could have hoped, actually. Very understanding, even though the two of them don't really get along. Kaylee's too much like you. She told Lizzy that she ought to pull the stick out of her ass. She has your smart mouth."

I grinned. "I love that girl. I really do."

"I was worried it was Kaylee coming between us," Kyle said. "That maybe she couldn't handle being a stepmother. I don't think that's it though. It doesn't make any sense."

"And I repeat, talk to her. And promise me, no more shenanigans."

"Because that's your department?" he quipped.

"Exactly. And for the love of grief, stay away from Lacey L'Amour. The chick is bad news swathed in Prada."

"She's not the one with a dead body in her freezer." He scowled, looking ready to ask another question, but the door opened, and Detective Darryl Brown strode in. "Sheriff, I'll take it from here. Has she spoken to anyone else?"

Kyle shook his head. "Just me. Have you found Malcolm Jones yet?"

"No." The detective gripped the door handle reflexively.

Though they spoke cordially enough, Darryl wasn't Kyle's biggest fan. I think it had something to do with Kyle's silver-spoon background. Darryl had to earn the football scholarship that had sent him to Notre Dame and then the degree that made him a detective. I was glad to see him on the case. He was a no-nonsense sort of guy. He'd find out who'd killed Rochelle without letting personal bias fog the investigation.

"May I use your office, Sheriff? Since you brought Miz Buckland here instead of to the city police department?"

Kyle nodded. "Of course."

The men locked eyes, Brown obviously expecting Kyle to leave. Kyle folded his arms over his chest, clearly having no intention of moving.

So not good. I'd thought the city police would remove me from the sheriff's station. Brown looked as though he wanted to and was torn between wasting time transporting me to his turf and catching a killer as soon as possible.

I looked back and forth between their silent standoff and then piped up. "I want a lawyer."

Both men swiveled their heads to stare down at me.

"What?" Brown asked as Kyle sputtered, "Why?"

"I want a lawyer. I refuse to say another word until one gets here." I folded my arms and stared at the battered desk. It was a Hail Mary stall tactic, but at least a lawyer could tell me whether or not Kyle must be present while I talked to the detective.

"Miz Buckland—" The detective was interrupted from shouts in the other room.

Kyle stood and rounded the desk.

"What is it?" Brown asked, following Kyle out.

Kyle barked out, "Andy, stay here," and then shut the door.

I didn't wait, just circled Kyle's desk, picked up his landline, and then dialed my own cell number. Since I had Kyle's number programmed into my phone, Jones would know who was calling.

Jones answered on the first ring. "I'm sorry, Sheriff. Andrea isn't here—"

"It's me," I breathed, turning away from the door. Hearing his voice gave me something to cling to. "I don't have a lot of time."

"What's wrong?"

"It's Rochelle." I took a deep breath. "Malcolm, I'm sorry, but she's dead."

"I know," he said.

"What?" I shrieked. "What do you mean you know?"

There was no sound on the other end of the phone. "Malcolm? Hello?"

I turned back, wondering if the call had been dropped. I saw Detective Brown standing there with the unplugged wall jack in one hand, a dark glower on his face.

"We," he said in a dangerous tone, "we have a great deal to discuss."

Mediterranean Chicken Couscous

You'll need:
1 1/4 cups low-sodium fat-free chicken broth
6 oz couscous
3 cups chopped cooked chicken
1/4 cup chopped fresh basil
4 oz tomato-basil feta cheese
1 pint grape tomatoes, halved
1 1/2 tablespoons fresh lemon juice
1 teaspoon lemon zest
1/4 teaspoon freshly ground black pepper
Garnish: fresh basil leaves and toasted pine nuts

Heat broth until it begins to boil. Place couscous in a large bowl, and stir in broth mixture. Cover, and let stand 5 minutes. Fluff couscous with a fork; stir in chicken and next 6 ingredients. Serve warm or cold. Garnish, if desired.

** Andy's note: Substitute 4 teaspoons of dried basil if you don't have fresh on hand.

CHAPTER SIXTEEN

———

"Well, at least he didn't arrest you," Donna said.

"Through no fault of my own." I laid my head back against the seat, breathing in the new-car smell with faint hints of Donna's perfume. I might never move again, I was so tired. "Kyle was pushing for it when he found out Jones had my phone."

"You don't think he ran, do you?" Donna asked. "Steve said they still haven't found him."

"He didn't run. He didn't do anything that would force him to run." Though I spoke the words, they held no real conviction.

Donna eyed me skeptically. "Well, here's the thing, Andy. You said he knew about Rochelle's murder. How could he know and not turn himself in for questioning?"

"Because Kyle has it out for him. He was trying to argue with Detective Brown that because he insisted Jones needed to have his marriage annulled, Jones decided it was easier to just kill her."

"And dump her in your walk-in?" Donna's brows went up. "That's a little farfetched."

"I didn't say it made sense, only that it was Kyle's theory. You and I know he's full of it. Jones isn't a killer, and he has an alibi for the time of the arsons." I took a deep breath to vocalize the worry that had been gnawing away at me for hours. "I'm scared I did this to her."

We were stopped at a light on the corner of Treasure and Green. Slowly, Donna turned to look at me, her expression blank. "I think I'm missing a step in your thought process. The whole town knows you're territorial about Jones, but come on,

Andy. How on earth could finding that poor woman's body be your fault?"

"There are a few things I haven't told you. Only because I was sworn to secrecy."

"Should I pull over for this?" Donna asked. We were passing the bank, and without waiting to hear my answer, Donna veered into the lot and backed into an empty space. "Okay, tell me everything."

So I did. It was easier the second time around, after telling Detective Brown all the gory details. Like Donna, he'd listened attentively as I spilled my guts. Unlike Donna, he hadn't asked if I'd been mixing medications.

I ended with, "You have to understand—Lizzy was terrified her father was the arsonist. She couldn't turn him in."

Donna shook her head. "I get that. God knows I used to protect my dad when he went on a bender and passed out with a lit cigarette burning away. It's only luck that he didn't burn the house down. You know yourself that you do crazy things for family. What I want to know is, why you didn't tell Jones? And don't give me some cockamamie story about how you wanted to protect Lizzy."

Lying to an old friend is never easy. There were times I'd been convinced that Donna knew me better than I knew myself. Times before Jones. I cleared my throat. "It's because I have daddy issues, okay?"

Donna scowled. "Daddy issues?"

I blew out a breath, too emotionally spent to be having such a conversation, but seeing no way to avoid it. "My mom never told me who my father was, and until a few years ago, Jones didn't know who his father was either. It's different from somebody who grew up knowing their parents. You build all these fantasies about who the parent was and why they couldn't be with you like the other kids' parents. It's something to cling to when all the other kids talk about going fishing with their dads on the weekend, or talking about how their fathers bought them their first car. I had it better than most because I had Pops, but it wasn't the same."

Donna put her mitten-covered hand over mine. "Why didn't you ever tell me any of this?"

I sniffed, refusing to cry. "It sounds so stupid and self-pitying. At least I had Nana and Pops. Jones grew up without any father figure. All he's ever had is the fantasy. And to find out that his father is a mean drunk is bad enough, but an arsonist and a murderer? It isn't fair."

"You wanted to protect him." Donna's eyes were wide.

I gave a hollow laugh. "And look at where that got me. Now Rochelle is dead, and Jones is a suspect himself. And thanks to me, his father is also being questioned. I've made a total mess out of it."

"But you provided Jones with an alibi for the times of the arsons, right?"

"Yeah. The assisted living facility's fire happened when he brought me to the hospital. And we were both home alone when the first one was lit. Of course, since I tried to obstruct the investigation, they aren't eager to take my word for it." I frowned, then jumped in my seat. "Turn the car around."

"What?" Donna blinked at my sudden burst of energy. "What's wrong?"

"We weren't alone at the time the first fire was set. Mr. Tillman stopped by, and he and Jones had an argument. You know what that means, right? He couldn't have set fire to the florist shop."

"Whoa, Andy, slow down a second." Donna held up her hand in classic hold-your-horses fashion. "Maybe he hired someone else to set the fires."

"But why would he leave all the gasoline cans on his property? That's like a flaming arrow pointing right back to him."

Donna shook her head. "Steve always says that criminals aren't as smart as they think they are. Most are caught because they make stupid mistakes. He probably thought no one else knew about the place in the woods."

"Well, in a few hours everyone will know." My second wind had dissipated, and I sagged in the seat. "Poor Rochelle. She should have left town when she finished investigating me. If I had just told Jones the truth, none of this would have happened."

"She was investigating *you*?" The last word went up an octave, and then Donna muttered, "I'm way behind."

"Flavor TV hired her after Jones dropped my case. But with all the lawsuits, they ended up dropping it too. Some guy with a PO box in Atlanta hired her, and she said she'd taken the case because she'd already done most of the preliminary background work."

"Who was her employer?"

"She never met him. He went by the name Jacob Griffin. It could be a real person or an alias. Rochelle just didn't know."

"But what would he want with information on you?"

I shook my head. "It could be anything. Maybe one of his relations was in the audience during my debut, and he wanted to know more about me, try to file his own lawsuit. Or it could be something else entirely."

Every part of me hurt and throbbed. Donna cast me a sympathetic glance. "Do you want me to take you to the pasta shop? Or should I take you home?"

"Home, if you'd be so kind. Pops and Aunt Cecily must have taken the car hours ago."

Donna scrunched her nose up and pulled the Escalade back out onto Treasure Street. "I shudder at the thought of either of them behind the wheel. This town has had more than its share of tragedy lately."

I was only half listening, my mind wandering back to Jones. "Donna, do you think it's odd that Malcolm didn't want me to call the police after I got that phone call?"

She didn't say anything for a minute. All the streetlamps had come on, and one lit her face as we drove beneath it. "Andy, look, I know you're beat, and I wasn't going to say anything."

"But?" I prompted.

"But, you're right. I mean, what kind of man finds out his girlfriend has received a death threat and doesn't go right to the police?"

I swallowed. It was difficult around the lump in my throat. "The kind with something to hide."

* * *

Pops and Aunt Cecily and even Roofus greeted us at the door. For a moment, no one said a word, and then Aunt Cecily nodded once. "Okay then. Pasta shop will be closed tomorrow. Who is wanting dinner?" Without waiting for an answer, she shuffled off toward the kitchen.

Pops slung an arm around me. "It's all right, Andy girl. Just remember that like a stone, this too shall pass."

In spite of the dour circumstances, I laughed. "Charming, Pops, really."

My grandfather turned to Donna. "Pretty as a picture as always, Mrs. Muller. You staying for supper?"

Donna shook her head. "I can't. The twins have a play coming up, and I have to supervise the making of costumes." Pops's eyebrows went up. "What's the play about?"

Donna grimaced. "The food pyramid. It's for their gymnastics class. Pippa is going to be a carrot, and Hailey is a cabbage. Try telling either one of them that veggies don't require a metric ton of pink sparkles. This is a slow-motion disaster in the making. My sunroom looks like Tinker Bell threw a party and forgot to clean up after."

"I remember when Andy had to be a sheep in the church's production of the Nativity. You couldn't have been more than five at the time. Her nana made her a vest and glued cotton balls to every visible inch of it. Musta worked on that thing for a month. Then what does our girl do? Wears it up on stage for five seconds and then whips it off and pitches it into the audience on her way off the stage."

"It was itchy," I said in self-defense. "Not to mention hideous."

"I won't argue with you there. And your nana laughed harder than anyone else. You get your sense of humor from her."

"God help us." Aunt Cecily crossed herself, but I saw the trace of a small smile.

Donna gave me a quick hug, threatened to string me up if I didn't call her the second anything happened, and took her leave. Pops led me over to the table and urged me to sit. I protested, saying I would get the dishes, but he waved me off. "Have you heard anything from your young man?"

I shook my head. "No. And if he comes by here, don't let him in."

Aunt Cecily set a bubbling cauldron of gravy on the table. "Why not?"

"Because…" This was hard to explain, mostly because I didn't understand it myself. "He needs to cooperate with the police. That was his ex-wife."

"They were not married, yes?" Aunt Cecily asked.

"No, I mean, yes. I mean, no. They were never really married because she was already married."

Pops nodded. "Malcolm told me."

I'd just taken a big sip from my wineglass but froze at his words. Wine slid down my windpipe, and I choked. Aunt Cecily leapt to her feet and pounded me on the back while calling me "*Sciocca ragazza*," a foolish girl.

"Me? Why am I foolish?" I managed to wheeze the question.

Aunt Cecily gave me a patient look. "Eugene, you must leave us *per un momento*."

I was shocked when Pops actually got to his feet and left. "What's this about?"

Aunt Cecily studied me for a moment before asking, "Do you no trust your man?"

I thought about when I'd seen him in the bar with Lacey and how I'd freaked out. Even though I knew he loved me and was faithful to me, I'd acted like a total jealous shrew. I thought about how I'd moved out suddenly after discovering that Jones had hidden Rochelle's investigation from me. Had I learned anything from that?

"I do," I said slowly. "I do trust him. But I don't understand why—"

Aunt Cecily held up a thin withered hand, cutting me off. "A child asks why over and over. But it is not always necessary to understand the why. Know what you know, and do what you do. Trust in your man and in your blood and in God, but most import, in yourself. You are smart and strong woman. You are a Rossetti. And Rossetti woman work hard, and we give thanks. It is that simple. Now we eat."

It was probably the longest speech I'd ever heard my great-aunt utter. Her life in a nutshell.

I kinda wanted to be her when I grew up.

Pops rejoined us at the table, and we ate our pasta and gravy in silence. It was the best meal I had in days, if not weeks.

"I'm changing the menu at the Bowtie Angel," I announced when the food was done.

Pops cast a wary glance to Aunt Cecily.

She narrowed her eyes at me. "You still make the pasta?"

"Always." I nodded once.

She folded her thin arms and looked me up and down. "All right. Come, I want to watch that television show with the judges and the cooks."

Pops offered to do the dishes, said it helped the arthritis in his hands to soak them in the hot water. Aunt Cecily and I settled on the couch, a bottle of wine between us. I checked the DVR and selected the latest episode of *Sliced*. It was a repeat, but I didn't care, glad I could shut down my brain for a while.

"Why do they no never make the pasta right?" Aunt Cecily asked. "*Lui è un pazzo.*"

"You would be the best judge ever," I told my great-aunt with complete sincerity. "You'd terrify them all."

"*Proprio così,*" she agreed, accepting my words as the truth.

We all turned in early, exhausted from the events of the day. Worry for Jones and the memory of Rochelle's sightless eyes kept me from sleeping. Who had killed her? Was it the arsonist? If so, he or she would be on to me and Lizzy next.

I wanted to call Lizzy, to see how she was holding up. I wondered if the police had searched the Tillman estate yet or if her father had been arrested.

Shoot, I'd never called Detective Brown to tell him that Mr. Tillman had come to see Jones at the time of the first fire. Donna had convinced me to call him with the information, but I'd been so out of it that I'd forgotten.

I sat up, reaching for lamp beside the bed.

In the darkness, fingers curled around my wrist.

Everything But The Kitchen Sink Gravy

You'll need:
1/2 pound lean ground beef
1/2 pound mild Italian sausage
1/2 pound spicy Italian sausage
1/2 pound ground turkey
1 whole carrot, peeled
2 cans tomatoes, crushed
2 cans tomatoes, pureed
1 small can tomato paste
2 cloves garlic, crushed
1/2 cup dry red wine
1 teaspoon oregano
9 fresh basil leaves, torn
Handful of fresh Italian flat-leaf parsley, chopped
1 medium yellow onion, diced
Handful of pepperoni, cut small
1 teaspoon sea salt
1/4 cup grated Parmesan

Brown each meat, and drain grease. Add tomatoes, wine, vegetables, pepperoni, cheese, carrot, and spices to same pot or transfer to Crock-Pot for a slower cook. Give it approximately 3 hours on the stovetop or 8 in the Crock-Pot. Remove carrot, and serve over hot pasta.

**Andy's note: This is really a very basic gravy recipe that leads to a hearty sauce. It's called Everything but the Kitchen Sink Gravy because that's exactly what you put in it—everything but the sink! I've been known to throw frozen meatballs, shredded cooked chicken, and even kielbasa into the pot. As long as it has plenty of time to simmer, it's always a treat.

CHAPTER SEVENTEEN

———

"Andrea," called a familiar voice with a sexy accent before I could scream. "It's me, love. Don't shout down the household."

I knew that voice, and only one person called me by my full first name. "Malcolm?"

The bedside lamp clicked on, and I flinched at the sudden flood of light. Though my retinas had been seared, I'd seen enough to know that yes, it was Jones in my bedroom. "Jeez-a-lou! You scared the ever-lovin' wits out of me! How did you get in here?"

"Your grandfather gave me a key," Jones murmured in a soft voice, which only made me aware of how loud I'd been. "I apologize for frightening you, but I needed to talk to you, and it couldn't wait until morning."

Slowly, my eyes adjusted to the light, and I got a good look at him. He wore a black coat over a black turtleneck and the kind of cargo pants that had a zillion and one pockets. There were leaves in his hair and mud on his clothing. His hand was like ice where it connected with mine. "You're freezing. What happened?"

"The police are looking for my SUV, so I left it at my sister's house."

"You walked all the way here from Lizzy's?" That had to be at least five miles, and he'd done it in the dark, and unlike his sister, he done it sans skis. "Crazy man, what were you thinking? I know it's below freezing out there, and Donna said there's a storm in the forecast. Do you want to die of exposure?"

Jones shivered. "I couldn't let them detain me for questioning, not until I knew you were all right."

"All right is overstating things a bit, but at least I'm still breathing." His cold skin reminded me of finding Rochelle, and it was my turn to shiver. "Oh, Malcolm, it was awful."

He pulled me close, hugging me to him.

It took several moments for me to rein my emotions in and even longer for me to tear myself from him. "Come on. Let me get you something hot to drink. And then you can tell me about how you found out about Rochelle."

The door to the guest bedroom was shut, and the sound of Pops's snoring filtered through the room. Roofus actually lifted his head at the sight of Jones, his tail thumping against the hardwood floor in greeting.

"Some watchdog you are," I huffed at the ancient beagle.

"He knows me," Jones said as he reached forward to pet Roofus. The dog growled a warning, and Jones retracted his hand hastily.

"Yeah, you two are obviously besties." I shuffled to the kitchen and pulled two mugs down from the cabinet. "Coffee or herbal tea?"

Jones took his filthy coat off and set it by the door before lowering himself onto the couch. "Tea, please. I'd like to get a little sleep tonight before I have to talk to the police."

I filled the kettle, set it on the stove, and turned the gas on. Though I was dying to pepper him with questions, I waited until the two cups of hot liquid were ready before joining him on the couch. "I'm glad to hear you aren't planning to dodge the law forever."

He held the warm mug in his hands but didn't make a move to drink from it. "Dodging the police investigation was never my intention. I was out of town most of the day."

"So how did you find out about Rochelle?"

"From Lizzy. I'd called her earlier to ask about the evidence she'd found linking our father to the arson case, so she knew I had your cell phone. Speaking of which—" He handed me his mug, then dug in his front pocket. He extracted my cell phone and set it on the coffee table.

"Did your friend manage to trace the call?" Now that I knew Rochelle had been killed, thinking about the phone call in which I'd heard it happen was even more unsettling.

Jones nodded. "He did pinpoint the location. There's a defunct lumber mill on the edge of town. I found a discarded burner phone there. It was obviously the crime scene."

"Oh god." I closed my eyes, and it was all too easy for me to envision the scene he described. Poor Rochelle, she must have been terrified. Then another thought pushed the vision out of the way. "The police need to know—"

Jones had anticipated my reaction. "I already called in an anonymous tip to the police, but I wasn't comfortable turning myself in for questioning unless you're with me."

"That must have been what caused the flurry of activity at the sheriff's office the day before. You sure know how to stir the pot, Malcolm."

Jones didn't smile as he studied me. "Whoever is behind all this has put a target on you, Andrea."

Shoot, I should have just had the coffee. It was unlikely I'd ever sleep again. "Why though? All because I told Lizzy to hire Rochelle? Why is the killer coming after me and not your sister? I mean, she was the one who hired Rochelle."

Jones shook his head. "I don't know. But it's a safe bet that it isn't my father, even though he's been arrested for the arsons."

I took my hand in his and squeezed. "I'm so sorry."

"Don't worry about him. He has a high-priced law firm to help get him out of it. God only knows what he was doing with all that gasoline. It looked as if he were anticipating an apocalyptic disaster."

"I didn't just mean your dad," I spoke softly. The guilt that had been looming over me all day had expanded, growing and morphing until I was afraid it would swallow me whole. It wasn't just about Rochelle either. Jones was a person of interest in a murder investigation, had been to the crime scene. What if he left evidence there? Hair, blood, a boot print, tire tracks. People had been convicted on less, and he'd been dodging the police. He could be charged with his ex-wife's murder, and no jury in the world would believe he was innocent.

My voice shook, and I fought hard to bury my fear. "I meant all of it. Rochelle and Lizzy. Me keeping you in the dark. I feel like I've set you up for this huge fall."

He stared off into space for a long moment. "As far as Rochelle goes, I'm sorry too. I'm glad you insisted I let her have her say, so there was nothing left unfinished between us. And Lizzy would have told me something eventually. As for you..." He turned so he faced me directly, blue gaze boring into me, seeing all the fear I'd tried to hide.

Though I wanted to look away, I couldn't. His gaze was mesmerizing. "I know I'm nothing but trouble—"

He interrupted me with a searing kiss. The contact stole my breath and scattered my thoughts, reducing me to a witless, panting creature.

Jones pulled back long enough to murmur, "You're worth all the trouble." Then he kissed me again.

And really, what more needed to be said?

* * *

"Lacey L'Amour is behind all this," I said to Jones as we drove into town. "It's too much of a coincidence that she just shows up, and then all of a sudden buildings start going up in flames all over town."

Jones was behind the wheel. For once his *slower than molasses in January* driving was a bonus, since neither of us was in a hurry to reach the police station. He cut his gaze to me, then refocused on the road. "Do you have any actual evidence to prove your theory, or are you just saying that because you don't like her?"

I made an indignant noise. "I don't like her because she's been hitting on my boyfriend and because I am an excellent judge of character. Lacey stands the most to gain if the Bowtie Angel goes out of business for good. That's motive."

Jones nodded slowly. "All right, I'll give you that. But if she was the arsonist, why wouldn't she just burn the pasta shop down?"

Perish the thought. Instinctively, I crossed myself before saying, "The fire would destroy the building, but that wouldn't be enough to drive the Buckland-Rossetti clan out of business. We'd rebuild and come back stronger than before with the support of the entire town. Linking the pasta shop to a murder though, that's different. She's out to ruin our reputation, so rebuilding isn't an option. She's already tried to hire Mimi away, and she sabotaged our first health inspection. In fact, I wouldn't put it past her to specifically hire your ex-wife and bring her to town to make trouble. If Rochelle dug up dirt on me, Lacey would use it, but even if she didn't, having your ex here was sure to cause trouble for me, to take my eye off the prize. But when Lizzy hired Rochelle to unmask the arsonist, Lacey knew it was only a matter of time until Rochelle put it all together. Don't you see? She's behind all of it."

"There are two problems with your theory," Jones said. We'd reached the traffic light at the edge of town, and he turned to face me fully. "One, why would Lacey burn down both the florist and the assisted living if she was targeting you? And two, if you're right and she was the one to hire Rochelle to investigate you, she must know about Kaylee. But if she does, why has she been keeping it to herself?"

"I don't know," I admitted. I liked my hypothesis too much to just let it go without a fight. "Maybe because of Kyle. The two of them have been spending time together. She might not want to hurt him by revealing the truth."

Jones shook his head. "You can't have it both ways, Andrea. You can't say she's a sociopath who'll burn down half the town to get at you, and claim she cares too much about the engaged man who has been using her to make his fiancée jealous to ruin his reputation. Now I'm not saying she isn't involved at all," he continued when I'd opened my mouth to protest. "But I don't think she's the mastermind behind the arsons."

We were only a few minutes out from the police station. My knee bounced nervously as our destination drew closer. "What if the crimes aren't related? We've been assuming that Rochelle's death is because of her involvement with the arson case. But you work more than one case at a time, right? What if there's something else going on?"

Jones nodded thoughtfully. "It's not impossible. If the killer was clever, perhaps he or she isn't really coming after you. Instead, he's using the two of us as a distraction to get the police off their trail."

"Right. The police are so busy investigating us, and the real killer literally gets away with murder."

He cleared his throat and murmured, "That sounds like something my father would do."

I sucked in a sharp breath. "But he was with us at the time of the first arson."

"Andrea, my father isn't the sort of man who soils his hands. He has underlings who do the dirty work for him." His tone was filled with bitterness as he added, "Like the lawyer who checked on my welfare twice a year and sent my mother money to provide for me. He didn't even write his own checks."

We'd arrived at the police station. Jones parked at the far end of the lot, but neither of us moved.

"Whatever happens," I told him softly. "We'll deal with it. Together, okay?"

He looked at me and smiled, though it didn't reach his eyes. "For what it's worth, I'm sorry."

I blinked. "Why?" If he handed me another bunch of roses, I was going to beat him with them.

He shook his head. "Because my life is a mess, and it's spilling over onto you. My father, Rochelle, Lizzy, all of it. I really wanted us to be a normal couple, but all of this refuse from my past keeps coming up, interfering with our relationship, your business. I feel like it's all my fault and you'd be better off if you had nothing to do with me."

"Malcolm, I'm the one with a long-lost daughter and a crazy stalker here. Don't take so much on yourself. You can't control other people's actions, especially not those of people who lie to you. And for what it's worth, I think you're worth it." I repeated his words from the night before back to him.

A real smile cracked his stony countenance. "All right, let's just hope neither of us gets arrested today."

I made a face, mumbling "You aren't kidding" before popping the car door. We walked hand in hand into the police station.

Beaverton was barely large enough to have its own police department. In fact, it hadn't when I was growing up. All matters of law enforcement had fallen on the overworked sheriff's department. The slow but steady population increase over the past decade had brought in enough citizens to justify the expense of forming both a fire department and a city police force. There were four detectives, including Darryl Brown, a handful of sergeants, and a baker's dozen collection of officers, all under the supervision of Chief Leroy Fontaine, who answered directly to the city council and Mayor Eli Randal II.

Donna had mentioned that there were quite a few homes on the market for winter, more than there had been at the same time a year earlier and even more in the week since the arsonist came to town. I wondered what would happen if the population of Beaverton fell below the necessary number for city status. Would the brave men and women who'd been trained as police officers, like Donna's husband, Steve, lose their jobs? That would perpetuate the cycle because the area lacked any major employment opportunities. More people would pull up stakes, which would hurt the whole town.

I'd have fewer customers, who I now had to share with Lacey L'Amour, if I ever managed to open again. Theo and the health department might shut the pasta shop down for good.

Shoving all my worries aside, I sat by Jones's side while we waited for Detective Brown to come fetch him. It wasn't until Jones put his hand over my knee that I realized it had been bouncing like mad.

"It'll be all right, love. I didn't do anything wrong."

My teeth sank into my lower lip. Maybe it was my own jaded point of view, but knowing that Jones hadn't done anything wrong didn't change the fact that Kyle had it out for him. And even though the murder investigation wasn't Kyle's case, he still had a lot of pull.

"Mr. Jones." Detective Brown made his way toward us. "I see you got my messages."

"I'm happy to help however I can." Jones rose and offered his hand to Darryl. The two men shook, but it wasn't a friendly gesture, more like something you'd see between army-navy rivals before the big game.

"If you'll come with me."

I jumped up, but Brown shook his head. "Wait here please, Andy."

"But—" I began.

Jones tilted my chin to meet his gaze. "I'll be all right. See you in a bit?"

The last thing I wanted was to spend time by myself ruminating on all that had happened and fretting over whether the detective would arrest my man. But Jones was right. He was innocent, and he hadn't done anything illegal. Besides, it didn't look like I'd been given much of a choice.

After resettling myself in the hard plastic chair, I fidgeted uncomfortably. Steve Muller stopped by and handed me a cup of coffee. It was bitter and had that nasty mineral essence, like when the pot hasn't been washed in a while, but it helped warm my chilly and aching hands.

A commotion from the front of the building caught my attention. Male voices raised in agitation, and a woman screeched indignantly. Curious and in need of a distraction, I set my paper cup down on the floor and went to investigate.

Several teenagers were being led into the station house, followed by older men and women who were doing the majority of the shouting. The kids looked scared, eyes big as they took in the bustle around them. There was nothing especially unique or vicious looking about them. I wondered if they'd been caught skipping school or maybe shoplifting. I recognized Joey Randal, the mayor's nephew, in the mix. The entire Randal family was about as complicated as plain white bread. It couldn't be too bad with Joey in the mix, probably just normal teenager stuff.

Then my blood flash froze as I recognized a familiar pink-and-black backpack.

Kaylee stood in the middle of the pack of miscreants, wide eyed and looking on the verge of a breakdown.

"What is this?" I demanded of a nearby officer. "What did she do?"

"She's under arrest. They all are." The officer gave me a matter-of-fact glance, obviously believing I was one of the irate parents.

"On what charge?" I snapped, eyes darting to Kaylee.

The guy scowled down at me. "Who are you?"

It was on the tip of my tongue to say "Her mother," but I bit it back. Where was Barbara? She should be here demanding answers, not me.

A hand landed on my shoulder.

I whirled and was actually relieved to see the sheriff's uniform. "What's going on here?"

Kaylee called his name, and I was stunned to see Kyle turn away from her as he pulled me aside. "It seems Beaverton has its first gang."

"Gang? You can't be serious. It's a bunch of kids. Besides, Kaylee wouldn't join a gang."

"I'm afraid it's the truth." His expression had gone stony. "It seems part of their initiation is to burn down a building. And our daughter was found with them."

No-Bake Ziti

You'll need:
3 oz prosciutto
1 pound extra-lean ground beef
1 large onion, chopped
2 cloves garlic, minced
2 fresh tomatoes, diced
24 oz spaghetti sauce
1 1/2 cups water
3 cups ziti, uncooked
1 cup mozzarella, shredded
1/4 cup grated cheese for topping

Brown prosciutto in large deep skillet until crisp; remove from skillet. Drain on paper towels. Add ground beef, onions, and garlic to skillet; cook until meat is browned, stirring occasionally.

Crumble prosciutto. Add half to meat mixture in skillet with the tomatoes, spaghetti sauce, and water. Mix well. Cover, and bring to boil.

Stir in pasta, and let simmer, covered, on medium-low heat 20 minutes or until pasta is tender, stirring occasionally. Remove from heat.

Top with cheese and remaining prosciutto. Let stand, covered, 5 minutes or until cheese is melted. Top with grated cheese, and serve.

**Andy's note: This is a quick, flavorful dish that won't heat up the house on a hot summer day.

CHAPTER EIGHTEEN

————

A gang in Beaverton? That made as much sense as serving cheese with a fish course—the two concepts just didn't mix. And Kaylee as part of it? She was only sixteen. Of course kids sometimes got involved with gangs at a younger age than that, but she was new to town and had spent all her free time at the pasta shop. When would she have even come across this alleged gang?

The whole idea was ludicrous. Too many things just didn't add up. I stood back and watched as the police and sheriff addressed the irate throng of parents.

"My son ain't part of a gang, Kyle Landers," a woman called out in a two-pack-a-day voice. "You've known me and Lance since high school, for cryin' out loud! You reckon we'd let Dalton run wild like that?"

I blinked, stunned. Holy macaroni, the woman was Dotty Roberts. I remembered Dotty and Lance from my time at Beaverton High. They'd been as tight in high school as Kyle and I had been. And their son was Kaylee's age, the older boy in the mix.

The last sixteen years hadn't been kind to Dotty. She'd always been petite, but her small frame didn't seem to carry an ounce of extra weight anymore. Her skin sagged over knobby bones, and she had dark circles under her eyes. The inch and a half of black-and-white roots that had grown only made her bad dye job worse. I barely stifled a shudder at my own narrow miss. I would probably have looked just as used up with a teenage kid driving me around the bend if Kyle and I had gotten married right out of high school.

My gaze slid to Kaylee, and I realized maybe I hadn't escaped that fate entirely.

The sheriff put his hands in the air, patting it in a classic simmer-down gesture. "Now you all know this isn't personal. We need to talk to the kids and to each of you, one at a time. A legal guardian must be present during each interview."

Of course, neither Kyle nor I counted in Kaylee's case. We were her parents, but no one knew that, and we were not her legal guardians. I fished my phone out of my pocket, fully intending to call Barbara and half-surprised she wasn't present already, shouting down the injustice of it all. Then again, Barbara wasn't exactly a shouter. I did another scan of the room to be sure I hadn't overlooked her on the first pass.

Kaylee's adoptive mother was a large-animal vet. They owned a horse farm, which they were trying to sell. Had she gone out of town to handle some real estate business? We'd talked a few times over the phone, and the demure but quiet woman got on better with animals than she did with people. After the week I had, I could understand the appeal.

Someone touched my shoulder, and I turned to see Jones taking in the chaos. "What's happening out here?"

"The usual. All hell breaking loose." Barbara's voice mail picked up, the prerecorded message telling me she was out on a medical emergency, and I hung up and sent her a text message with all the pertinent details.

Kyle sent me a look as he escorted the first kid and his parents to the interrogation room.

"Do you want to stay?" Jones asked.

I was torn. As much as I wanted to be there for her, I wasn't her legal guardian, and my presence on top of Kyle's might only make things worse for her. As though she read my mind, Kaylee looked my way. I saw horror and then defiance flash across her face before she turned away. It was obvious she didn't want me there.

But hadn't I missed out on enough of her life already? Maybe my showing support was what she needed, even if it wasn't what she wanted.

Tough toenails, kid. I'm done playing by your rules. I blew out a breath and then squared my shoulders before turning to face Jones. "Yeah, I'll stick around for a bit."

"Do you want company?" he asked.

I studied him for a minute, trying to read his expression. Outwardly he looked as calm and cool as always, but there was a restlessness to him, lurking just beneath the surface. "I do, but I get the feeling there's somewhere else you need to be. Did everything go all right with Detective Brown?"

Jones shrugged one shoulder. "About what I expected. Don't leave town. He'll be in touch. With an additional warning that I should keep out of the investigation."

I narrowed my eyes at him. "Why do I get the feeling you're going to ignore that last one?"

"Because you are both beautiful and clever. Text me if you need me." Jones brushed a quick kiss across my lips and left before I had a chance to ask where he was going. The man always left me wanting more. It was practically his trademark.

The initial pandemonium of the room had died down. I was surprised to see Kyle reemerge from the interview room. He looked over at Kaylee, hesitated, and then came to stand beside me.

"I don't know what to do for her," he confessed. "When I heard about it on the radio, all I could think was that I needed to be here for her. Now that I am, I'm afraid to single her out in any way."

I huffed out a breath. "Believe me—I'm having the same problem. I just tried to get a hold of Barbara, but she didn't pick up."

Kyle grimaced. "She's out on an emergency call, at least according to her office. No cell service there. They sent someone out to get a hold of her, but she can't be there right away."

I looked back at Kaylee, who sat alone on the edge of a wooden bench, hair hanging over her face. At least they'd taken the handcuffs off her. "She looks so scared and alone."

She did, too. While the other kids were surrounded by angry family members, Kaylee's solitary corner remained quiet. She stared down at her pink-and-black sneakers, her teeth biting into her lower lip.

"It'd go better if you were the one to go over to her," Kyle said.

"Why do you think that? Because I'm the woman?" I asked.

"No, because you're her employer, and I'm the sheriff. As much as I want to offer her comfort, I don't want to draw attention to her."

I swallowed and then nodded. "Wish me luck."

Kaylee didn't look up as I approached, didn't say anything when I sat beside her on the bench.

"Can I get you anything?" I asked.

"I want my mom," she whispered.

"Kyle's trying to reach her through her office, and I sent her a text message. I'm sure she'll be here as soon as she finds out what's going on."

Her lip trembled, and she bit it again, trying to keep from crying.

I huffed out a breath and put my arms around her. Screw the gossip—my kid needed support. And she was my kid, in all her dumbassery. Barbara was her mom, but she was mine too, and it was about time I laid claim to her.

She didn't even hesitate, just fell against me, sobbing for all she was worth.

I whispered soothing things and petted her curly dark hair. Told her over and over again that it would be all right, that she'd make it through all of this.

I lost track of time, when she finally pulled away. "Sorry, I didn't mean to snot all over you."

"Snot isn't a verb," I corrected her and fished a tissue from my pocket.

That got me an eye roll and a watery laugh. "You know what I meant."

"I do." Since the ice was officially broken, I decided to jump in with both feet. "Did you know about the gang?"

She shook her head. "No. There was talk, but kids are just stupid like that, you know? They say all sorts of stuff that isn't true. I thought they were some cool guys hanging out. And they wanted to hang with me. I don't have any friends here."

I opened my mouth to protest, then realized I was being an idiot. She meant friends her own age. "When did you start to hang out with them?"

"Just over the weekend."

I had to ask the next part to know what we were dealing with, even though I was terrified of the answer. "Did you find out they were setting the fires?"

A tear slid down Kaylee's cheek. "I didn't want to be a rat."

I groaned inwardly so she wouldn't hear it. "Kid, this is so not cool."

"But I didn't *do* anything." There was a half-hysterical note in her voice. "I swear I didn't."

"I believe you. But you should have told someone. Me, Kyle, Aunt Cecily, Pops, your mom, anyone. People died because of what they did, not to mention thousands of dollars' worth of property damage." I stopped myself there before I went all maternal and lectured her. She knew she'd screwed up. Taking out my worry on her wasn't going to help either of us. Instead, I took a deep breath and changed tactics. "Will you tell Kyle what you know about everything? Maybe he can help you."

"Dalton's gonna hate me." She looked across the room to where Dotty sat with a sullen-faced teenager. The kid was the spitting image of Lance, all shaggy dark hair, high cheekbones, and pouty lips. I was beginning to get a clearer picture of why she'd wanted to hang out with them in the first place.

Freaking hormones.

Well, kibitzing over reality wasn't going to help. "He might."

She glared at me. "Thanks a heap."

I shrugged. "I'm not about to lie to you. Loyalty is great, but you have to make sure the person you're loyal to is worthy. And you have to look out for yourself first. A real friend gets that and wants to protect you, not put you in danger." Again, I bit off the rant before it could take over. Frothing at the mouth wouldn't win me any points with the cops or Kaylee.

Her lips parted as if she were about to say something, then pressed shut as she glanced away. A full minute passed. I saw the station house clock on the wall behind her. Then finally, she nodded. "Can we not talk about this anymore?"

"Whatever you want, kid. You want to sit here in silence, we can do that."

She smiled, but it faded fast.

I put my hand on her arm. "Talk to me. Tell me what it is that makes you pull back like that."

Her eyes were locked on my hand on her arm. "Are you ashamed of me?"

My mouth dropped open. If she'd picked up the bench and whacked me with it, I couldn't have been more surprised. "What?"

She shifted, clearly uncomfortable. "You and Kyle. You both insisted I not tell anybody that I'm your daughter. Is that because I embarrass you?"

"Kaylee, of course not. How could you even think..." Then I thought about it myself and would have slapped my own forehead for being such an idiot. "Honey, no. Believe me when I say we would both love to shout from the rooftops that you're our kid."

She didn't look as though she believed me. "Then why haven't you? Why does it have to be this big secret?"

"It doesn't. Not if you don't want it to be. We, as in me, Kyle, and your mom, thought it would be easier for you if no one knew about your relationship to us. Not many people knew I'd even had you, you know? Beaverton is a small town, and once the truth is out, then everyone will know. There'll be all these nosy questions and people wanting to intrude. Are you sure you want that?"

She looked away, but I caught a flush creeping up her cheeks. "I don't want to cause you any more trouble."

"Kaylee," I instructed, "look at me."

She did, and I saw the gleam of hope in her eyes.

My heart was beating hard as I asked her again. "Do you want me and Kyle to shout from the rooftops that you're our kid?"

Slowly, she nodded.

I pulled out my cell phone and dialed.

"Who are you calling?" She looked half-horrified at the phone. "The press?"

"No, nothing like that. Just reinforcements."

Pops and Aunt Cecily arrived a few minutes later. There was a great deal of bilingual cussing and several Italian hand gestures that were almost as vulgar. Pops threatened to sue the pants off anyone in shouting distances. Aunt Cecily threatened to put The Eye on the entire gang so all their dangly parts would shrivel "like the raisins." It was loud and dramatic and more than a little humiliating, but by the time Barbara arrived, my kid knew she had a family who cared.

Certifiable though we all were.

Kyle pulled me aside. "What's going on here?"

"Kaylee needs her family around her right now."

The sheriff glared at me. "So what, you're just coming out with it now? Need I remind you that you were the one who didn't want the entire town to know?"

"No. You don't. I remember. But what all of us failed to consider was how Kaylee would feel about it. She came here looking for her family, Kyle. And as freaking dysfunctional as we are, we've been pushing her away."

Kyle shook his head. "This isn't the time. She's in so much trouble already, and if it comes out that she's my kid—"

"That's the problem though, Kyle. It will come out. One way or another, and if you wait, you'll only dig yourself deeper. This is what she wants. It's what I want, and I know it's what you want. Embrace the zaniness of our family reunion."

Kyle sighed, his shoulders sagging in defeat. "When my parents hear about this..."

But then he stopped complaining, squared his shoulders, and went to claim his daughter fully.

"Sheriff?" Detective Brown called. "I need to talk to you."

I put a hand on Darryl's arm. "Give him a second. He's bonding with his daughter."

"His what now?" The detective did a double take as he looked at me.

"It's a long story."

"Does it have anything to do with my murder investigation?"

I winced. "Maybe?"

Darryl gripped my arm. "You and your boyfriend are gonna be the death of me. I swear you are."

Resigned to another long interview, I could only hope that wasn't how this would all play out.

Italian Chicken And Sausage Sauté

You'll need:
6 chicken breasts, skinned and boned, salt and pepper
2 tablespoons olive oil
1 Italian sausage link—crumbled and cooked
1/4 teaspoon cayenne pepper
3/4 cup chicken broth
1/2 cup flour
2 medium zucchinis, sliced 1/2 inch thick
1 tablespoon margarine
3/4 cup dry white wine
2 large cloves garlic, minced
1 (7 oz) jar roasted red peppers, drained and sliced
1 tablespoon fresh parsley, chopped
1 teaspoon dried oregano, crushed

Cut chicken into bite-size chunks. Sprinkle with salt and pepper. Roll in flour to coat. Set aside.

In a 12-inch skillet, heat oil. Add zucchini; cook and stir over medium-high heat for1 to 2 minutes or until slightly browned. Remove zucchini with a slotted spoon, and set aside. Add margarine to skillet, and melt. Add cayenne pepper. Add chicken, and cook until no longer pink. Add wine, and heat to boiling. Boil uncovered 2 minutes. Add Italian sausage, red peppers, garlic, oregano, and basil. Reduce heat, cover, and simmer for 20 minutes. Add zucchini, and simmer 2 minutes more. Serve over pasta; garnish with parsley to serve.

CHAPTER NINETEEN

———

"Malcolm?" I called out as I let myself into Jones's place.

"Be up in a minute." His voice floated up from the basement.

"I'm hitting your wine rack with a vengeance," I replied. He didn't respond, so I assumed he was cool with my plan. And if not, well, too bad.

I moved around the kitchen with a familiar ease, extracting the electric corkscrew gizmo from its charger and picking out my vintage. It seemed to be a merlot kind of day, and I checked the pantry to see if he had any food in stock that would go with my selection.

"Now this is nice," Jones said a few minutes later when he found me sautéing sausage and onion, "to find you back here, cooking for me."

"Don't get too excited—it's nothing fancy. Your fridge is severely understocked, and I'm beat, so we're having a whatever-you've-got breakfast casserole to help sop up the insane amounts of alcohol I intend to consume. Would you dice those peppers, please?"

He did, but not before giving me a searing kiss.

We prepared the meal in a companionable silence. Tucked away from the rest of the craziness and insulated from the disasters, it was easy to see how I'd fallen into such a comforting pattern. Jones was easy to be with, regardless of the baggage he brought to the table.

"Penny for your thoughts?" Jones asked as I put the casserole in the oven to bake.

"I was thinking how effortless it would be to just be here with you all the time. I've been more relaxed here in your kitchen than I have anywhere else in the past few weeks. Why do we let other things overcomplicate us?"

Jones set my wineglass down and took my hands in his. "It would be rather remarkable to insulate ourselves from the rest of the town."

"Don't stop at the town. The whole world's gone nuts. A gang in Beaverton, I never thought I'd see the day. Those kids caused a lot of trouble and hurt a lot of people."

"Will Kaylee be all right?" Jones asked.

"I think so. Kyle said the DA is making noise about trying some of the older boys as adults. That'll mean hard time, especially if they are charged with manslaughter or even murder in the second degree. Kaylee is too young, and she has an alibi for both of the arsons, so the most they can charge her with is conspiracy. That'll probably mean some fines and community service. And of course Aunt Cecily will be keeping a very close eye on her from now on, which is a whole different level of punishment." I shook my head. "Why do smart girls get stupid over boys?"

Jones smiled. "Are you talking about Kaylee or yourself?"

I shrugged "Six of one, half dozen of the other. That child is her mother's daughter."

"Well at least you know one good thing that came out of all this. Your theory about the arsons being unrelated to Rochelle's death was correct."

I hopped up onto the island counter. "What happened during your interview with Detective Brown, by the way?"

Jones pushed some hair out of my face, then sighed. "Nothing much. I haven't been cleared as a suspect yet. I don't have an alibi for the time of death, but since I proved I filed for an annulment earlier in the week, that takes motive off the table."

"Rats, so we're back to square one?"

"Not exactly. How long have we got until that casserole's done?"

I peeked in the oven. "About another fifteen minutes. Why?"

"I want to show you something." Jones took my hand and led me downstairs.

His laptop screen saver was up, a black-and-white picture of me from last Thanksgiving. I cringed every time I saw it. I was so not-photogenic. Charisma didn't usually come across in stills. That particular shot wasn't too hideous. He'd captured me in profile, a glass of wine in my hand and a soft smile tugging up my lips. I wondered what I'd been thinking about in the shot.

Him most likely, or Kaylee, from before I'd actually had her in my life again. Then again, it might have been contemplation of dinner—I did go a little gaga over eggplant parm.

Jones tapped the screen, and a document appeared. I frowned as I sat in the desk chair, Jones standing behind me. Dates and times, names, the occasional "see attached" file. "What's this?"

"The police have Rochelle's computer, but I got to thinking about it. What do you do when you're done transcribing recipes?"

"Save them," I responded immediately.

One dark eyebrow went up. "To where?"

"The cloud." Then it hit me, and I looked back at the screen. "Oh? So this stuff was in Rochelle's cloud drive?"

Jones nodded. "I still had access to it, since our investigative company e-mail address was linked with a free-mail account. And most of those come with cloud storage anymore. Rochelle was horrible about passwords. She never changed them. Claimed she couldn't remember the new ones."

"Did you tell Detective Brown about that?" I asked, settling myself in the desk chair.

Jones shook his head. "Not about the cloud. I didn't know until now that she even used it."

I worried my lower lip. "But if the police find out you're accessing this stuff…"

His hands landed on my shoulders, thumbs kneading the knots in my neck. "Relax, Andrea. I know how to cover my tracks."

The massage felt good but didn't do much for my anxiety. "You like living dangerously, don't you? Tempting fate at every opportunity."

His hands stilled. "Don't fret, love. I don't do anything illegal."

"But the cops won't be happy—"

His hand covered my mouth as he leaned down to whisper in my ear. "It's not my job to make them happy. It's my job to uncover the truth."

The warmth of his breath made me shiver. "Just promise me you'll be careful. It's not just the cops. If whatever information Rochelle was killed over is in these files, and whoever wants it hidden knows you have them, you could be putting a big old bull's-eye on your back."

Jones turned the chair until I faced him. "Better me than you. I know how to handle myself."

I huffed out a breath. Stubborn man. "Okay, let's do dinner, and then we'll get to work."

"We?" Jones asked, both eyebrows going up.

I nodded. "Yes, we. If you insist on doing something not quiet illegal but foolhardy, you need someone watching your back. Rochelle didn't have that, and I'll be damned if I let you try to handle all this on your own."

"What about the pasta shop?"

I shook my head. "I can't think about that right now. Once this killer is unmasked, then I can focus on getting my business back on track."

Upstairs, the timer went off, and I pushed up from the chair, heading for the kitchen.

A hand snagged my arm. Jones wore a pained expression. "Andrea. It's your dream. You've been working so hard on that new menu. What about the other restaurants you were talking about? You need to keep making forward progress. Besides, you said you were exhausted."

The screen saver came back on with my picture. That was how Jones saw me, and someday I wished that could be me. "I've got my priorities in order. Come on—food first, then we're going to catch a killer."

* * *

Catching a killer wasn't as easy as I thought it would be. Not that I'd really expected it to be all cut and dried, but Rochelle's documents made no sense to me.

"This all sounds the same to me." I blinked as I looked away from the laptop to where Jones was studying some of the pictures he'd printed out. "How am I supposed to know what's important? Half the time she doesn't even use names. Just says the client or the suspect."

"Look for buzzwords." Jones was frowning down at a color shot of people on a busy street.

I came to stand beside him. "Buzzwords?"

He nodded. "Missing persons, suspicious activity, fraud. Child custody cases. Things that would drive people to kill. Or would kill to protect."

I thought about it for a beat. "So not necessarily someone from Beaverton then. What are you looking for there?"

Jones was still frowning at the same photograph. "This man." He tapped the picture. "Does he look familiar to you?"

I blinked and stared down at him. "Maybe. I'm not sure. He might just have one of those faces."

"Perhaps. Are his eyes green or blue?" Jones was color-blind and had a hard time with blues and greens. Which to me made his skill with photography even more impressive.

"It's kinda hard to tell from the angle. Is he in another shot?"

Jones shuffled through the photos, then handed me one. "Here."

I didn't see the man at first, but I recognized the location. "Hey, that's the coffee shop I used to hit every morning when I lived in Atlanta. It's about a block from my old apartment. That might explain why the man's familiar."

"His eyes, Andrea." Jones took my spot at the computer and opened up a new window. He did some quick typing and then turned back to me.

I studied the photo. The new shot had the man getting out of a car, looking slightly away. "Blue, definitely blue. And you're right—he seems very familiar. Is it possible we both know him?"

"If that's the case, where do you think we know him from?" Jones took the photo and continued to type.

In Atlanta, there could only be one connection that both Jones and I would recognize. "You interviewed several of the audience members after the debut, right? Do you think he was in the audience, maybe someone you questioned?"

"I think it's likely, though I'll have to dig through the case notes to be sure." Jones punched a few more keys and then sucked in a sharp breath.

"What, what is it?"

"I input his license plate number at the DMV database. Look at the registration."

I looked and was filled with excitement. "Jacob Griffin. That's him. That's the man who hired Rochelle."

Jones shut down the laptop and collected the scattered photographs. "I'm going to Atlanta."

"Now?" I gaped at him. "It's like two AM."

"I'm not tired." Jones was a man on a mission, one headed for the stairs at a dead run.

"I'm coming with you." I followed him up to the first floor.

Jones stopped and set the laptop bag down on the kitchen counter. "You can't."

My chin went up in classic defiant Buckland style. "Watch me."

He looked pained. "Andrea, from what we know, this is the man who hired Rochelle. He lives in Atlanta and might have been in the audience and might have a serious grudge against you. Enough of a grudge to kill Rochelle and set you up for murder. What do you think will happen if you show up on his doorstep?"

I folded my arms across my chest. "Then we should turn it over to Detective Brown. If you try to leave without me, I'll go right to him and tell him what we found, and he'll have the Atlanta cops at Griffin's door before you hit the county line."

Jones set his jaw. "You're being exceedingly stubborn about this."

"I believe in playing to my strengths. Either we both go, or neither of us go. You decide."

Jones huffed out a breath. "Famous last words. All right, you can come. But I'm driving. You had too much wine."

"Fair enough." I knew a win when I heard one. After slinging on my coat, I rushed for Jones's SUV, lamenting that there wasn't enough time to make a thermos of coffee.

The drive between Beaverton and Atlanta took about six hours. For the first two, I was too pumped to sleep and peppered Jones with nonstop questions about what he planned to do when we found Griffin. His standard answer of "We'll have to see" got old real fast.

When the sun finally came up, I started texting my friends back home. First was to Donna, to let her know I hadn't been abducted. Then to Mimi, asking her to call Aunt Cecily and Pops at a decent hour and let them know I was seeing to some out-of-town business. Let them read into that what they would.

I thought about it for a beat and then asked Jones, "Do you want me to let Lizzy know where we're going?"
Jones shook his head. "I don't want to get her hopes up until we know more."

I nodded and then shot Lizzy a *Talk to you soon* text.

She didn't respond, not that I'd expected her to, though I had hoped.

"Thank you for trying with my sister," Jones said quietly.

"It's the least I can do for you," I said, meaning it. "Although if you told me a year ago that Lizzy and I would be chumming around together, I wouldn't have believed it."

"I think she and Kyle are going to, what's that American phrase, call it quits?"

I'd been drinking from a bottle of water and choked when he said that. "You mean break up? Why?"

Jones shrugged. "She wouldn't tell me."

I shifted uncomfortably in my seat. No way was I actually feeling guilt over my role in their relationship's demise. "Well, Kyle has been doing some pretty idiotic stuff lately. But I know he loves her to the point of insanity. Can you talk her out of it?"

Jones made a half-strangled noise, as if I'd ask him to tear one of his arms out of the socket. "You're not serious."

"I feel bad for them."

"Andrea, Kyle despises me. He tried to have me arrested for bigamy. Why would I want to do him any favors?"

"Because it's the right thing to do. Look, if it was the other way around, I'd talk to Kyle for you."

"The difference being, I would never ask you to meddle in someone else's relationship." His tone was acerbic.

"You are such a guy. Fine, I'll fix them myself."

"Some things can't be resolved," Jones cautioned me. "Please think before you meddle."

"I always think first," I told him. "Just sometimes, I think better of it later."

Jones shook his head. "Let's agree to disagree on this one and change the subject. Anyway, we'll be there soon."

"What's our plan of attack?" I asked. "We could be dealing with a murderer here."

"I'm planning to stick to the truth as closely as possible and let him infer the rest. I'll call Griffin first and have him meet me somewhere public."

It sounded easier said than done. "How will you finagle that?"

"I'll tell him I'm her business partner and that I haven't heard from her in a few days and that I know she was working for him. Remember, Rochelle never met Griffin in person. If he didn't kill her, he might not know she's dead. If he did, he'll want to find out what I know about him. Either way, I'm gambling that he'll be curious enough about how I found him to take the meeting."

I just shook my head. "You're playing a very dangerous game here, Malcolm. If Griffin did kill Rochelle over my case, he's going to want you gone."

"Open the glove compartment," he instructed me.

I did and withdrew the small zippered bag within. After unzipping it, I peered in at the contents. "What's all this?"

"Listening devises. I'm going to plant a bug on Griffin and wear a transmitter. You'll be able to hear everything we're saying, and we can find out where he's headed after our meeting.

If we gather enough evidence, we can take it straight to the police."

He made it sound so simple. But I had faith that my man knew what he was doing. "And if he's innocent?"

Jones shook his head. "Then we've come a long way for nothing. One problem at a time, love."

Jones picked the coffee shop by my apartment as the designated meeting place. We parked in the Laundromat parking lot across the street so I'd have a clear view of the door to the coffee shop from the car. The call went exactly the way Jones had predicted it would—the meeting set up for 10:00 AM.

"I wish I had time for a coffee. You don't know how long it's been since I had a double half-caff with a shot of espresso and foam." My hometown had its charms, but a decent coffee place wasn't one of them.

Jones gave me a quick kiss. "Business before pleasure. I'll bring you something if you stay in the car."

"You'd stoop to bribery?"

Jones raised one eyebrow. "I would have handcuffed you in my darkroom if I wasn't worried another teen arsonist would strike while I was away."

"It's a good thing you didn't go that route," I told him. "My wrath would know no bounds. Good luck."

I watched as Jones crossed the street and entered the coffee place. He took a table near the plate-glass window overlooking the street and spoke softly into the microphone. "Can you hear me?"

We'd tested his transmitter with him outside the car, but the program he had running on his laptop made it sound as if he sat in the car next to me. Though I doubted he could see me, I gave him a thumbs-up through the windshield. Then there was nothing to do but wait.

Ten minutes later, I was beginning to believe Griffin was going to stand us up, when he rounded the corner. I recognized him immediately, a tall man with dark hair streaked with silver. It fell in such a way I knew he had visited a decent stylist or barber not too long ago. He was tall with wide shoulders encased in an expensive coat over a steel-gray suit. Most men who dressed like that would have been on their way to the office. Maybe Griffin had been before Jones's phone call.

I held my breath, hoping Jones wasn't putting himself in danger.

The man entered the coffee shop and looked around. Jones rose, and through the transmitter I heard him say, "Mr. Griffin?"

Griffin offered the hand but didn't smile. "Mr. Jones, I presume?"

He had a smooth, cultured voice, carefully accentless but deep and just a little bit gruff. Though it was an idiotic notion, I couldn't keep from thinking that the man didn't sound like a killer.

"I'm sorry, but I don't know if I can help you. I've never met your partner in person."

"Anything you can tell me would be helpful." Jones pressed. "I need a place to start, so maybe I can follow her trail. Tell me, what was my partner doing for you?"

Griffin stared at Jones for a moment. "I assume this will stay between the two of us."

"Of course." Jones didn't so much as twitch. "Just us."

In spite of my apprehension, I smiled to myself. Just them and the woman recording the entire conversation from the van.

Griffin took a deep breath. His words knocked my world off its axis and sent me careening into the void. "I hired her to send me information about my daughter."

Whatever-You've-Got Breakfast Casserole

You'll need:
1 pound mild Italian sausage
1/2 small sweet onion, chopped
3 mini sweet bell peppers of varying color, seeded and chopped
10 oz fresh spinach, rinsed and chopped
1 cup all-purpose flour
1/4 cup grated Parmesan cheese
1 teaspoon dried basil
1/2 teaspoon salt
8 eggs
2 cups milk
1/2 cup shredded mozzarella
1/2 cup shredded aged cheddar

In a large skillet, cook sausage and onion over medium heat until meat is no longer pink; drain. Transfer to a greased 3-quart baking dish. Sprinkle with half of the peppers; top with spinach.

In a large bowl, combine the flour, Parmesan cheese, basil, and salt. Whisk eggs and milk; stir into flour mixture until blended. Pour over veggies.

Bake, uncovered at 425 for 15 to 20 minutes or until a knife inserted near the center comes out clean. Top with cheese

**Andy's note: Perfect for a brunch or brinner (breakfast for dinner). And turn up the heat with a bottle of Tabasco on the table. Great pairing with a pitcher of Bloody Marys.

CHAPTER TWENTY

His daughter. Jacob Griffin had hired Rochelle to find his daughter. Me. I was his daughter.

If the men kept talking, I couldn't hear them over the roaring in my ears. I was his daughter? How was that possible?

Well, of course I knew *how* that was possible. He and my mom, well, they...yeah. Thirty-three years ago they'd been a couple. Or maybe not a couple. Maybe it was a drunken hookup. Mommy dearest had never said. She'd run home to Beaverton and never mentioned him, at least not to me.

Nana had always told me to be grateful I had Pops because he was the best man out there. Pops, who coincidentally had suffered an excruciating arthritis flare-up the second I asked him if he knew Jacob Griffin. Maybe it was just happenstance, but I didn't think so. Pops had known Griffin, at least by name. Knew the man was my father.

And there he sat, across the street in plain view, with my boyfriend. I looked at him again, really looked. Jacob Griffin was my father.

I'd opened the door to the coffee shop before I was even aware of moving. And I looked down at the men, both wide eyed at my sudden appearance. Jones made a strangled sound, but I barely noticed. All my attention remained fixed on the other man.

"You're my..." My throat closed up around the word, choking me to keep it from escaping. "You and my mom..."

"Yes, I knew your mother." Griffin rose slowly, moving as if I were a deer he didn't want to startle. "Andrea Sophia Rossetti Buckland."

I nodded, swallowed as best I could, and managed to croak, "That's me."

No wonder we'd both thought Griffin looked familiar. He looked like me. The nose, the small upturned nose. His was broader, but it fit his face. The chin too, with just the tiniest point, and around the eyes, too. The resemblance was right there for anyone with working vision to notice. Like me, pictures didn't capture his charisma, the assessing flicker of his gaze as he studied me head to toe. Was that why I hadn't recognized him sooner?

"I've seen you before," I breathed. "Here, I mean."

He nodded. "I've been following your career. A mutual friend told me you were a chef in Atlanta. I've been following your career over the past several years. I saw you on Flavor TV."

"You did?" I whispered, amazed that he'd been paying attention, essentially following my career. Then made a face and said in a much different tone, "You weren't in the audience, were you?"

He shook his head, a small smile on his lips. "I had business in Luxembourg during your premiere, or I would have been there."

"I'm glad you weren't," I murmured with heartfelt sincerity, then winced when I heard the way the words sounded. "I mean, that is..." Why was I stammering like a half-wit?

Jacob Griffin grinned at me—it was a crooked gesture though, utterly genuine. "I know what you meant."

His teeth were perfect, white and even. The grin changed him from the business professional to a real man, and a good-looking one at that. His expensive clothes fit him just so, complementing his coloring. I suddenly felt very self-conscious, wishing I wasn't sporting a wrinkled sweatshirt and jeans with a small hole in the knee.

"Would you sit down?" he asked, gesturing toward the table.

"Andrea." Jones was tugging on my arm, trying to drag me from the table. "I need to speak with you right now."

I'd almost forgotten he was there. "Can't it wait?" I asked, my gaze straying back to Jacob Griffin. To my father.

"No," Jones insisted. "It'll only take a moment."

I was about to dig my heels in when Griffin murmured, "I'll just go get us all some coffee." He turned away, and I was finally able to focus on Jones.

"He's my...." Again, my voice died on the word.

"You need to be careful," Jones whispered, shooting a look to the counter where Jacob Griffin stood. "We don't know this man or even if what he claims is true."

I made a face at him. "Jones, he looks like me. More than Pops or Aunt Cecily or even my mom did. You saw all the pictures."

"I'm not denying that. If anyone can understand what it's like to want to know your father after a lifetime of imagining, it's me. But don't forget—he's never approached you directly. There has to be a reason for that. Even under the best of circumstances, I would advise you to maintain a bit of distance, but we came here looking for a murderer. This doesn't change anything."

"You don't understand," I began but then cut off when Griffin approached with three cardboard cups.

"I assume the two of you know one another." He looked from me to Jones.

"I'm surprised you don't already know about our relationship." Jones made no motion to reach for the coffee cup. "Since you hired someone to spy on Andrea."

I huffed out a breath but didn't try to apologize. Now that the initial shock was wearing off, my brain had begun to chug along again. Though I knew Jones was only trying to protect me, he was allowing his poor relationship with his own father to sour the meeting.

That didn't mean he was wrong to be cautious.

Griffin looked from me to Jones and back, his face open and relating confusion. "No, it never came up. You said you were a private investigator. That you worked with Rochelle?"

"I did." Jones nodded. "I was also married to her."

"Before he met me," I rushed to add. God, why did I feel the need to justify my relationship to this man? It was the oddest sensation, like when I didn't want Aunt Cecily to know I'd screwed up a batch of homemade pasta, or to admit to Pops that I dented the car. Their good opinion mattered to me.

Under the table, Jones's hand brush against mine. I gripped it hard, taking the reassurance he offered while trying to give some of my own.

Jacob frowned at us. "Rochelle never mentioned that in her reports."

It was on the tip of my tongue to ask if he knew about Kaylee, but I bit it back. Careful, I had to be careful and not do anything to endanger my daughter.

"Why would you pay a PI for information?" Jones probed. "Why not just approach Andrea yourself?"

Griffin cleared his throat and looked away. My grip on Jones tightened as I waited for him to answer.

He exhaled and then looked at me, his expression unreadable. "Because of your mother."

"What about her?" I whispered. It was all well and good to tell myself that I was going to maintain some distance, but I'd craved answers about my parents my entire life.

Griffin's chin lifted, and he squared his shoulders, looking me right in the eye. "I felt guilty for abandoning you to her care. I knew she suffered from depression, and it only got worse after you were born. I left her, but I should have taken you with me. It's a choice I've had to live with every day of my life, one that I've regretted. I had to know that you were all right, but at the same time, I didn't feel as if I had any right to insert myself into your life."

At his words, my heart seized up and flash froze inside my chest. I couldn't breathe, couldn't think. His honesty floored me.

"Andrea," Jones spoke, but it sounded like it was coming from a great distance. "Are you all right?"

"I have to go." Stumbling from the booth, I lurched through the coffee shop, ignoring everything else while Griffin's words circled and dove down like pecking buzzards, shredding me.

If not for Jones, I probably would have walked right into traffic. A strong arm went around me, and he guided me across the street to his SUV. He half lifted me to deposit me in the seat. Through a veil of tears, I could still see Jacob Griffin sitting in the coffee shop window.

Our eyes met.

"Drive," I whispered to Jones. "Please. I need to not be near him."

Bless the man—he drove. But the distance changed nothing. "We're exactly the same," I croaked.

"What?" Jones cast me a worried look. "What do you mean?"

"What I did to Kyle, to Kaylee. That's exactly what he did to me. He left me to go live his own life. I'm no better than he is. We're exactly the same."

"You're not." Jones hit the gas and sped through to make the green light. He changed lanes without looking. Behind us a car horn blared as he cut off a Monte Carlo. Jones didn't so much as flinch as he maneuvered the giant vehicle into a parking garage. He snagged the nearest available space, threw the mammoth gas-guzzler into park, and then unfastened my seat belt.

"You're not," he repeated as he pulled me across the parking break and onto his lap. "You're nothing like him. You did what was best for Kaylee as well as yourself. You didn't leave her with a deranged woman. You made sure she would have better than what you could have given her. Andrea, do you hear me? You are nothing like him."

I clung to him and his words, wishing that they were true, fearing that they weren't.

* * *

I slept during the entire trip back to Beaverton and still felt both physically and emotionally exhausted by the time we got back to Jones's house.

Lizzy's Audi was parked in the driveway, and something smelled good when Jones opened the door. "I ordered takeout from Lacey's," Jones's sister said.

A day earlier I would have refused to eat anything Lacey L'Amour had prepared, but cast in the light of the day's revelation, our feud seemed both juvenile and pointless.

"Did she know it was for me?" I opened the Styrofoam take-out dish. Filet mignon and ratatouille, and it both looked and smelled good enough to eat.

"Not unless she's psychic." Lizzy shrugged. "Why?"

"Good, then she probably didn't spit in it." Too tired to care either way, I grabbed a fork from the island and dug in.

"For the record, I didn't either," Lizzy murmured. "But I thought about it."

"We both appreciate your restraint." Jones gave his sister a one-armed hug. His gaze drifted back to me, his expression worried. "Any news?"

Lizzy shook her head. "Town's been quiet for a change. Daddy's back home."

"Did you ever find out what he was doing with all those gasoline cans?" Jones asked.

Lizzy made a face. "Apparently, he's joined a survivalist's club. He claimed the gas was for after the Apocalypse hit. He's been squirreling canned goods in the basement along with bottled water, but he didn't want to keep the gas on the property. I really don't know if this is better or worse than if he was an arsonist. That's why I've been hiding here for the day."

Jones made a disgusted noise. "Better, though everything is relative. Especially with relatives."

A sort of half-hysterical noise escaped my throat, and both Jones and Lizzy whipped their gazes to me. I waved them away and slid off the stool and approached the fridge. Several bottles of water stood in anal-retentive rows, and I moved them around, just to give myself a minute to recover.

"A bunch of people stopped by—Bee from the post office, Freddy Harris, Mrs. Bradford, and Mayor Randal."

"Here?" Jones raised an eyebrow. "Why?"

I could answer that one. "It's the gossip committee. Everyone is looking for the scoop now that word is out about Kaylee being my and Kyle's long-lost daughter."

Lizzy shifted on her barstool. "And Kyle and I broke up."

No one said anything for a minute. I opened a bottle of water and took a swig.

"I'm sorry," Jones murmured, placing a hand on Lizzy's.

"Not as sorry as Kyle," I said.

Lizzy frowned at me. "What do you mean?"

"The man is stupid for you," I told her. "I mean, come on. Fake flirting with my arch enemy to get me to fink him out. That falls neatly into the *it's just so darn crazy it might work* category. He was never like that with me or with anyone else. You brought forth his special streak of idiot."

Jones cast me a *what the blazes do you think you are doing?* kind of look, but Lizzy's lips actually twitched as if she was holding in a smile. "It was ridiculous."

"Like romantic comedy sort of ridiculous. A full-blown boom box over the head playing our song in the middle of the night kind of ridiculous." I nudged her a little. "The kind where the audience roots for the guy to get the girl because they know he'll never be truly happy without her."

But Lizzy was shaking her head. "I can't—"

"Don't make any decisions right now." Though Jones was speaking to Lizzy, his gaze locked on me. "If it's right, it will all work out."

Lizzy opened her mouth and then shook her head as though she'd changed her mind. "I'd better head home."

Jones walked her to the door. I finished my dinner—it was better than I'd ever have thought possible from Lacey, though I'd never say so aloud—and then checked my phone messages. The first was from Detective Brown, letting me know the investigators were done with the Bowtie Angel and I was free to come and go as I pleased. Well, that was sort of good news. That meant Mimi could move back into her apartment. She'd been staying with Pops and Aunt Cecily at the A-frame. I almost called her to let her know, but the idea of her being alone in the pasta shop after a body had been dumped there bothered me.

Jones returned and sat down next to me. "You're frowning," he observed.

I forced a smile. "We can get back into the pasta shop."

"Do you want to go now?" Jones asked.

I sort of did, but he looked exhausted. "Yeah. You need to rest though."

He shook his head, but I rolled over the top of him. "Malcolm, go lie down before you fall down. I promise I won't leave the house without waking you."

He studied me a moment, then nodded. "You swear on Mimi's cannoli cake?"

"Cross my heart and hope to die."

He made a face at my inappropriate word choice and then pushed back from the island. "Can I convince you to lie down with me?"

"If I do, you won't get any sleep."

He grinned. "You speak the truth, my lady." He brought my hands to his lips and kissed them before heading into the bedroom.

I tidied the kitchen and wiped down the counters. Thought about opening some wine but decided against it. Sleeping was out of the question, and there was nothing decent on television. I found myself downstairs, poking through Rochelle's files again.

Though we hadn't officially cleared Jacob Griffin—it was easier for me to still refer to him as Jacob Griffin than in terms of any personal connection—of the murder, neither Jones nor I got the sense that he had anything to gain from Rochelle's death. If the gang had been behind the arsons, then they hadn't killed Rochelle either. That was the first thing Detective Brown had done—find out if any of the gang members had alibis for the time of Rochelle's death. And across the board, they'd all had solid ones.

So who'd killed her and why? Could it be personal? Some other case that had gone horribly wrong? If so, why had the killer called to warn me off? Why not just leave Rochelle's body at the lumberyard instead of moving it to my walk-in?

Try as I might, I couldn't see Lacey as the killer. For one thing, she'd been busy opening her restaurant. I knew firsthand just how time consuming that could be. And secondly, she had nothing to gain from Rochelle's death.

I clicked open the file folder Rochelle had marked Beaverton. Inside there were two subfolders, one marked Griffin and the other marked Arson. I clicked on the Griffin folder first and began to read.

Within the first few paragraphs, it became clear that
Rochelle had kept plenty of information about me to herself. My
relationship with Jones, Kaylee's birth certificate listing me as
her mother, and that she'd moved to Beaverton. The document
mostly focused on my career, something that it sounded as
though Griffin already knew about. She'd done her best to
protect both Jones and Kaylee from an unknown. Whatever her
reasons, I was grateful to her for that.

I opened the arson folder and began to read. At first the
document made little sense. There was a lot of legalese as well
as names and dates like in the earlier transcripts. She hadn't
gotten far enough to do a summary report and translate her
findings into normal people speech.

I was about ready to throw in the towel when a name
caught my eye. I blinked and then read the sentence again.

"No way," I breathed.

"I'm afraid so," a male voice said from behind me. It
wasn't Jones's smooth New Zealand accent but a Southern twang
I recognized all too well.

I spun on the chair, but something crashed down on my
head. The force sent me to my hands and knees. Starbursts of
light exploded behind my eyes as waves of pain rolled through
me.

"It's you," I gasped a second before the next blow
knocked me out cold.

Orzo Casserole

You'll need:
1 cup orzo
3 oz prosciutto
1 medium onion, chopped
3 garlic cloves, chopped
1 bell pepper, chopped
Six baby bella mushrooms, washed and sliced thin
Drizzle of extra virgin olive oil
Pinch salt
Pinch black pepper
2 tablespoons flour
2 cups chicken broth
1/4 cup milk
2 1/2 cups Parmesan cheese
1/2 cup Panko bread crumbs
3 tablespoons melted butter
1/2 teaspoon paprika
1/2 teaspoon chili powder

Preheat oven to 375 degrees. Pour orzo in 9 x 9 baking dish.

Heat a sauté pan over medium-high with a few tablespoons of olive oil. Add the onions, mushrooms, and pepper, and cook for 2 to 3 minutes, until translucent. Add the garlic. Season with salt, and cook until fragrant.

Sprinkle with flour, and stir to coat onions, pepper, and garlic. Cook for 1 minute to toast flour. Whisk in the chicken stock, and cook for 3 to 4 minutes or until the mixture thickens slightly.
Add milk and 2 cups of cheese, and stir together. Adjust seasoning to taste. Pour over the orzo.

In a medium bowl, combine the remaining ingredients, and stir. Sprinkle over the baking dish. Bake for 30 minutes until bread crumbs are golden. Serve warm.

**Andy's note: A great dish to make ahead and store in the fridge, perfect for a packed-to-the-brim sort of day.

CHAPTER TWENTY-ONE

———

Considering the way my head throbbed even before I opened my eyes, I was fairly sure I had another concussion. My thoughts were thin and slippery, like overcooked angel hair soaked in olive oil, as I tried to recall what had happened. Bits and pieces stuck together, mostly images and feelings. Jones kissing me before turning in, me leafing through Rochelle's files and finding...

My eyes flew open, and I stared up at the profile of Mayor Eli Randal the Second.

He hadn't noticed I was awake yet. Maybe I could use that to my advantage. Maybe there was some suitable weapon nearby, something that would help me turn the tables. I didn't think he had a handgun, but there was no way to be sure.

The room around me was dark, but I recognized right away that I was no longer in Jones's darkroom. I was half sitting, half leaning against something hard. A desk maybe, or a cabinet. Though there wasn't much light, I could make out sleek tile beneath my feet and the press of cool metal against my back. A refrigerator. I was in somebody's kitchen. Not mine or Jones's or even the Bowtie Angel's.

"Where?" The word came out as a croak, and even that made my pulse pound in my temple. And then I realized I'd ruined my chance to take him unawares.

Randal turned to face me, his soft doughy face as amiable as always. "Good, you're awake. I need you to sign something for me."

Was he nuts? "So you hit me on the head? That's not the way you get votes, Mayor."

He made a tsking sound, the kind I heard him make to some of the children who cut across his home on Oak Summit Drive after school let out. "Now, Andy, you've made more than enough trouble for me already. You and your boyfriend and that private investigator you hired."

It all came back in a rush. Rochelle's notes about the business that had been torched, and the line in the town law about any property in the town limits that had not been developed in a set amount of time after a catastrophic incident would revert back to the town to auction off.

And her notice that both the owners of the flower shop and the assisted living facility had been members of the Beaverton Chamber of Commerce. The group of business owners who were always chaired by the mayor, who knew the town bylaws like the back of his hand.

Rochelle had suspected that Mayor Randal was behind the arsons, though she'd lacked any real evidence to support her theory.

The fact that he'd conked me on the head was pretty damning though.

"Sign this." Eli thrust a clipboard at me. Though I had no intention of doing what he said, I wanted a closer look at the paper. I lifted my right hand, but it stopped about halfway to the clipboard. There was a clank behind me, and I looked up to see the metallic glint of a handcuff linking my arm to the refrigerator.

Maybe I hadn't lost my chance at escape, only because I'd never really had one.

"Use the other hand." Randal was starting to sweat like a cheese that had been left out on a hot day. "It doesn't need to be perfect, just legible."

"How did you even get into Jones's house?" I asked.

He shrugged. "That was simple enough. I just asked to use the facilities and unbolted the door to the cellar from the inside. Lizzy was so inundated with company, she didn't even notice I slipped downstairs. Never underestimate the power of misdirection."

Using my left hand, I brought the clipboard down to eye level. It read, Last Will and Testament, and my full name was typed in the space below.

"A will?"

Randal nodded. "To make it legal that upon your death, the Bowtie Angel reverts to the town."

This was all a real estate scam? When had I stumbled into an episode of *Scooby-Doo*?

Then his words registered. "Upon my death," he'd said. I wasn't supposed to make it out of this mystery kitchen alive.

"I've already left a suicide note on your boyfriend's computer," Randal muttered, mostly to himself.

"You're out of your mind if you think Jones would ever believe I committed suicide. He won't stop looking, and he'll expose you."

Randal perched on a black chair, looking like an overfed Atlas as he stared down at me. "I disagree. He knows how unstable you are. You broke up with him over nothing, moved out on a whim, started a bar fight, and got yourself thrown in jail by your ex-boyfriend. Combined with the fact that the health department has shut your pasta shop down and that your daughter will be tried for destruction of private property, I think he'd believe you cracked under the pressure. And even if he doesn't, I have other plans for him."

The words sent a cold chill through me, and the shaking only made my headache worse.

"What about Rochelle? The entire town knows she was murdered."

"And found on your property. There's some serious nepotism in the police department— you should have been arrested already." A line formed between his eyebrows. "I should look into that."

"But they already found the crime scene. Sooner or later Detective Brown will link it back to you."

Randal blinked as if I'd interrupted him mid-thought. "Of course they won't. When you're found dead, everyone will assume you and Jones killed Rochelle together, but you cracked under the strain of it all. With no more murders or arsons to contend with, the good people of Beaverton will have no reason to ask questions."

"So you're okay letting your nephew and his friends take the rap for the fires? Was there ever really a gang?"

His fishy lips twitched. "Not in the strictest interpretation of the word. My nephew actually believes he concocted the idea on his own, and my brother has already hired some of the best lawyers in the state to represent him. He'll get off with a slap on the wrist while his peers take the brunt of the blame. Sign the paper, Andy."

"This will never hold up in court," I said. "Aunt Cecily and Pops know I would never leave the pasta shop to the town over my own flesh and blood."

"It's already notarized. I convinced Alfred Hennessey to do it in exchange for a bottle of whiskey and fixing his DUI." Randal shrugged. "There's nothing they can do, regardless of what they believe."

I shook my head, stalling for time. My only hope was that Jones would realize I was no longer in the house and come looking for me. Once I signed the papers, I was as good as dead. "Why though? Why is it so important to have all this land turned over to the town? What are you going to do with it?"

He blinked as though I'd startled him. "Why, franchise it all, of course."

"Franchise? This is all for a Starbucks?"

"Starbucks, McDonald's, Subway, Pizza Hut, you name it. Beaverton proper open to the highest bidder."

"But how can you? I thought the chamber of commerce denied the franchises."

"The old chamber of commerce did. The motion lost by three votes." He held up his hand and started to tick names off. "Inga Bradford, Freddy Harris, Cecily Rossetti, and Lacey, L'Amour."

"Lacey? She just moved to town. What does she have to do with any of this?" It dawned on me exactly where I was. "Oh my god, this is Lacey's restaurant. You're going to torch it?"

Randal shrugged as though it couldn't be helped. "I tried to talk her to my side of things. Tell her we all stand to gain from opening the town to franchises. No one wants to drive thirty miles for fast food. But she was as obstinate as you usually are. Besides, I think you setting fire to your rival's restaurant fits right in with your character."

Considering the source, the slight didn't faze me. "So you've destroyed all the businesses who opposed you? And what about the innocent people who've died? Those kids you manipulated, who've destroyed their futures? Don't they matter at all?"

"Not especially." His tone was flat. No hint of regret or remorse. A lunatic. Our mayor was a complete sociopathic lunatic.

He cleared his throat and then continued as if I wasn't already pants-peeing terrified. "Both the florist and the assisted living facility were severely underinsured. The pasta shop is different. If the kids had burned it down, you would have just rebuilt. Your family is as stubborn as they come, and you've been a thorn in my side from day one."

There was no hate or malice in his eyes, and that scared me more than everything else. He didn't see us as people, only obstacles to be overcome by whatever means necessary. Destruction of property, fraud, murder—he'd do anything to have his way. This wasn't personal. It was business to him.

"What if…" I searched frantically through my mental hard drive, looking for anything I could say that would convince him not to kill me. "What if I just closed the pasta shop? What if we all just moved away?"

He smiled at me, but there was no amusement in it. If not for the sweat soaking his underarms and glistening on his face, I would have guessed he was a cyborg. "Come now, Andy. You don't kid a kidder. Your family would never move away from Beaverton. And even if they agreed, it's not like I can let you live after telling you all this."

My voice shook only a little as I asked the next question. He hadn't asked me to sign the paper again, and I needed to stall as long as I could. We were in the heart of town. Someone had to come by eventually. God alone understood why that paper was important to him. It's not like psychopaths had supervisors. After arson and murder, forgery should be no biggie. "I still don't understand why, though. Why is it so important to you to have franchises all over town?"

For the first time, his expression changed with genuine emotion. Rage. His tone was deadly quiet as he hissed, "Do you know what it's like to have a family legacy hanging over your head?"

"I do," I said, before thinking better of it.

He sent me a sharp glare, and I pressed my lips together. Apparently, he didn't want me relating to his angst. "You have *no* idea. The Randals were a founding family. We've been part of Beaverton since before the Revolutionary War. Each generation is expected to be instrumental in bettering the town. So don't tell me you understand my position. You, who got to leave this town and then were foolish enough to return. You had freedom there for the taking, and you turned your back on it."

"You don't have to stay here," I insisted. "Eli, you don't have to be mayor anymore if you don't want to be. There's nothing holding you to it. Go out and find your bliss."

He rose from the chair and straightened his shirt over his doughy frame. "I never shirk my responsibilities. I am doing what I must for Beaverton. It's my destiny. Now, let's be done with this. Sign the paper, Andy."

"No." Though it took effort, I lifted my chin and stared him straight in the eye. "I will never sign that."

He sighed as if I'd disappointed him, then shrugged. "Fine then, I'll force your daughter to do it."

My eyes went wide. "You wouldn't."

He raised an eyebrow, as if I dared him.

"Leave her alone. Kaylee has nothing to do with this."

"The way I understand it, she has everything to do with it. When your Aunt Cecily turned the Bowtie Angel over to you, there was a clause that if anything should happen to you, the pasta shop will go to your next of kin. And the whole town knows that's Kaylee. Sign the papers, Andy, or I'm going after her."

I signed the papers.

* * *

Eli left me chained to the refrigerator. The key to my handcuffs sat on the metal workstation that he had nudged about six inches beyond my reach. "To make it look like you put it down and then kicked the bench away so you couldn't back out at the last minute."

The man had covered his tracks well.

He'd set the fire in the storeroom, the innermost part of the building. No one passing by on the street would see it before it was too late. The small space was packed with plenty of flammable materials like oils and grease, which would make the fire burn harder and be that much more difficult to put out. Smoke had started to seep out from underneath the storeroom door. An insidious trickle at first, it was growing into a bigger cloud by the minute. Soon the entire door would be consumed by flames, and then the choking smoke would billow forth, suffocating me well before the fire got to me.

I coughed. Then stretched for the key again. I had to get out of here. For Pops and Aunt Cecily, for Kaylee, and Jones.

"Damn you, Malcolm Jones," I wheezed. My wrist was raw where the skin along the cuff had scraped away. "Where the hell are you when I need you?"

The smoke was growing thicker. I coughed again and stretched, reaching for the key. I wanted to live, damn it. I wanted to live. To bring Mayor Randal down, but also so I could know my daughter and spend the rest of my life with the man I loved. I couldn't stand the thought that my loved ones would believe I'd offed myself. It would destroy Aunt Cecily and Pops, good Catholics that they were. They believed suicide was a mortal sin, and the grief over not just losing me but envisioning me in hell might kill one or both of them.

Kaylee would be scarred for life and might be in danger if she questioned what Randal was doing.

And Jones. Would he be blamed for Rochelle's murder in the end? Worse, would he think I didn't love him enough to fight for my life? For our lives? I couldn't let that happen.

I gave another vicious yank, driven by desperation. The refrigerator budged. Gripping the handle, I yanked again with all my strength.

The fridge groaned and then toppled forward. I yelped and tried to get out of the way, but it crashed down onto my tethered arm. Pain exploded, pain unlike any I'd ever known.

I was stuck with one arm pinned under the monstrous appliance. Worse, the metal workstation had been knocked over, and the key was nowhere in sight. The air was only slightly cleaner down below, and I sucked in as much oxygen as I could.

"Help!" I shrieked, then coughed again. The pain had darkness wavering in my periphery, but I mustered enough strength to shout again. "Help me! Somebody!"

There was no answer. I could hear the fire now, see the flames licking through the closed door as the blaze consumed it. I tried to shift, to struggle, but the pain in my arm almost made me pass out.

Maybe unconsciousness would be a mercy. But that would mean I'd given up. And I couldn't—I could *not*—give up, no matter what.

"Anybody!" I screamed again, coughing, gagging on the acrid tang of smoke. "Help me!"

The swing door to the kitchen burst open, and a man's shape stood silhouetted by the lights from the other room. At first I thought it was Eli Randal, come back to stuff a gag in my mouth. But the shape was too tall to be the mayor.

"Andrea," the man said. "Where are you?"

"Jones?" I gasped.

But as he drew nearer, I saw that it wasn't Jones, but the only other man who used my full name.

"Dear God," Jacob Griffin said. "Andrea, what—"

"Handcuffed. Key fell. Over there." I pointed to where the workstation had gone down.

Griffin immediately crawled to where I indicated. There was a clanging, barely audible over the roar of the fire. Then he was back, key in hand. "We've got to get this off you."

I tried to tell him that I was handcuffed to the fridge, but could manage nothing but a cough. Griffin put his shoulder into the side of the massive appliance and shoved.

White hot pain, so intense I was sure a part of me had caught fire, enveloped me, robbing me of consciousness. The last thing I heard was my father's voice. "Don't worry. I'm going to get you out of here."

"Please," I gasped, struggling not to lose consciousness, afraid I'd never wake again.

Another male voice came from somewhere nearby. "Andrea!"

Jones. I couldn't call to him. I was coughing almost nonstop, every jarring making my arm ache even worse. Unable to look at it, I turned my face into Griffin's jacket.

"I've got her." Griffin was huffing for breath. Between carrying me and the smoke, his lungs must've been burning, but he still managed to call out. "There's a fire. We're coming out!"

Then cold January night air licked my skin, and familiar hands touched my face. "Andrea, what happened?"

Between coughs, I managed to gasp, "Mayor."

"We need to get her to the hospital." Jones's hands moved over me as he assessed the damage. "She might need surgery on that arm."

"There's an ambulance on the way." I recognized Kyle's voice. "Did she say the mayor did this?"

I gave a weak nod, but it was too much. Relief filled me as I sank into the blackness
once more.

Vegetarian Lasagna

You'll need:
8 lasagna noodles
1 14 oz can tomatoes
1 cup celery, chopped
1 cup green pepper, chopped
2 bay leaves
1 egg, beaten
1/4 cup Parmesan cheese
1 10 oz package frozen chopped broccoli
1 15 oz can tomato sauce
1 cup of red onion, chopped
1 1/2 teaspoon dried basil
1 clove garlic, minced
2 cups low-fat ricotta cheese or cottage cheese
1 cup mozzarella cheese, shredded

Cook lasagna noodles and broccoli separately according to their package directions; drain well, and set aside.

For sauce, cut up canned tomatoes. In a large saucepan, stir together chopped, undrained tomatoes, tomato sauce, celery, onion, green pepper, basil, bay leaf, and garlic. Bring to boil. Reduce heat, and simmer uncovered for 20 to 25 minutes, or until sauce is thick. Stir occasionally. Remove bay leaf.

Meanwhile, in a bowl stir together egg, ricotta cheese, Parmesan cheese, and 1/4 teaspoon pepper. Stir in broccoli. Spread 1/2 cup sauce in the bottom of a 9 x 13 pan. Top with half of the noodles, half of the cheese-broccoli mixture, and half of the remaining sauce. Repeat layers, ending with sauce.

Bake uncovered at 350 for 25 minutes. Sprinkle with mozzarella and bake 5 minutes more or until cheese melts. Let stand 10 minutes.

**Andy's note: Perfect for freezing and reheating for those crazy-busy days.

CHAPTER TWENTY-TWO

———

Every part of me hurt. From my head to my mangled arm and down to my smoke-damaged lungs, there wasn't much left of me that was undamaged.

Secretly, I was glad for the pain. It meant I was still alive. Though it made it a bear to get any rest that wasn't hopped up on whatever clear liquid was running through my IV.

Jones sat asleep in the chair next to me. He was scruffy as hell, having refused to leave my side since my surgery in case I needed anything. I was dying for a drink of water but loathe to wake him. Maybe I could reach the cup myself. I glanced at the plaster cast on my arm—it went from shoulder to palm, with only my fingers peeking out—and decided not to chance it. The giant refrigerator had all but crushed the bone, and I didn't want to undo the orthopedist's careful reconstruction.

A familiar face peered around the corner. I smiled at Donna and gritted my teeth as I tried to sit up a little.

In an instant, Jones was awake and by my side. "What do you need?"

"Help me sit up. And some water would be great."

He adjusted the bed and then aimed the straw at my lips. I sucked gratefully until the cup was empty, but waved away his offer for more.

Donna put her hand on Jones's shoulder. "Malcolm, go home."

His gaze slid to me, and he started to shake his head, but in typical Donna fashion, she steamrolled him. "I'm saying this as a friend. You stink, literally. The hospital staff has considered a health and comfort quarantine. Go have a shower and a hot meal. I've got the day shift, and Eugene and Cecily will stop in for lunch. Andy will be fine for a few hours. Go."

His smile was rueful. "I am rather ripe, aren't I? All right. But I'll be back later on." Reaching down, he stroked my face. His anxiety at the thought of having me out of his sight was palpable. He'd told me how afraid he's been when he'd discovered I was gone, vanished without a trace. He'd called Kyle directly, and the entire sheriff's office had been out hunting. But it wasn't until Lacey L'Amour's security monitoring company had reported the fire that anyone had thought to look there. If not for Jacob Griffin arriving in town in the dead of night, I might not have made it out.

"I'll be fine," I reassured him. "Go on, stinky man. I'll see you in a bit."

He caressed my cheek tenderly, then gave me a soul-shattering kiss before turning to go.

Donna took Jones's chair. She wore a black workout outfit with hot pink and electric-blue stripes, and her face was sans makeup.

"Going casual today?"

She shrugged. "No sense getting all dolled up and making you feel worse about the hospital stay than you already do. Besides, I figured you'd need a chance to vent, as every time you complain, Jones hops up like he needs to do something about it ASAP. So go ahead—let loose."

"The food here is the pits," I grumbled. "And the wardrobe leaves much to be desired."

Donna raised an eyebrow. "That's the best you've got?"

I settled back as best I could against the pillows. "Give me time to warm up at least. I might pull something if I go into full-throttle bitchfest."

Donna's lips quirked. "We wouldn't want that. Okay, so what do you know, and what can I fill you in on from the outside?"

"I know the mayor's been arrested." A shiver racked me, which in turn only made my broken arm throb. "Detective Brown stopped by yesterday. He said they found the handgun that had killed Rochelle and the burner phone Randal used to call me in his potting shed. There was also DNA evidence that Rochelle had been in his SUV. No jury in the world will let him walk."

Donna nodded. "And Kyle said that the mayor's nephew admitted that Eli had suggested the initiation ritual and had pointed out which buildings they should torch. Since Joey was supposed to be the leader, none of the others knew about the mayor's involvement or his intentions. That might get a few of the older kids a reduced sentence at least. And Kaylee is just getting community service. And her juvenile file will be sealed."

I sagged in relief. "Good. I was worried. Any news on the pasta shop?"

Donna grinned. "Cecily is handling it. You could almost feel sorry for the board of health."

I smiled back, but then had to ask, "What about Lacey's restaurant?"

She shook her head. "I haven't heard a word about it. The fire and damage was extensive though, at least according to Steve. She won't be able to reopen anytime soon."

"This may sound nuts, but I feel sort of bad for her."

A knock sounded on the door, and I looked up to see Jacob Griffin standing in the doorway. He looked from me to Donna and back again. "If this is a bad time, I can come back."

I wasn't sure what to say to him. The man had saved my life. Hell, he'd given me life. Yet he was a total stranger. I opened my mouth, but Donna rose smoothly. "Actually, I was on my way to go grab a cup of coffee. You want anything?"

Griffin pulled a face. "Not from here."

My friend laughed, then turned to face me. Soundlessly, she mouthed, "Be nice," and then slipped past him.

Griffin moved further into the room but didn't sit down. I shifted, though considering the catheter and the IV, I couldn't go far. An awkward pause ensued.

He went with the obvious. "How are you feeling?"

"Okay, all things considered."

"When do you get out of the hospital?"

"I don't know. A few more days." Any longer than that and I very well might chew my own arm off.

"Good. That's...good."

More uncomfortable pauses.

"Thanks," I said to him finally. "For saving me, I mean."

He frowned. "You shouldn't have to thank me for that. It's what any decent person would do."

"Not the guy who put me there."

"I said decent," he growled. "How the hell did that maniac get elected in the first place?"

I tried to shrug and instantly regretted the motion, hissing in pain, shutting my eyes reflexively. It was kind of a stupid reflex, because without any sight, all I could focus on was the searing agony.

Griffin moved by my side and put his hand on my good arm. "Are you all right? Do you need me to call someone?"

The wave of nausea abated, and I cracked an eyelid. "No, I just need to be still for a bit."

His hand was warm and comforting where it rested on my arm. I wasn't sure if it was right for me to accept his comfort, but at the moment I'd take all I could get.

"Why are you here?" I whispered. "In Beaverton. After all this time, why come here now?"

He stared down at me a moment. "Well, the cat was out of the bag, so to speak. You knew about me. And I didn't like the idea of just letting things stay the way they were between us. I figure you have questions, and I have answers. I'd like to get to know you, Andy. Directly this time, not through third parties. And I want you to know me. I'm not asking you to like me, just to be open."

I stared up at him. Damn, that was a reasonable request, and I'd feel like a total shrew if I denied it. I cleared my throat and asked, "Does that mean you're staying in town?"

"For a while at least. Anyway, my wife is already settled here. I don't think she'd like to be uprooted right now."

"You're married?" I squeaked. It had never occurred to me that he'd be married. Hell, he could have a whole passel of kids for all I knew.

Griffin looked surprised. "Recently, actually. I thought the two of you were already acquainted."

"Oh, zat we are, dahling." Lacey L'Amour minced into my room and put an arm around my father's shoulders. The diamond-encrusted wedding band on her left ring finger caught the horrible fluorescent lights. "Isn't zat right, Andee?"

My eyes slid shut again. "I think I'm going to be sick."

* * *

It took a week before I was cleared to leave the hospital. On my request, Jones had held up Rochelle's burial until I could attend. I felt I owed it to the other woman to be there to honor her memory.

The small graveside service took place on a blustery February morning. Kaylee and her mom were there along with Donna and her husband, Pops and Aunt Cecily, Mimi, Lizzy, and Jones. Jacob Griffin had offered to pay for Rochelle's funeral, since she'd been in town on his errand, but Lizzy had turned him down. I was grateful to her, since that meant Mr. and Mrs. Griffin had no reason to attend. That was one situation I didn't want to think about. Kyle showed up in his sheriff's uniform, but he spent more time casting longing looks at Lizzy. Eventually Aunt Cecily shooed him off.

Since he was the only one who'd known her, Jones spoke to honor his ex. It was brief but heartfelt, and I think it gave him a sense of closure to honor her memory and help put her to rest. Everyone was gathering at the Bowtie Angel afterward, but Jones insisted on driving me home to rest.

"Where is home?" I asked him as we drove. "I don't really know anymore."

"Well, in this case, it's the A-frame, since I promised to let Roofus out." He turned up the road toward my rental. "For me though, home is wherever you are, Andrea."

My eyes, which were already red rimmed, filled with tears. "Don't make me cry again. I feel as though I'm half drowned already."

I'd expected him to smile and make some glib comment. Bantering was our way. Instead, his knuckles turned white where they gripped the steering wheel. Suddenly, he pulled over to the side of the road and turned to face me.

"What?" I asked, concerned. "Malcolm, what's the matter?"

He huffed out a breath and cast me a sidelong look. "Marry me?"

I blinked. "Say what now?"

He sighed. "Andrea, I know this isn't the right time or place. This isn't how I wanted to propose to you. When I proposed to Rochelle, I did everything right, the way it was supposed to be done. And look how that turned out."

I couldn't contain a grimace.

"But that isn't us. Our relationship has never been tidy. It has never made any sort of sense. We're chaos personified, and I wouldn't want it any other way. I don't have a ring for you, but that doesn't change the fact that this feels right to me, right now. I know I want you to be my wife. Marry me?"

I sat there, unable to blink, to move, to breathe. I felt as if I were floating somewhere far distant and watching the two of us, wondering what would happen next.

"Okay," I breathed and then slammed back to full awareness.

His lips twitched. "Is that a yes?"

"Technically, I think it's more of a why the hell not, but that's what you get when you propose on the way home from your ex's funeral." I slapped him on the arm. "Idiot, you are an idiot, and I love you, Malcolm Jones."

He leaned over and claimed my lips, careful of my casted arm. "Let's go home and eat something exceptionally bad for us."

One thing was for sure, the man with the smoking-hot accent knew the quickest route to my heart.

Cannoli Cake

You'll need:
1 package vanilla cake mix
4 eggs, brought to room temperature
1/2 cup miniature chocolate chips

Frosting:
16 oz Mascarpone cheese
3/4 cup confectionary sugar, sifted
1/4 cup half-and-half
2 teaspoons almond extract
1 teaspoon vanilla extract
1 cup sliced almonds
1/2 cup miniature chocolate chips

Prepare and bake cake mix according to package directions along with extra eggs. Mix in 1/2 cup miniature chocolate chips. Cool for 10 minutes before removing from pan to wire rack to cool completely.

In a large bowl, beat the Mascarpone cheese, confectioners' sugar, half-and-half, and extracts on medium speed until creamy (do not overmix).

Frost sides and top edge of cake with 2 cups frosting.

Press almonds and remaining chips into sides and top of cake. Refrigerate until serving.

**Andy's note: Mimi would faint if she knew I used a boxed mix, so we'll just make this our little secret.

ABOUT THE AUTHOR

Former navy wife turned author Jennifer L. Hart loves a good mystery as well as a good laugh and a happily ever after is a must. When she's not playing with her imaginary friends or losing countless hours on social media, she spends her free time experimenting with both food and drink recipes and wishing someone else would clean up. Since she lives with three guys and a beagle, that's usually not the case. Her works include *The Misadventures of the Laundry Hag* series and *Murder Al Dente*.

To learn more about Jennifer L. Hart, visit her online at www.jenniferlhart.com

Enjoyed this book? Check out these other fun reads available in print now from Gemma Halliday Publishing:

www.GemmaHallidayPublishing.com

CPSIA information can be obtained at www.ICGte
Printed in the USA
LVOW06s2145071215

465864LV00001B/36/P